NEW YORK REVIEW BOOKS
CLASSICS

W9-BTZ-643

THE LATE MATTIA PASCAL

LUIGI PIRANDELLO (1867–1936) was born in Agrigento, Sicily, the son of a rich mining contractor. Having studied at the universities of Palermo and Rome and taken a degree in philology at Bonn, the young Pirandello turned to writing poetry and stories, achieving his first literary success in 1904 with his novel *The Late Mattia Pascal*. During World War I, Pirandello began to write for the stage, winning an international following with plays such as *Six Characters in Search of an Author* (1921) and *Henry IV* (1922). In 1934, he received the Nobel Prize for Literature. Pirandello was the author of novels, essays, stories, and more than fifty plays, as well as an influence on writers as different as Eugène Ionesco and T. S. Eliot. Commenting on his work in 1920 he wrote:

> I think that life is a very sad piece of buffoonery; because we have in ourselves, without being able to know why, wherefore or whence, the need to deceive ourselves constantly by creating a reality (one for each and never the same for all), which from time to time is discovered to be vain and illusory.... My art is full of bitter compassion for all those who deceive themselves; but this compassion cannot fail to be followed by the ferocious derision of destiny which condemns man to deception.

CHARLES SIMIC is a poet, essayist, and translator. He teaches American literature and creative writing at the University of New Hampshire. He has published five books of essays, a memoir, numerous translations, and sixteen collections of poetry, the most recent of which, *The Voice at 3:00 A.M.: Selected Late and New Poems*, was published in 2003. Among the many literary awards he has received are a MacArthur Fellowship and the Pulitzer Prize.

THE LATE MATTIA PASCAL

LUIGI PIRANDELLO

Translated by
WILLIAM WEAVER

Introduction by
CHARLES SIMIC

NEW YORK REVIEW BOOKS

New York

This is a New York Review Book
Published by The New York Review of Books
1755 Broadway, New York, NY 10019

Translation copyright © 1964 by William Weaver
Introduction copyright © 2005 by Charles Simic
All rights reserved.

Published in Italian as *Il Fu Mattia Pascal*

Library of Congress Cataloging-in-Publication Data
Pirandello, Luigi, 1867–1936.
  [Fu Mattia Pascal. English]
  The late Mattia Pascal / Luigi Pirandello ; translated by William Weaver ;
introduction by Charles Simic.
      p. cm. — (New York Review Books classics)
  ISBN 1-59017-115-2 (trade paper : alk. paper)
  I. Weaver, William, 1923– II. Title. III. Series.
  PQ4835.I7F813 2004
  853'.912—dc22

                                        2004017966

ISBN 1-59017-115-2

Distributed to the trade by Publishers Group West

Printed in the United States of America on acid-free paper.
10 9 8 7 6 5 4 3 2 1

www.nyrb.com

Contents

Introduction

Everyone who loves to read and spends time browsing in libraries and bookstores knows the excitement of coming across an unfamiliar book that seems full of promise. Something about the writing is so captivating; it beckons like a table already set. As it happens, one is very rarely wrong about a hunch like that. That was my experience with *The Late Mattia Pascal*. I knew a number of Pirandello's plays and stories, but never realized what an extraordinarily fine and original novelist he was until I read this book. First published in 1904, it was a great success in Italy at the time and was widely translated. Pirandello wrote it in Rome, working mostly at night while his wife lay prostrate in bed unable to move her legs after hearing the news of her father's bankruptcy. What he thought of his own life we may surmise from the novel.

It is a story of a man who runs away from an unhappy marriage only to discover on his way home after an absence of two weeks that people there have mistaken a body found in the waters of a millrace in advanced state of putrefaction for his body; Mattia Pascal, they concluded, has committed suicide. Delighted by this stroke of luck, he sets out to construct a new identity for himself until the disguises and lies he is forced to employ entangle him into another absurd and miserable relationship. He fakes suicide and returns to his hometown, where he finds that his wife has married his best friend and borne him a child. Twice dead, twice born, Mattia Pascal spends the rest of his days in a provincial library writing his memoir and mulling over the paradox that outside of the oppressive institutions of family, marriage, and love, there can be no life worth living.

This sounds like a gloomy tale, but that is not the way Pirandello tells it. He has a light touch and this translation by William Weaver does it full justice. "I have made a habit of laughing at all my misfortunes and torments," his hero says. Pirandello's characters tend to behave foolishly, which is to say, they are like most people we know. They scheme, cheat, fall in love, hate, make idiotic decisions, bad-mouth others, and occasionally have truly wise things to say. Whatever they are, they are unpredictable: like the eyebrows of one of the characters which he describes as always being ready to slip away. Most of Pirandello's stories and plays have a comic slant. In his polemic with Benedetto Croce, which began after he wrote an essay on humor, and which lasted many years, he rejected the philosopher's opinion that humor was an indefinable psychological state, a pseudo-concept, and not an aesthetic category. He thought there ought to be room for the comic and tragic in the same work. Pirandello called Copernicus one of the greatest humorists because he dismantled the image man had created of himself. In his hands the earth became a tiny ball, a grain of sand thrown at the universe. For the inventor of Mattia Pascal, the theory of laughter is a theory about reality.

Luigi Pirandello was born in 1867 in Agrigento, Sicily. His father was a former soldier under Garibaldi who made a fortune as a mining contractor. Pirandello's childhood was not a happy one. The atmosphere at home was permanently tense. His father was a moody man who suspected, correctly, that things were kept from him by the members of his family who lived in fear of his frequent rages at any real or imaginary challenge to his authority. As for his mother, Pirandello's biographer Gaspare Guiduce describes her as a mere shadow, a nervous one at that. After attending universities in Palermo and Rome, Pirandello did graduate work in philology in Bonn, Germany, with his father's generous support.

His first extended piece of writing was a dissertation in German about the Sicilian dialect in his hometown. This was rather unusual, since most of the young men from his part of Italy were sent abroad to study mining or engineering.

When it came to marrying, his behavior was much more conventional. He married a girl his father had picked out for him, a daughter of a business partner. During their courtship, they were allowed to see each other only in the presence of three or four other people. The women talked; the men sat in silence. Pirandello's future bride was forbidden to look her future husband in the face. They had three children. After years of suspicions that her husband was cheating on her and trying to poison her, his wife was declared insane and was committed to an institution for the rest of her life. In *The Late Mattia Pascal* all families have their troubles. As the Sicilian novelist Leonardo Sciascia said of Pirandello,

Love always retains a smell of death—not the idea of death, but the physical putrefying aspect of death. It is either tarnished by madness or poisoned by incomprehension and betrayal. Never do his characters abandon themselves to the emotions and the senses and there is not one woman, however beautiful, to whom the author does not give some repulsive characteristic.

Pirandello began as a poet, but then started writing stories, novels, and plays. His theatrical success didn't come till 1917 with the staging in Milan of *Right You Are (If You Think You Are)* and especially with *Six Characters in Search of an Author, Henry IV*, and *Tonight We Improvise*, the plays he wrote from 1921 to 1930. Famous directors regularly staged them, and in 1934 he won the Nobel Prize for Literature. But while Pirandello's plays were being produced all over Europe, Mussolini refused financial support to his Arts Theater in Rome, and Italian theatrical companies tended to ignore his work. Pirandello joined the Fascist Party in 1924 out of loyalty for the nationalist cause, but he remained an unconventional, unsettling writer. He was an anarchist at heart who did not believe in God, and though he hated democracy he displayed a genuine compassion for the weak. "Our spirits have their own private way of understanding one another, of becoming intimate, while our external persons are still trapped in the commerce of ordinary words, in the slavery of social rules," he writes. The most moving passages in *The Late Mattia Pascal* are the portraits of various characters the narrator encounters in his travels around Italy. What his compassion and humor have in common is a regard for individual quirkiness, the large and small fictions we uphold to maintain our human dignity.

Pirandello is a highly self-conscious and deliberate writer, but his aesthetics are without a system or preestablished formulas. In "A Warning on the Scruples of the Imagination," as he called the afterword to the 1921 reprint of *The Late Mattia Pascal,* he elaborates:

> For life, happily filled with shameless absurdities, has the rare privilege of being able to ignore credibility, whereas art feels called upon to pay attention to it. Life's absurdities don't have to seem believable, because they are real. As opposed to art's absurdities which, to seem real, have to be believable. Then, when they are believable, they are no longer absurd. An event in life may be absurd; a work of art, if it's a work of art, cannot be.
>
> It therefore follows that to criticize, in the name of life, a work of art for being absurd and unbelievable is sheer stupidity. In the name of art, yes. But not in the name of life.

My father used to tell us a story about taking my great-grandfather, a village blacksmith, to see Pirandello's *Six Characters in Search of an Author* in Belgrade in the late

1920s. To their surprise, as they walked into the theater, the curtain was already raised and there was no scenery. Eventually a few people dressed in everyday clothes started strolling around the stage and chatting about a play they were going to rehearse when they were interrupted by the arrival from the back of the auditorium of a family of six in deep mourning who demanded that they be allowed to tell their stories. When an actor disguised as a member of the audience and seated a few rows away yelled something at the stage, grandpa, who had no idea what was going on, stood right up. At his next outburst, he told the man to shut up and start behaving himself. The audience assumed that this was just more of Pirandello's tricks and applauded. According to my father, who remained silent throughout, the people continued to regard the disruption as part of the play even as grandpa, who continued shouting at the man, was being dragged out by the ushers.

Pirandello might well have been amused. The play breaks down; identities collapse and are reinvented. Life is always a comedy and a tragedy in the making. Mattia Pascal puts a wreath of flowers on his own grave. The tragedian yearns to stop time, to stand face to face with eternal truth; the comic spirit delights in a world forever made new by human folly. As Pirandello recognized, the two are often found under the same roof.

—CHARLES SIMIC

I. Foreword

One of the few things—perhaps the only one—that I know for certain is that my name is Mattia Pascal. I used to take advantage of this. Every now and then a friend or acquaintance was foolish enough to come to me asking for some suggestion or advice. I would shut my eyes slightly, shrug, and answer:

"My name is Mattia Pascal."

"Yes, yes, I know that much."

"And does it seem so little to you?"

To tell you the truth, it didn't seem a great deal to me either. But at that time I had no idea what it meant not to know even this much. I mean, not to be able to answer as before, when necessary:

"My name is Mattia Pascal."

Now some of you may feel like pitying me (pity costs very little), imagining the horrible suffering of a poor wretch who suddenly discovers that . . . that nothing, no father, no mother, no past or present. And some of you may also become indignant (that costs even less) about modern corruption, vice, the terrible times we live in, and all the harm that these can cause a poor innocent creature.

Well, go right ahead. But I feel it my duty to warn you that this isn't exactly my case. In fact, I could draw you a whole family tree, with the origins and ramifications of my line, and I could show you that I not only knew my father and mother, but can name my ancestors also and recount their deeds over a long period of time, even if not all of these were praiseworthy.

What am I talking about then?

This: my own case is far more strange and different. So different and strange that I am thinking of narrating it.

For about two years I was rat hunter, or if you prefer, librarian, of the library that a certain Monsignor Boccamazza left to our city when he died in 1803. Obviously this Monsignor was not familiar with the character and habits of his fellow citizens, or perhaps he hoped that, with time and accessibility, his bequest would kindle a love of reading in their spirit. So far, as I can personally testify, this love hasn't been kindled; and I say this in all praise of my fellow citizens. To begin with, the city authorities displayed so little gratitude to Boccamazza that they wouldn't erect a monument to him, not even a bust, and for many, many years they left the books piled up in an enormous damp cellar. From there the books were taken—you can imagine in what condition—and stored in the remote little church of Santa Maria Liberale, which for some reason or other had been deconsecrated. Here, without any discrimination, the books were entrusted, as a kind of benefice or sinecure, to some idler with influential friends. For two lire a day, he would sit and look at them. In fact he didn't even have to look at them; all he had to do was bear for a few hours a day the smell of mold and old age.

This fate befell me, too. From the very first day I conceived such a low opinion of books, printed or in manuscript (like some very ancient volumes in our library) that ordinarily I would never have decided to take up writing myself. But, as I said before, I feel that my story is truly strange and may serve as a lesson for some curious reader who might prove that the pious hope of Monsignor Boccamazza wasn't unfounded. That is, if such a reader happened to come to this library, to which I am bequeathing my manuscript on the condition that no one open it until fifty years after my *third, last,* and *definitive* death.

For the moment (and God knows how much it pains me), I have died already twice, but the first time was a mistake, and the second . . . well, you may read for yourself.

THE LATE MATTIA PASCAL

II. Second Foreword (Philosophical)
By Way of Being an Apology

The idea, or rather the suggestion that I should write this book was given me by my reverend friend, Don Eligio Pellegrinotto, the present librarian of the Boccamazza collection, to whom I will entrust this manuscript as soon as I have finished it, if I ever do.

I am writing it here in the deconsecrated church by the light that comes from a lantern up there in the dome. I sit in the apse, which is reserved for the librarian and is closed off by a low wooden railing, while Don Eligio sighs and goes on with the task he has heroically assumed of putting a little order into this veritable Babylon of books. I'm afraid he will never achieve anything. Before him, nobody bothered to give even a fleeting glance at the books' spines to form a rough idea of the volumes that the Monsignor had donated to the city; it was believed that all, or almost all of them, dealt with religious matters. Now Pellegrinotto consoles himself with the discovery that there is an enormous variety of subject matter in the Monsignor's collection, and since the books were taken at random from the storeroom and piled up in here in haste, the confusion is indescribable. Vicinity has forced among these books some singular friendships: Don Eligio told me, for example, that he had a hard time detaching the three volumes of an extremely licentious treatise, *Concerning the Art of Loving Women*, written in 1571 by Anton Muzio Porro, from a *Life and Death of Faustino Materucci, Benedictine of Polirone, Known to Many as "Blessed,"* a biography published in Mantua in 1625. The dampness had caused the bindings of the volumes to stick fraternally together. It is worth noting that the second volume of the licentious treatise discusses at length the life and amorous adventures of monks.

Perched all day long on a lamplighter's ladder, Don Eligio Pellegrinotto rummages among the shelves of the library. Every now and then he picks out a book and elegantly drops it down on the big table in the center of the nave. The church echoes, and a cloud of dust rises, as two or three spiders run off in fright. I hurry up from the apse, climbing over the railing; first I use the book to chase the spiders off the dusty table, then I open the volume and glance through it.

So, little by little, I have developed a taste for this kind of reading. Now Don Eligio tells me that my book should be composed along the lines of those that he is digging out of the library. According to him, it should have their special flavor. I shrug my shoulders and answer that such an effort is not for me. And besides, there is another reason which discourages me.

Covered with sweat and dust, Don Eligio climbs down the ladder and goes for a breath of air in the little garden that he has managed to cultivate here behind the apse, protected by a fence of stakes and spikes.

"Ah, my dear Reverend," I say to him, sitting on the low wall, my chin on the knob of my cane as he tends his lettuces, "this doesn't seem to me a time for writing books, not even in jest. For literature, as for everything else, I can only repeat my usual motto: *A curse on Copernicus!*"

"Oh, oh, what does Copernicus have to do with it?" Don Eligio exclaims, straightening up, his face flushed under his big straw hat.

"Copernicus has everything to do with it, Don Eligio. Before, when the earth didn't turn. . . ."

"Come now! The earth has always turned!"

"No, that's not true. Man didn't know it, and therefore it was as if it didn't turn. For many people it doesn't turn even today. I told this scientific fact the other day to an old peasant, and you know what he answered? He said it was only a

good excuse for drunkards. For that matter, you can't deny
that Joshua stopped the sun. But we'll skip this. What I say is
that when the earth didn't turn and man was dressed in Greek
or Roman clothes and looked so elegant in them and was so
aware of his own dignity, I can imagine that a detailed narration, full of tiny incidents, was agreeable. Doesn't Quintilian
say—as you taught me yourself—that history should be made
to be told and not to be experienced?"

"I can't deny that," Don Eligio answers, "but it's also true
that since, as you say, the earth has taken to turning, books
have become more and more detailed, filled with the most intimate particulars."

"Oh, I know! *The Count rose betimes, at exactly half past
eight . . . his wife, Madame la Comtesse, wore a lilac-colored
dress, richly adorned with laces at her throat . . . Teresina was
dying of hunger . . . love was breaking Lucrezia's heart. . . .*
For heaven's sake! What do I care about any of that? Are we
or are we not on a kind of invisible top, spun by a ray of sun-
shine, on a little maddened grain of sand, which spins and
spins and spins, without knowing why, never reaching an end,
as if it enjoyed spinning like this, making us feel first a bit of
heat, then a bit of cold, making us die—often in the awareness
that we have committed only a series of foolish acts—after
fifty or sixty spins? Copernicus, my dear Don Eligio, Copernicus has ruined humanity forever. We have all gradually become used to the new idea of our infinite smallness, and we
even consider ourselves less than nothing in the universe,
despite all our fine discoveries and inventions. What value can
information about our private troubles have, when even mass
disasters count for nothing? Our stories are like the biogra-
phies of worms. Did you read about that little calamity in the
Antilles? It's nothing. The earth, poor thing, grew tired of
spinning meaninglessly the way that Polish clergyman wanted,
and so it made a little gesture of impatience and puffed a bit
of fire out of one of its many mouths. Who knows what caused
that fit of pique? Perhaps the stupidity of men, who have

never been so boring as they are now. That's all. Several thousand worms roasted to death. And the rest of us go on. Who even mentions it now?"

Don Eligio Pellegrinotto, however, points out that no matter how hard we try to uproot and cruelly destroy the illusions that Nature has generously provided for our own good, we never succeed. Luckily, man is easily distracted.

This is true. Our city authorities, on certain nights indicated by the calendar, don't have the street lamps lighted and often—if the night is cloudy—we are left in the dark. This means that basically even today we believe that the moon is in the sky only to give us light at night, like the sun in the daytime, and the stars are there to afford us a magnificent display. Naturally. And we often gladly forget that we are infinitesimal atoms; instead we respect and admire one another and are even capable of fighting for a scrap of land or of grieving over certain things which, if we were really aware of what we are, would seem incalculably trivial.

Therefore, because of this distraction furnished by Providence and, as I have said, because of the strangeness of my case, I will tell about myself, but as briefly as I can, giving only the information I consider necessary.

Some of this information, to be sure, will not do me honor; but I am now in such an unusual condition that I can consider myself already outside of life and therefore without obligations or scruples of any kind.

I will begin.

III. The House and the Mole

At the beginning I said that I had known my father, but I spoke too soon. I didn't know him. I was four and a half when he died. He went off one day in a fishing boat of his to Corsica for certain business dealings and he never came back, killed by a malignant fever in three days at the age of thirty-eight. Nevertheless, he managed to leave us in easy circumstances: his wife and his two children, Mattia (that would be —and was—myself) and Roberto, two years my senior.

Some of the old men in the village still take pleasure in hinting that my father's wealth (which should no longer bother them, since it long ago passed into other hands) had origins that were . . . well . . . mysterious.

They say that he won it playing cards in Marseilles with the captain of an English merchant ship. This captain, after losing all the money he had with him, no small amount, also gambled away a large cargo of sulphur he had taken on in far-off Sicily for a merchant in Liverpool. (They even know the name of the city! Why not the merchant's as well?) When the empty ship set sail, the unlucky gambler drowned himself on the high seas, so the vessel landed in Liverpool relieved also of the weight of its captain. Luckily, it had for ballast the spitefulness of my fellow townsmen.

We owned various houses and farms. A wise and adventurous man, my father never had a permanent headquarters for his dealings. He was always traveling on his boat, buying merchandise of every kind where he found prices best and immediately selling it again where he could make a profit. Since he was never tempted into enterprises that were too grandiose or risky, he invested his earnings from time to time in land and houses here, in his own village, where perhaps he hoped soon to retire and enjoy his hard-earned comfort, peaceful and happy with his wife and children.

First he bought the stretch of land known as the Two Rivers, a rich plantation of olives and mulberries. Then the Hen Coop farm, also well-cultivated and with a fine stream which was later used for the mill. After that he bought the Spur, the best vineyard in our neighborhood, and finally San Rocchino, where he built a charming villa. In the town, besides the house where we lived, he bought two other houses and a whole block, now run-down and used as an arsenal.

His unexpected death spelled our ruin. My mother, incapable of administering the inheritance, had to entrust it to a manager. This man had received many kindnesses from my father, who had even bettered his material conditions, and my mother thought that he would at least feel some gratitude which—like his zeal and honesty—would cost him no sacrifice, since he was paid a generous salary.

My mother, that sainted woman! Shy and serene by nature, she had had little experience of life and of human dealings. When she spoke she seemed a little girl. She spoke with a nasal accent and she even laughed through her nose, because she pursed her lips when she laughed, as if she were ashamed. Frail by nature, after my father's death she was always in poor health, but she never complained of her suffering and I believe that she never thought about it, accepting it with resignation as a natural consequence of her loss. Perhaps she had expected to die of grief, and therefore she had to thank God for keeping her alive, even in pain, for the sake of her children.

With us, her tenderness was almost another illness, filled with alarm and anxieties. She wanted us always near her, as if she were afraid of losing us; and if one of us strayed off a little, she would send the maids to search through the large house.

She had abandoned herself blindly to her husband's guidance, and without him, she felt lost in the world. She never left the house any more except early on Sunday mornings to go to Mass in the church next door, accompanied by our two old maidservants, whom she treated as part of the family. At home, she lived only in three rooms, leaving all the others to the scarce attention of the servants and to our mischief.

In those rooms, the faded curtains, all the old-fashioned furniture gave off that special odor of aged things, like the breath of another time; and I remember that more than once I looked around with strange consternation at the silent immobility of those old objects which had stood there for so many years without any use, without life.

Among the people who most often visited my mother was a sister of my father's, a shrewish old maid, dark and proud, with a pair of ferrety eyes. Her name was Scolastica. When she came, she never stayed long because, as she talked, she would become furious at something and run off without saying good-by to anyone. As a boy, I was afraid of her. I used to stare at her, wide-eyed, especially when I saw her spring up in a rage and stamp her foot on the floor, shouting at my mother:

"It's hollow underneath. Can't you hear? The mole! The mole!"

She was referring to Malagna, our manager, who was secretly digging the graves beneath our feet.

Aunt Scolastica (I learned later) wanted my mother to take a husband again, at all costs. Usually sisters-in-law don't have such ideas and don't give such advice. But my aunt had a bitter, spiteful sense of justice; and it was for this reason, I believe, more than for love of us, that she couldn't bear to see Malagna stealing with impunity. Since my mother was utterly blind and helpless, Aunt Scolastica could think of no remedy but a second husband. And she even had a candidate, in the person of a poor man named Gerolamo Pomino.

This man was a widower with a son, who is still alive and is named Gerolamo like his father. He is a great friend of mine, indeed something more than a friend, as I will soon explain. From the time he was a child, he used to come to our house with his father, and he was the desperation of my brother Berto and myself.

His father, as a young man, had long aspired to the hand of Aunt Scolastica, who would have none of him as, for that matter, she would have none of anyone else. This was not because she didn't believe in love, but because the most remote suspicion that the man she loved could betray her, even in thought, would have driven her—as she used to say—to commit some crime. They were all false, for her, all men, rogues and deceivers. Even Pomino? No, to tell the truth, not Pomino. But she had realized this too late. With all the other men she succeeded in discovering some betrayal and took fierce pleasure in it. Only with Pomino, nothing; on the contrary, the poor man had been martyrized by his wife.

Why then didn't Scolastica now marry him herself? What a question! Why, because he was a widower! He had belonged to another woman and perhaps he might think of her occasionally. And then because . . . well, really! You could see it a hundred miles away, despite his shyness: he was in love, in love with . . . it was obvious with whom poor Signor Pomino was in love!

As you can imagine, my mother would never consent. It would have seemed to her a sacrilege. But perhaps, poor thing, she didn't even believe Aunt Scolastica was speaking seriously; and when her sister-in-law flew into a rage, my mother would laugh in that special way of hers, as she laughed at the exclamations of poor Signor Pomino who was present at those arguments during which the old maid shamelessly sang his praises.

I couldn't count the times he must have exclaimed, wriggling in his chair as if it were an instrument of torture: "Oh, merciful heavens!"

He was a neat, carefully dressed little man with mild blue eyes; I suspect that he used face powder and even had a weakness for putting a little rouge, just a touch, on his cheeks. He was very proud of having reached his age with all his hair, which he combed very carefully, parting it in the middle, and which he was always touching with his hands.

I don't know how our affairs would have gone if my mother, not for herself surely but for the future of her children, had followed Aunt Scolastica's advice and married Signor Pomino. They couldn't, however, have gone worse than they did, entrusted to Malagna (the mole!).

When Berto and I were grown, a great part of our possessions had already gone up in smoke; but we could have at least saved the rest from the clutches of that thief, and this would have allowed us to live without hardship, if not in luxury. We were both idle; we didn't want to bother our heads about anything, and as adults, we went on living the way our mother had accustomed us to live as children.

She hadn't even wanted to send us to school. A certain Tweezer was our tutor. His real name was Francesco, or Giovanni, Del Cinque; but everybody called him Tweezer, and he was so accustomed to the nickname that he even called himself Tweezer at times.

He was repulsively thin and terribly tall. He would have been even taller, but his body bent, just below his nape, drooping like a stalk that has grown beyond its strength. He had a slight hump, from which his neck seemed to struggle painfully, like the neck of a plucked chicken. His huge, protuberant Adam's apple was always bobbing up and down. Tweezer made an enormous effort to keep his lips and teeth shut tight, repressing, hiding, biting back a harsh, nervous little laugh he had. But his effort was, partially at least, in vain: the laughter trapped behind those clenched lips escaped through his eyes, more harsh and mocking than ever.

He must have seen many things in our house with those eyes, things that neither Mamma nor we boys ever saw. But he didn't speak up, perhaps because he felt it wasn't his duty to speak, or because—more probably, I think—he enjoyed himself secretly, venomously.

We could do anything we wanted with him; he allowed us to have our way. But then, as if to pacify his conscience, he would betray us, when we least expected it.

One day, for example, Mamma told him to take us to church. It was just before Easter, and we were to go to confession. After confession, a short visit to Malagna's sickly wife, then straight home. You can imagine how much fun that would be! As soon as we were in the street, we suggested an escapade to Tweezer: we would buy him a fine bottle of wine, if he would give up the idea of taking us to church and to Malagna's and let us go instead to Hen Coop farm to hunt birds' nests. Tweezer agreed with delight, rubbing his hands, his eyes flashing. He drank his wine, and then we went out to the farm. For nearly three hours he larked with us, helping us to climb trees, climbing them himself. But that evening when we came home, as soon as Mamma asked him if we had been to confession and to Malagna's:

"Well, Madam . . . I'll tell you . . ." he answered as boldly as you please. And then he told her everything we had done down to the tiniest detail.

We took our revenge on him for these acts of treachery, but it was of no avail. Still I remember that our tricks were nothing to joke about. One evening, remembering how Tweezer used to enjoy a doze on a seat in the entrance hall while he waited for supper, Berto and I furtively crept from our beds, where we had been sent early as a punishment, and found a narrow lead pipe a few inches long. We filled it with soapy water from the laundry tub and, with this weapon, cautiously approached him, put the pipe to his nostrils and—whoosh! He jumped almost to the ceiling.

You can easily imagine how far our studies progressed with a tutor like him. But the fault wasn't all on Tweezer's side. In his effort to teach us something—anything—he didn't bother about method or discipline and tried a thousand different

devices to hold our attention in some way. With me he often
succeeded, since I was of a more impressionable nature. But
his store of learning was curious, capricious, typical of him.
He was an authority on all kinds of pedantic verse, medieval
doggerel, macaronic poetry, strange burlesques and archaisms.
He would go on about alliterations and appositions, end
rhyme and internal rhyme, iambics and dactyls. And he composed more than his own share of foolish verses.

I remember one day at "San Rocchino," when he made us
recite over and over again a poem of his called "Echo," as we
faced the hill opposite us. It went:

> Has she a heart, my lady fair as snow?
> —*No.*
> What is she made of, what is her device?
> —*Ice.*
> Then tell me, Echo, my prize if I am true.
> —*Rue.*

He set us to solving all the ottava rima *Enigmas* of Giulio
Cesare Croce, the sonnets of Moneti, and poems, also in son-
net form, by some no-good who had the nerve to conceal himself behind the pen name of Cato of Utica. Tweezer had cop-
ied them all out in tobacco-colored ink on the yellow pages of
an old notebook.

"Listen to this one! Listen! It's by Stigliani. It's so beautiful . . . Can you guess the answer? Listen!"

> Both at one time, am I one, and two.
> Double I render what before was one.
> My one with your five gives two work to do,
> Against the many found upon man's crown.
> I am all mouth, upwards from my waist,
> And bite worse toothless than with teeth.
> I have two warring and opposed tastes:
> Fingers are in my eyes; and eyes are at my feet.

I can see him still, as he recited, joy bursting from his face, his eyes half-shut, his fingers delicately joined together.

My mother was convinced that what Tweezer taught us was enough for our educational needs, and she may have thought, when she heard us reciting the riddles of Croce or Stigliani, that we might even be growing too learned. But Aunt Scolastica felt differently. Since she failed to pass off her beloved Pomino on our mother, she started persecuting Berto and me. Thanks to our mother's protection, we paid no attention to our aunt, who became so furious that if she could have done it without being seen or heard, she would happily have skinned us alive. I remember once, when she was running off in one of her rages, she encountered me in an abandoned room. She seized my chin and held it tight in her fingers, saying: "Isn't he the handsome little man? Isn't he? Isn't he?" Then, as she spoke, she moved her face closer and closer, until her eyes were staring into mine. She uttered a kind of grunt then and let go of me, growling through her clenched teeth: "Dog-face."

She was especially hard on me, even though I certainly paid far more attention to Tweezer's crazy teaching than my brother Berto did. But she must have been irked by my calm, irritating face, with the huge, round spectacles that had been forced on me to straighten one of my eyes which, I don't know why, tended to gaze off in a different direction, on its own.

Those glasses were a torture for me. At one point I threw them away and let my eye look where it liked. Anyway, even if the eye had been straight, it wouldn't have made me handsome. I was bursting with health, and that was enough for me.

Perhaps, if a man were able to choose a nose suited to his face, or if when we saw a poor man burdened with a nose too big for his sunken cheeks, we could say: "That nose would suit me. I'll take it . . . ," perhaps, in that case, I might have changed my nose gladly, and my eyes, too, and other parts of me. But since I knew that this couldn't be done, I was resigned to my features and paid no attention to them.

Berto, on the other hand, handsome of face and body (compared to me, at least) couldn't tear himself away from the mirror, and preened and patted himself and wasted endless amounts of money on the latest neckties, the most exquisite perfumes, the finest linen and clothing. To spite him one day, I took from his wardrobe a shiny new dress coat, an elegant black velvet waistcoat, and an opera hat, then went off hunting in this attire.

Batta Malagna, in those days, was always coming to my mother to complain over the bad harvests, which were forcing him to incur onerous debts to meet our excessive expenses and to pay for the many repairs our farms constantly needed.

"Another hard blow," he would say every time, as he came in.

The fog had killed off the olives at the Two Rivers. Or phylloxera had destroyed the vines at the Spur; new American vines would have to be planted, since they were immune to the disease. That meant more debts. Then he advised us to sell the Spur, then the Two Rivers, then San Rocchino. All we had left were the houses and Hen Coop farm, with the mill. My mother was expecting him to come some day and announce that the stream had dried up.

It's true that we were idle and that we spent money recklessly; but it's also true that there will never be a more thieving thief than Batta Malagna on this earth. That's the least that I can say, considering the kinship that I was later forced to enter into with him.

He artfully saw to it that we never lacked for anything as long as my mother was alive. But that comfort, the free rein to every whim which he allowed us to enjoy, was useful in concealing the abyss ahead. When my mother died, it swallowed me up. But only me, since my brother was lucky enough to marry a rich wife in good time.

Whereas my own marriage . . .

"Don Eligio! Will I really have to talk about that, too? About my marriage?"

Up there, on his lamplighter's ladder, Don Eligio Pellegrinotto answers: "Of course. Naturally. But in a clean way . . ."

"Clean? You know perfectly well that . . ."

Don Eligio laughs, and the whole deconsecrated church laughs with him. Then he advises me: "If I were in your shoes, Signor Pascal, I'd first read a novella or two by Boccaccio or by Bandello. . . . To catch the right tone . . ."

Don Eligio thinks only of the tone. Uff! I'm just writing all this down as it comes.

Courage, then! Let's get on with it!

IV. This Is How It Started

One day, when I was out hunting, I saw a haystack,
dwarf-like, potbellied, with a saucepan on the top of its center pole. I stopped, fascinated.

"I know you," I said to the pile of straw, "Yes, I know
you . . ."

And all of a sudden I cried out: "You're Batta Malagna!"

I picked up a pitchfork lying there on the ground and stuck
it so zestfully into the stack's belly that the pan on top almost fell down from the pole. There was the living image of
Batta Malagna when, sweating and panting, he would go
around with his hat over one eye.

He seemed to be losing everything. On either side of his
long, fat face, his eyes and eyebrows seemed ready to slip away;
and his nose, too, drooped down over his silly mustache
and his goatee. His shoulders slid away from his neck; his
limp, enormous belly almost reached the ground. It was so
close, in fact, to his squat little legs, that his tailor—to cover
those legs—had to cut his trousers very liberally, and when you
saw Batta from a distance, it looked as if he were wearing a low
dress, his paunch dragging.

With a face and a body like that, how Batta Malagna managed to be a thief I'll never know. I should think that even
thieves would have to have a certain ease and stature, which
he seemed to me to lack. He used to walk slowly, with that
hanging paunch, his hands always clasped behind him; and
apparently with great effort he would produce a little whining voice. I'd like to know how he explained to his own conscience the thefts that he was carrying out against us all the

time. Since, as I've said before, he wasn't in real need, he must have given himself some excuse, some justification. What I say is this: perhaps he stole simply to have some pleasure in life, poor man.

In his heart of hearts, he must have been sorely tried by his wife, one of those women who know how to command a husband's respect.

He had made the mistake of picking a wife from a rank above his own, which was very low. Now if that woman had married a man of her own station, she probably wouldn't have been nearly so troublesome with him as she was with Batta, to whom she naturally had to demonstrate on every possible occasion that she came from a good family, and that in her home they did things in such and such a way. And Malagna obediently did things that way, too, just as she said, so that he too would look like a gentleman. But what an effort it was for him! He was always sweating. Always.

Moreover, just after their marriage, Signora Guendalina fell ill, with a disease of which she couldn't be cured, since the cure demanded a sacrifice beyond her strength. She would have had to give up those little truffle pastries she liked so much, not to mention other delicacies of the same nature and, worst of all, wine.

She didn't drink a great deal, naturally; she was of gentle birth, after all. But according to the doctors, she shouldn't have drunk a drop.

Berto and I, as young boys, were sometimes invited to dinner at the Malagna home. It was great fun to hear Batta, with all due respect, preach a sermon to his wife on continence, while she ate, or rather devoured, with downright voluptuousness, the most succulent dishes.

"Now myself," he would say, "I can't conceive how a person, for the brief pleasure the palate enjoys in swallowing a morsel like this—(*gulping down the morsel in question*)—should then suffer torments for a whole day afterwards. What's the use? I'm sure that, in that case, I'd feel ashamed of myself. Rosina!—(*calling the maid*)—Give me a little more! Mmm, this sauce is good!"

"I'll sauce you!" his wife snapped, venomously. "That's enough of that! The Lord should make you feel what it means to suffer from stomach trouble. Then you'd learn to have more consideration for your wife."

"Consideration? Why, Guendalina!" Malagna exclaimed, pouring himself some more wine.

His wife's only reply was to stand up, take the glass from his hand, and throw the wine out of the window.

"Why?" he moaned, amazed.

And his wife answered: "Because wine is poison to me! When you see me pour a drop into my glass, take it from me and pour it out of the window, just as I've done. Can't you understand?"

Malagna, smiling but mortified, looked first at Berto, then at me, then at the window and the glass. Finally he said: "Heavens, are you a child? Should I use violence? No, no, my dear . . . You should be rational, use self-control . . ."

"How?" his wife would shout. "With temptation always before my eyes? Watching you drink all that wine, licking your lips, and holding your glass up to the light, just to spite me? Don't tell me! If you were a different kind of husband, you wouldn't make me suffer . . ."

In the end, Malagna went even that far. He stopped drinking wine, to set his wife an example and to keep her from suffering.

And then . . . he stole. Of course, he did! He had to do something, didn't he?

But a short time later, he found out that Signora Guendalina was drinking wine on the sly. As if her husband's not knowing about it were enough to keep the wine from doing her harm. So Malagna also started drinking again, but outside the house, so as not to mortify his wife.

He went right on stealing, however. What he really wanted from his wife was a special compensation for the endless afflictions that she heaped on him; he wanted her one day to make up her mind to bring a son into the world. There it was! Then the stealing would have a motive. To what lengths won't we go, for the sake of our children?

But his wife wasted away from one day to the next, and Malagna didn't dare mention to her this ardent longing of his. Perhaps she was also sterile by nature. He had to be so considerate of her illness, too. And—God preserve us—what if she were to die of childbirth? Not to mention the risk of a miscarriage.

He resigned himself.

Was he sincere? He couldn't have made a greater display of sincerity when Signora Guendalina died. He wept for her, oh yes, he wept a great deal, and always remembered her with such respectful devotion that he would never put another lady in her place. Mind you, he could have found one easily enough, rich as he had become. No, he took a farmer's daughter: healthy, plump, strong, and jolly, selected solely because she seemed certain to produce the desired offspring. If Batta acted somewhat hastily . . . well, you must bear in mind that he wasn't a youngster any more and he didn't have any time to waste.

Oliva was the daughter of Pietro Salvoni, our farmer at Two Rivers. I'd known her well before her marriage.

Thanks to Oliva, I'd raised many hopes in my poor mother's heart: the hope that I had finally come to my senses, that I was beginning to take an interest in our land. Mother was beside herself with pleasure and satisfaction, poor thing.

But one day our terrible Aunt Scolastica opened her eyes for her: "Silly, haven't you noticed that he's always going to Two Rivers?"

"Yes, they're harvesting the olives."

"Don't be a fool: he's only after one Olive!"

After that, Mamma gave me a thorough talking-to: I

should beware of committing a mortal sin and leading a poor girl into temptation, to her eternal perdition, etc., etc.

But there was small danger of that. Oliva was pure; her purity was unshakable, in fact, because it came from the awareness of the mistake she would be making if she gave in. This awareness, on the other hand, freed her from any foolish pretense of shyness, of false modesty, so she could be very bold and frank.

How she used to laugh! Her lips were two cherries. And what teeth!

But never a kiss from those lips, not one. And from those teeth, only an occasional bite, to punish me when I seized her by the arms and refused to let her go until she let me kiss her at least on the hair.

No further.

Now, so beautiful, so young and fresh: the wife of Batta Malagna . . . Ah! Who is brave enough to refuse such strokes of luck? And yet Oliva knew very well how Malagna had become rich! She told me terrible things about him one day, and yet, precisely because of that wealth, she married him.

A year went by after the wedding, a second year, and still no children.

Malagna had always been convinced that his first wife had given him none because of her sterility or her long illness; he hadn't even the remotest suspicion that the responsibility might be on his side. And he began to grumble with Oliva.

"No signs?"

"No."

He waited another year, the third, again in vain. Then he started reproaching her openly; and finally, after still another year, now almost without hope, in his exasperation he began to maltreat her without any restraint. He shouted that her apparent healthiness was all a trick to deceive him, yes deceive! All he wanted her for was to have a child. That was why he had raised her to her present station, to a position that had formerly been occupied by a lady, a true lady whose memory he would never have offended, except for this reason.

Poor Oliva didn't answer him; she didn't know what to say. She often came to our house to unburden herself to my mother, who comforted her with kind words and urged her to keep on hoping, she was still young, very young: "Twenty?"

"Twenty-two . . ."

Well then! Couples had been known to have a child after ten years of marriage, even after fifteen.

Fifteen? But what about him? Batta was already old, and if . . .

Even during the first year Oliva had begun to suspect that, after all, between the two of them, the—How to say it?—the lack might be more his than hers, though he obstinately said it wasn't. But could it be proved? When she was married, Oliva had vowed that she would be a faithful wife; and now she refused to break that vow, even to regain her peace of mind.

How do I happen to know these things? Good question! As I said, she used to come to our house to unburden herself. And as I also said, I had known her before. Now I used to see her crying at the cowardly behavior of that repulsive old man, his stupid, provoking presumption . . . And . . . must I really tell everything? Well . . . the answer was no, and that's enough on the subject for the moment.

I quickly consoled myself. In those days I had—or thought I had—a head full of ideas. And I had money, which also inspires ideas that a young man without money wouldn't have. However, I had all too much help spending it from Gerolamo Pomino II, who was never sufficiently provided, thanks to his father's sage parsimony.

Mino was like our shadow, mine and Berto's in turn. And with his wonderful gift for aping, he changed according to whether he was tagging after Berto or after me. With Berto he became a dandy, and his father, who also aspired to elegance, loosened the purse strings a little. But Mino didn't last long with my brother. When Berto saw that even his walk was being imitated, he promptly lost patience, perhaps afraid of being made ridiculous, and maltreated poor Mino until he was driven off. Then Mino came back to me, and his father drew the purse strings tight again.

I was more patient with Mino because I had taken to enjoying myself at his expense. I repented afterwards. I realized that, in his admiring presence, I had outdone myself in some of my adventures, I had gone too far, exaggerated my feelings for the pleasure of dazzling him or getting him into trouble, for which naturally, I, also suffered the consequences.

Now one day when Mino and I were out hunting, we talked about Malagna. After I had narrated my former exploits with his wife, Mino told me that he had his eye on a girl, a cousin of Malagna's in fact, for whose sake he would go to any lengths. He was capable of anything, all right; and what's more, the girl herself didn't seem unwilling. But so far he hadn't even been able to speak to her.

"I'll bet you didn't have the nerve!" I said, laughing.

Mino denied the charge, but blushed too much in his denial.

"I've talked with the servant girl, though," he hastened to add, "and I've heard some good ones, too. You know something? She says that your friend Malagna—*Malanno* she calls him! Calamity!—is always hanging about the house, and she has a feeling he's planning some nasty trick, with the help of the old woman, his cousin, who's a witch."

"What kind of trick?"

"Oh, he's always going there to moan about his hard luck, about how he doesn't have any children. And the old woman, hard and sour as she is, tells him it serves him right. Apparently when Malagna's first wife died, the witch thought of making him marry her daughter and did everything she could to bring it off. Then, when she was balked, she said all kinds of things about the old monster, how he was an enemy of his own kin, betraying his own flesh and blood, etc., etc., and she even took it out on her daughter for not being smart enough to trap her uncle. Now the old man keeps saying how he regrets not having made his niece content . . . so who knows what treachery the mother may have thought up."

I covered my ears with my hands and yelled at Mino: "Shut up!"

I didn't look it, but in those days I was very ingenuous at heart. Still, when I learned about the scenes that had taken place—and were continuing—at Malagna's house, I thought there might be some grounds for the servant's suspicions. And, for Oliva's sake, I decided to see what I could find out, and I made Mino give me the old witch's address. Mino reminded me that the girl was for him.

"Don't worry!" I answered. "I'll leave her to you."

The next day, with the excuse of a bank loan which my mother happened to tell me fell due that day, I went to track down Malagna at the widow Pescatore's.

I ran all the way purposely, and burst inside, overheated and sweating.

"Malagna! The loan!"

If I hadn't already known about his guilty conscience, I'd have realized it beyond a doubt then, from the way he sprang to his feet, pale, overwhelmed, stammering: "Lo . . . loan? What loan?"

"The such-and-such bank loan, which falls due today . . . Mamma's sent me, she's so worried."

Batta Malagna fell back in his chair, exhaling in an endless *ah* all the fear that had gripped him for a moment.

"But that's been extended . . . all taken care of . . . My God, what a scare! . . . I renewed it for three months, paying the interest, of course. And you ran all the way here for such a trivial matter?"

He laughed and laughed, making his paunch shake. Then he invited me to sit down and introduced me to the women.

"Mattia Pascal. The widow Marianna Pescatore, my cousin. And her daughter Romilda, my niece."

He insisted I drink something, after all my running.

"Romilda, would you . . . ?"

As if he were in his own home.

Romilda stood up and looked at her mother as if conferring with her silently; then a moment later, despite my protests, she came back with a little tray bearing a glass and a bottle of vermouth. Annoyed at the sight of this, the widow promptly stood up and said to her daughter: "No, no, no . . . Give me that tray . . ."

She took it from Romilda's hands and went out, to come back in a short time with another tray, of lacquer, brand new; on it was some cordial in a magnificent decanter shaped like a silvered elephant, holding a glass barrel on his back, with a number of tinkling little glasses hanging around it.

I would have preferred the vermouth, but I drank the cordial. Malagna and the widow also drank some. Romilda didn't.

I stayed only a short while that first time, so that I'd have an excuse to come back. I said I was in a hurry to go home and reassure my mother about the loan, but I would come back in a few days to enjoy the ladies' company with more leisure.

From the way she said good-by I felt that the widow Marianna Pescatore received this announcement of my second visit with no great pleasure. She barely held out her hand: a cold hand, dry, knotty, yellowish; she lowered her eyes and pursed her lips. But her daughter made up for this with a friendly smile that promised a cordial welcome, and with a look, both sad and sweet, in those eyes which had made such a deep impression on me from the very beginning. Her eyes were of a strange green color, dark, intense, shaded by very long lashes. They were nocturnal eyes, between two bands of waved hair, black as ebony, which came down over her forehead and her temples, as if to set off the vivid whiteness of her skin.

The house was simple, but among the old pieces of furniture I noticed several recent additions, pretentious and clumsy in the display of their too-obvious newness: two great majolica lamps, for example, still intact, with globes of frosted glass in a strange shape, set on a humble console with a yellow-marble top, which also bore a grim mirror in a round frame, peeling here and there. In the room, that mirror seemed to open like a mouth yawning with hunger. And then, in front of the old and rickety sofa there was a little table with gilt legs and a top of brightly painted porcelain. Then a Japanese lacquer cabinet on the wall, etc., etc. Malagna's eyes rested on these new objects with evident pride, just as he had gazed at the decanter borne in triumph by his widowed cousin Pescatore.

The walls were almost entirely covered with old and not ugly prints. Malagna made me admire some of them, explaining that they were the work of Francesco Antonio Pescatore, his cousin, a distinguished engraver (who died, insane, in Turin, he added in a whisper). Then he showed me the engraver's portrait.

"He did it with his own hands, all by himself, standing in front of a mirror."

A short while before, when I had stared first at Romilda, then at her mother, I had thought: She must look like her father! Now, with his portrait before me, I no longer knew what to think.

I don't mean to make any offensive suppositions. In all honesty, I do believe the widow Marianna Pescatore capable of any wickedness. But how could I imagine a man—and a handsome one, at that—falling in love with her? Unless he was mad, even madder than her late husband.

I reported to Mino my impressions from that first visit. I spoke of Romilda with such warm admiration that he immediately was enflamed again, delighted that I had also liked her so much and that I approved.

I asked him what his intentions were. The mother, indeed, seemed a witch, but the daughter was an honest girl; I would have taken my oath on that. There was no doubt about

Malagna's evil aims; so the girl had to be saved, and as quickly as possible.

"But how?" Pomino asked, hanging spellbound on my words.

"How? We'll see. First of all we must investigate various things, we must study the situation, get to the bottom of it. You realize that we can't come to a decision like this on the spur of the moment. Leave everything to me. I'll help you. This adventure appeals to me."

"Yes . . . but . . ." Pomino then timidly objected, beginning to grow uneasy, seeing me so carried away. "You mean that . . . perhaps . . . I should marry her?"

"I haven't said anything, for the moment. Are you afraid to, by any chance?"

"No. Why?"

"Because it looks to me as if you're rushing things too much. Go slowly and reflect. If we discover that she really is what she should be: good, wise, virtuous (beautiful she certainly is, and you like her, don't you?) . . . Well then, suppose that she is really in serious danger, through that evil mother and that other monster . . . Suppose she is going to be a pawn in some vile bargain, some disaster . . . Would you hesitate to perform a noble deed, a holy mission of salvation?"

"Not I . . . Oh no!" Pomino said. "But . . . what about my father?"

"Would he object? On what grounds? Because of the dowry, is that it? There could be no other reason! Because— did you know this?—she's the daughter of an artist, an eminent engraver, who died . . . in the city, in Turin, yes, an excellent person! . . . But your father's rich, and you're his only son. To please you he could forget about the dowry. And besides, if you can't persuade him you needn't worry: a nice elopement will fix everything. Pomino, what is your heart made of? Straw?"

Pomino laughed, and then I promptly showed him how he was a born husband, the way others are born poets. I described in glowing, seductive colors the bliss of married life with his Romilda: her devotion, her attentions, the gratitude that she would feel for him as her savior.

And then I concluded: "Now . . ." I said to him, "you must find the way to make her take notice of you, so that you can talk to her or write her. Why, at a moment like this, a letter from you might seem a port in the storm, while that spider is weaving his web around her. In the meanwhile I won't stop going to the house. I'll keep my eyes open, and I'll try to find an opportunity to introduce you. Are we in agreement on this?"

"Yes."

Why was I displaying such eagerness to marry off Romilda? For no reason. As I said: it was for the fun of dazzling Pomino. I went on talking, talking, and all the difficulties vanished. I was impetuous, I made light of everything. Perhaps this was why women loved me, despite my slightly off-center eye and a body like a log. This time, however—I must confess—my enthusiasm also came from the desire to outdo that loathesome Malagna and destroy the trap he was setting. Then, too, there was the thought of poor Oliva and—why not?—the hope of doing a good turn for that other girl, who really had made a deep impression on me.

If Pomino was too timid to carry out my instructions, what fault is that of mine? And how am I to blame if Romilda, instead of falling in love with Pomino, fell in love with me, though I constantly talked to her about him? And finally, am I responsible if the widow Pescatore's treachery made me believe that my cleverness had soon overcome her distrust and even worked the miracle of making her laugh more than once at my scatterbrained remarks? Little by little, she seemed to lay down her arms. I found myself welcomed. I thought that, with a rich (I still believed myself rich) young man about the house, showing unmistakable signs of being in love with her daughter, the widow had finally abandoned her evil idea, if she had ever harbored one. You see: I had begun even to doubt its existence!

I admit, I should have suspected the fact that I never encountered Malagna again in her house and that, for some reason, she received me only in the morning. But who would have paid any attention to such things then? For that matter, it was only natural, because every day—to enjoy greater freedom of action—I suggested excursions into the country, and these are more pleasant in the morning. And also I had fallen in love with Romilda, though I continued to talk to her about Pomino's devotion. I was mad with love for those sweet eyes, that delicate nose, that mouth, everything, even a little wart that she had on the nape of her neck, and an almost invisible scar on her hand, which I kissed again and again and again . . . on Pomino's account . . . desperately.

Still perhaps nothing serious would have occurred, if one morning when we were at Hen Coop farm and had left her mother admiring the mill, Romilda hadn't felt that the joke about her timid, remote lover had gone on too long and if, as a result, she hadn't suddenly started sobbing, throwing her arms around my neck, trembling, pleading with me to have pity on her, to take her away anyhow, anywhere, so long as it was far from her house, far from that awful mother, from everything . . . at once, at once . . .

Far away? How could I immediately take her far away?

Afterwards, indeed, for several days, still intoxicated with her, I looked for a way, ready for everything, any respectable solution. And I was already beginning to prepare my mother for the news of my approaching marriage, now inevitable, a question of honor, but then—for no apparent reason—a very curt letter from Romilda arrived, telling me not to concern myself with her any more in any way, and never to come back to her house, since all relations between us were over forever.

No? How? What had happened?

That same day Oliva ran weeping into our house and announced to my mother that she was the unhappiest woman in the world, that the peace of her home was forever destroyed. Her husband had succeeded in proving it wasn't his fault that they had no children, and he had come to her, triumphant, with the news.

I was present at this scene. How I managed to control myself at that moment, I don't know. Only my respect for my mother restrained me. Choking with anger and disgust, I ran off and locked myself in my room, alone, tearing my hair and asking myself how Romilda, after what had occurred between us, could have lent herself to such an ignominious plot. Ah, worthy daughter of such a mother! The two women had not only basely deceived the old man, but me as well! Like her mother, Romilda had exploited me shamefully for her wicked ends, for her treacherous lust! And now poor Oliva! Ruined . . . ruined forever . . .

Still in a rage, that afternoon I went out, heading for Oliva's house, Romilda's letter in my pocket.

Oliva was in tears, packing her things. She would go back to her father, from whom until now she had prudently concealed all the torments she had been made to suffer.

"But what's the use of my staying here now?" she said to me. "It's all over! If he had at least taken up with some other girl, perhaps . . ."

"Then you know . . ." I asked her, "the girl he's gone with?"

She nodded several times, amid her sobs, then covered her face with her hands.

"A young girl . . ." she exclaimed, raising her arms in horror. "And the mother! The mother agreed to it! The girl's own mother, you understand?"

"I know . . ." I said. "Here. Read this . . ."

I handed her the letter.

Oliva looked at it, dazed. As she took it, she said: "What does it mean?"

She barely knew how to read. Her eyes asked me if it were really necessary for her to make such an effort at a time like this.

"Read it," I insisted.

She dried her eyes, unfolded the sheet of paper, and began to decipher the writing, slowly, syllable by syllable. After the first few words, she glanced at once at the signature, then looked at me, opening her eyes wide: "You?"

"Give it here," I said. "I'll read the whole thing to you."

But she pressed the paper to her breast.

"No!" she cried. "I won't give it back to you! I know how to use this now!"

"How can you use it?" I asked her, with a bitter smile. "Do you mean to show it to him? But there isn't a word in this whole letter to prevent your husband from believing what he is overjoyed to believe. They've trapped you good and proper, that's all there is to it."

"Oh, you're right, you're right!" Oliva moaned. "He came at me, threatening to beat me and he shouted that I should never dare question the honor of his niece!"

"Well?" I said, with a bitter laugh. "You see? You won't get anywhere by denying it. You mustn't! You must say yes, of course, it's true that he can have children, and then . . . You understand?"

Now why, a month later, did Malagna furiously beat his wife and, still foaming at the mouth, rush to my house and shout that he demanded satisfaction at once, I had to make amends because I had dishonored and ruined a poor orphan girl? He added that originally, to avoid a scandal, he had preferred to remain silent. Out of pity for the poor girl, and since he was childless, he had decided to keep the child, when it was born, as his own. But now God had finally given him the consolation of having *a legitimate child, by his own wife*, and he couldn't, no, in all conscience, he couldn't act as father for that other child that was going to be born to his niece.

"Mattia, make amends! Mattia, act!" he concluded, choking with fury. "And right now! Obey me at once! And don't force me to say another word, or do anything desperate!"

At this point, let's try to think rationally for a moment. I've been through all sorts of things in my time. To pass for an imbecile or for . . . worse . . . would be no great misfortune for me. As I've told you, I am outside of life, and nothing matters to me any more. So if, at this point, I choose to discuss the situation, it's merely for the sake of logic.

It seems obvious to me that Romilda hadn't had to do anything really evil, not to deceive her uncle at least. Otherwise why had Malagna promptly beaten his wife and reproached her for her betrayal, then come to blame me in front of my mother for dishonoring his niece?

In fact, Romilda insists that, shortly after our excursion that day, she confessed to her mother the love that was now an indissoluble bond between us. Her mother flew into a rage and shouted that she would never, never agree to her daughter's marrying an idler, already on the brink of ruin. And since Romilda, acting on her own initiative, had done herself the worst harm that could befall a girl, her mother now had only one course left: to exploit the situation as best she could. It was easy to imagine what she had in mind. When Malagna came at the usual hour, the widow went away on some pretext and left her daughter alone with the uncle. Then Romilda —she says—threw herself, weeping hot tears, at the man's feet, explaining her misfortune and telling what her mother wanted of her. She begged him to intervene and persuade her mother to a more honest course, since her heart belonged to another and she wanted to remain true to him.

Malagna was moved—up to a point. He reminded Romilda that she was still a minor, and therefore under the authority of her mother, who—if she wished—could take action against me, even legally. But in all conscience he, too, couldn't approve her marriage with a no-good like me, a brainless wastrel, and therefore he couldn't advise her mother to allow such a thing. He said the girl would have to sacrifice something to her mother's just and natural indignation, and this sacrifice, after all, would be the making of her. He ended by saying that all he could do—on condition that the maximum secrecy be observed—would be to provide for the infant, act as father to it, since he had no children of his own and had long wished for one.

Now I ask you: Can a man be more straightforward than that?

There it was: everything he had robbed from the father he would restore to the expected child.

What fault was it of his, if like a worthless ingrate, I then went and spoiled all his plans?

Two! Ah, no, by God! Not two!

Two children were one too many, from his point of view. Because, since Roberto—as I've already said—had made a good marriage, Malagna felt that the harm he had done wasn't so great that he should make amends doubly.

The conclusion was self-evident: in the midst of all these fine people, I was the one who had caused the damage. And therefore I was the one who had to pay.

At first I refused, indignantly. Then, exhorted by my mother, who already foresaw our family's ruin and hoped that by marrying her enemy's niece, I might somehow be saved, I gave in and married Romilda.

But over my head still hung the terrible wrath of Marianna, the widow Pescatore.

V. Ripening

The witch couldn't resign herself:

"You see what you've brought about?" she kept asking me. "Wasn't it enough for you to worm your way into my house like a thief, to seduce my daughter and ruin her? Wasn't that enough for you?"

"Ah, no, my dear mother-in-law!" I answered. "Because if I'd stopped there, I'd have been helping you, doing you a favor . . ."

"You hear?" she screamed at her daughter. "He's bragging . . . He dares to brag about his great feat with that other . . ." and here she added a string of horrible words on the subject of Oliva. Then, her hands on her hips, elbows akimbo: "What have you achieved, after all? Haven't you ruined your own child this way? Oh, but what does he care? The other one is his, too . . ."

She never failed to add this dash of venom at the end, knowing its powerful effect on Romilda, jealous of the child that was to be born to Oliva in ease and luxury, whereas her own would come into an insecure, straitened world, in the midst of all this warfare. Her jealousy was fanned by the news that the good ladies, our neighbors, came to bring her, pretending not to know anything; they kept telling her about her Aunt Malagna who was so pleased, so happy that God had finally answered her prayers. Ah, the Signora Oliva was like a flower, yes, she had never been so beautiful, so plump and healthy!

There was Romilda, on the other hand, always slumped in a chair, racked by constant fits of nausea, pale, disheveled, ugly, with never a moment of good health, refusing to talk or even to open her eyes.

Was this also my fault? Apparently. She couldn't bear the sight of me, or the sound of my voice. But the worst was yet to come, when—to save Hen Coop farm and the mill—we had to sell our houses in town, and my poor mother was forced to come share the inferno of my household.

Of course, the sale did no good at all. Malagna, with his heir on the way, now felt no restraint or scruple, and he achieved his final treachery. He made an agreement with the moneylenders, and without revealing his name, he bought in all our houses for a few pennies. So the debts that burdened the farm and the mill remained more or less as they were, and both were put into the hands of receivers by our debtors. We were out of it.

Now what was to be done? Almost without hope, I began looking for some kind of occupation, to provide for the family's most pressing needs. I was no good at anything, and the reputation I had won by my youthful exploits and my idleness certainly didn't inspire anyone to give me a job. The daily scenes I had to witness or take part in at home robbed me of the calm I needed to collect my wits and think about what was to be done.

I was truly horrified at the sight of my mother in contact with the widow Pescatore. The sainted old lady was no longer unaware of her wrongs, but in my eyes she was in no way responsible for them. She just couldn't grasp the full extent of human wickedness. She remained sitting in a corner, all closed in herself, hands in her lap, eyes cast down, as if she weren't quite sure she could stay there, as if she were expecting to leave any moment—God willing! And she didn't bother a fly. She smiled, piteously, every now and then at Romilda, not daring to approach her because once, a few days after she had come into our house, Mamma had hurried to help Romilda and had been rudely pushed away by the old witch.

"I'll do it. I know what's to be done."

Since Romilda really did need help at that moment, I remained prudently silent, but I kept my eyes open to make sure no one was disrespectful to my mother.

I soon realized that the guard that I kept over Mamma secretly irritated the witch and even my wife, and I was afraid that when I was out of the house, the two of them might maltreat her, to vent their annoyance and empty the bile from their hearts. I was certain, too, that my mother would never have told me about it. And this thought tortured me. Time and again I looked into her eyes, to see if she had been crying! She would smile at me, caressing me with her gaze, then ask:

"Why are you looking at me like that?"

"Are you all right, Mamma?"

She would make a fleeting gesture towards me and answer: "I'm all right, can't you see? Go to your wife. Go on. She's suffering, poor girl."

I finally wrote Roberto in Oneglia and asked him to take Mamma into his house for a while—not to be relieved of a burden that I would happily have borne even in my present difficulties, but solely for her own good.

Berto answered that he couldn't. He couldn't because his position with regard to his wife's family and even to his wife herself was very painful now, after our financial downfall. He was living on his wife's dowry and therefore couldn't also impose her mother-in-law on her. For that matter—he added —Mamma would perhaps have been in an equally awkward position in his home, because he too lived with his mother-in-law, an excellent woman, but one who might turn jealous in the inevitable friction between two rival mothers. So it was best for Mamma to stay at my house; there she would at least spend her last years in her own town and she wouldn't be forced to change her habits and her way of life. Berto also said how sorry he was that, for the reasons mentioned above, he couldn't offer me even a token financial assistance, though he would have liked to, with all his heart.

I hid this letter from Mamma. Perhaps if my embittered

spirit at that moment hadn't beclouded my judgment, I wouldn't have been so outraged. I could, for example, have considered, according to my naturally reflective nature, that if a nightingale gives away its tail feathers it can say: I still have my gift of song; but if you make a peacock give away its tail feathers, what does he have left? To destroy the delicate position that had probably cost Berto so much effort, the equilibrium that allowed him to live with a show of dignity on his wife's money, would have been an enormous sacrifice for him, an irreparable loss. Beyond his respectable appearance, his fine manners, his elegant-gentleman façade, Berto had nothing to give his wife, not even a crumb of affection, which would probably have compensated her for any trouble that my poor mother's presence would have caused. Well, that's how God made him; God gave him only a tiny scrap of a heart. What could poor Berto do about it?

Meanwhile our hardships were increasing, and I couldn't find any solution to them. Mamma's jewelry, precious keepsakes, were sold. Afraid that my mother and I would soon be forced to live on her dowry interest of forty-two lire per month, the widow Pescatore became grimmer and nastier every day. I could tell that her fury might break out at any moment; it had now been repressed for too long, perhaps because of Mamma's presence and manner. As that tempest of a woman saw me darting around the house like a fly without a head, she hurled looks at me that were flashes of lightning, announcing the coming storm. I would leave the house for a while to remove the electricity and prevent the explosion, but then I would begin to fear for Mamma and I would go home again.

One day, however, I didn't get there in time. The storm had finally burst, caused by an utterly trivial incident: two old maidservants had paid Mamma a visit.

One of them, who had been unable to save any of her earnings since she had to keep a widowed daughter with three children, had easily found a place elsewhere on leaving us.

But the other, Margherita, alone in the world, was more fortunate and could look forward to a comfortable old age thanks
to the little nest egg saved up during her years of service in
our house. Now it seems that talking with these two good-
hearted old women, Mamma little by little began to complain
about her wretched condition. Then Margherita, who had
suspected the situation but hadn't dared say anything about
it, promptly invited Mamma to come and stay with her. She
had two neat little rooms with a tiny flower-filled terrace
overlooking the sea; the two of them could live there together
in peace. Margherita would be happy to be able to wait on
Mamma again, to show the affection and devotion she felt
towards her former mistress.

Could my mother accept the offer of that poor old woman?
Whence the wrath of the widow Pescatore?

When I came home, I found the widow shaking her fists at
Margherita, who was bravely confronting the witch, while
Mamma, terrified, tears in her eyes, was clutching the other
old servant with both hands, as if seeking refuge.

At the sight of my mother in this situation, I lost my head.
I seized the widow Pescatore by one arm and sent her sprawl-
ing across the room. She was on her feet in a moment and
after me, ready to fight back. But when she was facing me,
she stopped.

"Out!" she cried. "You and your mother both! Get out of
my house!"

"Listen," I said to her in a voice that trembled from the violent effort I was making to control myself. "Listen: you
get out yourself! Here and now, on your own two legs, and
don't cross my path again. Get out, for your own good! Out!"

Weeping and screaming, Romilda rose from the armchair
and threw herself in her mother's arms. "No! Stay with me,
Mamma! Don't leave me! Don't leave me here alone!"

But that worthy mother thrust her away, furious: "You
wanted him, didn't you? Now keep him, this thief of yours!
I'm going away alone!"

But she didn't go away, obviously.

Two days later, after a visit—I presume—to Margherita, Aunt Scolastica appeared in a great furor, as usual, to take Mamma off with her.

This scene deserves to be narrated in full.

That morning the widow Pescatore was making bread, her arms bared, her skirt drawn up and tied around her waist so it wouldn't be soiled. She barely turned around when she saw my aunt come in and she went on sifting as if nothing had happened. My aunt didn't notice; for that matter she came in without greeting anybody, and went straight to my mother as if she were alone in that house.

"Get your clothes on! We're leaving at once! You're coming with me! I've heard what's going on! And here I am. Hurry up now! Collect your belongings!"

She spoke in jerks. Her proud beaklike nose in her dark, liverish face, seemed to quiver and twitch, as her eyes flashed sparks.

The widow Pescatore didn't utter a sound.

When she had finished sifting, when she had wet the flour and made the dough, she brandished it high above her head and slammed it down hard, purposely, on the kneading trough. This was her only answer to what my aunt was saying. Aunt Scolastica became more insistent, while the witch banged the dough harder and harder as if to say: "*Why yes!* —*Why, of course!*—*Naturally!*—*To be sure!*" Then, as if this weren't enough, she went to get the rolling pin and set it down there on the trough, meaning: I have this, too.

That was the last straw! Aunt Scolastica sprang to her feet, furiously took off the shawl she had around her shoulders and hurled it at my mother: "Take this! Leave everything else behind! Out of here this minute!"

Then she went over to confront the widow Pescatore. The latter, to avoid having Scolastica face to face, took a step backwards, menacingly, as if she planned to wield her rolling pin. Aunt Scolastica, with both hands, took the huge mound of dough from the trough, stuck it on the widow's head, and pulled it down over her face, and pushed at the mass with clenched fists, there . . . there . . . there . . . on the nose, the eyes, into the mouth, wherever it would go. After that, she seized my mother by the arm and dragged her off.

The next scene was all mine. The widow Pescatore, roaring with anger, ripped the dough from her face, from her sticky hair, and threw it at me, while I laughed, in a kind of convulsive hilarity. She seized my beard, scratched me all over. Then, as if she had gone mad, she threw herself on the floor and began to rip off her clothes, rolling over and over frantically on the tiles. Meanwhile in the other room, my wife (*sit venia verbo*) was retching amid piercing screams, as I shouted at the widow Pescatore, on the floor: "Your legs! Your legs! Don't show me your legs, for heaven's sake!"

I may say that, from that day on, I have made a habit of laughing at all my misfortunes and torments. At that moment I saw myself as an actor in a tragedy that could hardly have looked more comical: my mother had run out with that madwoman; my wife was in the other room busy . . . we'll skip that! Marianna Pescatore there on the ground; and I myself . . . not knowing where to turn for my daily bread. I was quite literally without bread for the morrow. My beard was all floury, my face scratched and wet—whether with blood or tears of laughter I didn't yet know. I went to the mirror to examine myself. The wet came from tears, but I was also thoroughly scratched. Ah that eye of mine, how I liked it at that moment! Out of sheer desperation, it had begun to look off in the wrong direction more than ever, gazing into the distance on its own account. And I ran out, determined not to go back into that house until I had found a way to keep my wife and myself, however poorly.

As I thought of my long years of foolishness with angry contempt, I came to the easy conclusion that my neighbors would not only fail to sympathize with my plight—they wouldn't even take it into consideration. I deserved no better. There was only one person who should have had pity on me: the man who had stolen everything we owned. But can you imagine Malagna feeling obliged to come to my aid, after what had happened between us?

Aid did come, however, and from the person I would least have expected to help me.

After staying out of the house all that day, towards evening I happened to run into Pomino. He pretended not to see me and tried to walk on.

"Pomino!"

He turned around and stopped, with a grim expression, his eyes cast down: "What do you want?"

"Pomino!" I repeated, in a louder voice, gripping his shoulder and shaking it, laughing at his sulkiness. "Are you serious?"

Oh, human ingratitude! He bore me a grudge. A grudge! Because of what he considered my treachery towards him. I couldn't convince him that, on the contrary, he was the one who had betrayed *me*, and that he shouldn't merely thank me, but should throw himself on the ground and kiss the place where I had trod.

I was drunk on the bitter hilarity that had seized me when I looked at myself in the mirror.

"You see these scratches?" I said to him, at a certain point. "She gave them to me!"

"Ro— I mean, your wife?"

"Her mother!"

And I told him the why and the wherefore. He smiled, but only faintly. Perhaps he thought that the widow Pescatore would never have given him those scratches; his condition was quite different from mine, and his was a different nature, a different heart.

I was then tempted to ask him why, if he was really so grieved, he hadn't married Romilda himself when he still had time, even running off with her, as I had advised him before his ridiculous shyness or his indecision had unfortunately caused me to fall in love with her. And there were other things, too, plenty of them, that I wanted to say to him in my emotional state at the time. But instead I held out my hand and asked him whom he was seeing those days.

"Nobody!" he sighed. "Nobody at all. I'm bored to death."

From the exasperation with which he uttered these words I all of a sudden began to understand the real reason for Pomino's sadness. He didn't so much regret the loss of Romilda as he did the companionship he now missed. Berto had gone off. Pomino couldn't hang around with me because Romilda was between us, so what could the poor fellow do?

"Get married, my boy!" I said to him. "Then you'll see how jolly married people are!"

But he shook his head, gravely, his eyes shut. He held up his hand: "Never! Never!"

"Good for you, Pomino! Stick to it! If you want company, I'm at your disposal, even till tomorrow morning!"

And I explained to him my resolution on leaving the house, and I described my desperate situation. Like a true friend, Pomino was moved, and he offered me what little money he had with him. I thanked him from the bottom of my heart, but said that such help was of no use to me: the next day I'd be back where I started. I needed a steady position.

"Wait a minute!" Pomino then exclaimed. "Did you know that my father's in City Hall now?"

"No, but I might have guessed."

"He's the City Councilor for Education."

"That I'd never have guessed!"

"Last night at dinner . . . Wait! Do you know Romitelli?"

"No."

"What do you mean, no? He works down there at the Boccamazza library. He's deaf, almost blind, senile, and he can hardly get around any more. Last night at dinner my father was saying that the library's in terrible shape and that

something should be done about it at once. There's the job
for you!"

"Librarian?" I exclaimed. "But I—"

"Why not?" Pomino said. "If Romitelli could do it . . ."

His reasoning convinced me.

Pomino suggested I have Aunt Scolastica talk to his father
about it. That would be the best course.

The next day I went to visit Mamma and I talked about it
to her, since Aunt Scolastica refused to lay eyes on me. So,
four days later, I became librarian. Sixty lire per month. Richer
than the widow Pescatore! At last I could crow over her!

For the first months it was almost fun with old Romitelli
who couldn't be made to understand that City Hall had put
him out to grass and therefore he shouldn't come to the library any more. Every morning at the same hour, not a moment earlier nor a moment later, I saw him appear on his four
legs (counting the two canes, one in each hand, which served
him better than his feet did). As soon as he arrived, he took an
old copper turnip from his pocket and hung it on the wall with
its impressive length of chain. Then he would sit down, the
canes between his legs, take his nightcap from another pocket,
his snuffbox, and a big handkerchief with red and black checks.
He would thrust a generous pinch of snuff into his nostrils,
wipe his nose, then open the drawer of the table and take out
one of the library's books: *Historical Dictionary of Musicians,
Artists and Amateurs, Living and Dead*, printed in Venice
in 1758.

"Signor Romitelli," I used to shout at him, seeing him
perform all these operations with the utmost calm, without
the slightest sign that he was aware of my presence.

But why was I shouting? He couldn't have heard a cannonade. I shook his arm, and he turned, blinked, pursing his
whole face to peer at me. He bared his yellow teeth in what
perhaps was meant as a smile, then he would lower his head
on the book, as if it were a pillow, but oh no! that was the
way he read, with the page an inch from his face. He read
aloud, with one eye closed:

Birnbaum, Giovanni Abramo . . . Birnbaum, Giovanni Abramo printed . . . Giovanni Abramo printed in Leipzig in 1738 . . . Leipzig in 1738 . . . a pamphlet in octavo . . . in octavo . . . entitled Impartial Observations on a Delicate Passage of the Critic-Musician. *Mitzler . . . Mitzler included . . . included this work in the first volume of his Musical Library. In 1739 . . .*

And he would go on and on like this, repeating names and dates two or three times, as if to memorize them. Why he read in such a loud voice I don't know. As I said, he couldn't have heard a cannonade.

I used to watch him in amazement. Why should a man in his condition, on the brink of the grave (in fact he died four months after my appointment as librarian), care what Birnbaum Giovanni Abramo had had printed in Leipzig in 1738 in octavo? If only this reading hadn't cost him such an effort! Apparently he was unable to do without those dates and those pieces of information about musicians (and he himself, so deaf!) and artists and amateurs, living and dead before the year 1758. Or did he perhaps think that, since a library is made for reading, and since no other living soul ever turned up there, the librarian himself was obliged to read? Perhaps he had just picked that book up at random, and he might as easily have chosen another. He was so senile that this supposition is possible, indeed much more probable than the first.

Meanwhile on the large central table there was a layer of dust at least an inch thick, so thick that—to compensate somehow for my fellow citizens' ingratitude—I could trace in big letters the following inscription:

TO

MONSIGNOR BOCCAMAZZA

HIS FELLOW CITIZENS

DEDICATE THIS PLAQUE

TESTIFYING

THEIR ETERNAL GRATITUDE.

From time to time, a book or two would crash from the shelves, followed by rats as fat as rabbits.

To me they were like Newton's apple.

"Eureka!" I shouted happily. "There's something for me to do while Romitelli is reading his Birnbaum."

To begin with, I wrote an elaborate official memorandum to the illustrious Cavalier Gerolamo Pomino, City Councilor for Education, requesting that, with the greatest urgency, the Boccamazza or Santa Maria Liberale Library be provided with a minimum of two cats, whose upkeep would not represent a financial burden on the city, since the above-mentioned animals would be able to feed themselves handsomely on the proceeds of their hunting. I added that it might be wise to supply the library also with half a dozen traps and the wherewithal to bait them, avoiding the word *cheese*, a vulgar word which—as a subordinate—I didn't feel it was proper to write to the Councilor for Education.

First they sent me two kittens, so miserable that they were immediately frightened by those huge rats and—to keep from dying of starvation—they immediately took shelter in the traps and ate up the cheese. I found them imprisoned in there every morning, scrawny and ugly, so mournful that they seemed to lack the strength or the will to mew.

I lodged a complaint and this pair was replaced by two big handsome tomcats, quick and earnest, who promptly set about doing their duty. The traps were useful, too, and they provided me with rats still alive. Now, one evening, irked by the fact that Romitelli refused to recognize my labors and my victories, as if he was obliged only to read the books as the rats were there to eat them, I decided to place two live rats in the drawer of his table before leaving the library. I hoped to distract him, for at least the following morning, from his habitual, boring reading. Not at all! When he opened the drawer and felt those two beasts slip past his nose, he turned towards me (I was exploding with laughter, unable to contain myself) and asked: "What was that?"

"Two rats, Signor Romitelli!"

"Ah, rats . . ." he said calmly.

They were at home there; he was used to them, and he went back to the reading of his dreary book as if nothing had happened.

In a *Treatise on Trees* by Giovan Vittorio Soderini one reads that fruits ripen "in part through heat and in part through cold; wherefore the heat, manifest in all, operates in a cooking fashion, and is the simple, first cause of ripening." Giovan Vittorio Soderini, however, was unaware that, in addition to heat, fruiterers have invented another *first cause of ripening*. In order to carry early fruit to the market and sell it at high prices, they gather apples or peaches or pears before they have reached the stage which makes them sound and flavorsome, and the vendors ripen them by the simple expedient of bruising them.

And this was how my spirit, still green, ripened to its maturity.

In a short time I became a different man. After Romitelli's death, I found myself here alone, devoured by boredom, in this remote little church, among all these books, terribly lonely and yet with no desire for company. I could have stayed here only a few hours each day, but I was ashamed to show myself, in my poverty-stricken state, in the streets of the town. I fled my house as if it were a prison; better here in the library, I used to say to myself. But what could I do? Yes, hunt rats, but would that be enough for me?

The first time I happened to find myself holding a book, taken at random, unconsciously, from one of the shelves, I shuddered with horror. Was I becoming like Romitelli? Was I beginning to feel obliged, as librarian, to read in the place of all the others who never came inside the library? I flung the book to the floor. But then I picked it up and—yes, that's right—I started reading, too, and also with only one eye, because that other eye of mine would have none of it.

I read in no order, a bit of everything, but especially books of philosophy. They weigh a great deal, and yet the man who is fed on them and digests them lives among the clouds. They made my brain—already confused—even more distracted. When my head was spinning, I would close the library and climb down a steep path to a little stretch of lonely beach.

The sight of the sea plunged me into a kind of dazed horror, which gradually turned into intolerable oppression. I sat on the beach and forbade myself to look at the water, hanging my head; but I could hear its crashing all along the coast, as I slowly sifted the heavy, thick sand through my fingers and murmured: "On and on, like this, until I die, with never any change, never . . ."

The immobility of my existence inspired me with sudden, strange thoughts, like flashes of madness. I sprang to my feet, as if to shake them off, and started walking along the shore; but then I had to look, there at the sand's edge, at the sea endlessly bringing its somnolent, flaccid waves. I could see the deserted sands, and I shouted with anger, shaking my fists: "But why? Why?"

And I got my feet wet.

The sea sent a wave or two farther on to the beach, as if to warn me:—You see, my friend, what happens when you start asking the why of certain things? You get your feet wet. Back to your library! Salt water will rot your shoes, and you don't have money to throw away. Go back to your library, but avoid those books on philosophy. You, too, should start reading how Birnbaum Giovanni Abramo had printed in Leipzig in 1738 a pamphlet in octavo. That kind of reading will be much more profitable for you.—

But finally they came one day to tell me my wife was in labor and I was to run home at once. I darted out like a deer, but it was more to flee from myself, to avoid being left alone even for a moment to reflect that I was about to have a child —in my situation—a child!

When I reached my door, my mother-in-law grabbed my

shoulders and spun me around: "A doctor! Hurry! Romilda's dying!"

A piece of news like that, point-blank, is enough to freeze you fast on the spot, isn't it? And instead: "Run! Hurry!" I couldn't feel my legs any more. I didn't know which way to turn, and as I managed somehow to run on, I kept saying: "A doctor! A doctor!" The people stopped in the street and wanted me to stop too, to explain what had happened to me. I felt them tugging at my sleeves. I saw pale, worried faces before mine. But I brushed everyone aside: "A doctor! A doctor!"

And meanwhile the doctor was already there, back at my house. When I returned, desperate and furious, gasping for breath, after having been to every pharmacy in town, the first little girl was already born, and they were battling to bring the other into the world.

"Two!"

I can see them still, there in the crib side by side; they scratched at each other with those little hands, so delicate and yet turned into claws by some savage instinct which filled me with pity and horror. Two wretched, wretched little creatures, more miserable than the kittens I used to find in my traps every morning. And like the kittens, these two hadn't the strength to cry. Still they clawed!

I moved them apart, and at the first touch of that tender, cold flesh, I shuddered again, an ineffable tremor of tenderness: they were mine!

One of them died a few days later. The other chose to give me time to love her, with all the passion of a father who, having nothing else, makes his child the reason for his existence. She cruelly chose to die when she was almost a year old, when she had become so pretty, with her little golden curls that I twisted around my finger and never tired of kissing. She would call me: *Papa*, and I would answer at once: *My child*, and again she would call: *Papa* . . . and so, on and on, for no reason, as birds call to one another.

She and my mother died at the same time, the same day,

almost the same hour. I didn't know how to divide my attentions and my grief. If the baby fell asleep, I would leave her and rush off to my mother, who cared nothing for herself, her own death, but asked about the baby, her grandchild, in torment that she couldn't see the little one again, kiss her for a last time. And it went on for nine days, this torment! Then after nine days and nine nights of constant vigil, never closing my eyes even for a moment—must I say it? Many would be ashamed to confess, and yet it's only human, utterly, utterly human . . . No, I felt no grief, not at that moment. For a long time I was in a frightful, dazed gloom, and I went to sleep. Of course I did. I had to sleep first. Then, oh yes, when I woke, grief assaulted me: angry, ferocious grief for my little daughter, for my mother, who were no more . . . And I almost went mad. A whole night I wandered about the town and the countryside, with God knows what thoughts in my mind. I know that, at the end, I found myself at our farm, the Hen Coop, near the millrace, and a certain Filippo, an old miller who was the caretaker, took me with him, made me sit down there under the trees and talked to me a long time about Mamma and about my father and about the happy days of the past, and he said that I wasn't to weep or to feel so desperate, because the baby's granny had hurried into the other world to take care of my little girl, the good granny, who would hold my baby on her lap and talk to her about me always and never leave her alone, never.

Three days later, Roberto—as if to pay for my tears—sent me five hundred lire. To see that Mamma had a proper burial, he said. But Aunt Scolastica had already taken care of that.

For a while that five hundred lire stayed between the pages of an old book in the library.

Then I spent the money on myself, and—as I am about to tell you—it was the occasion of my *first* death.

VI.   *Click, Click, Click*

In the room, only that little ivory ball, tripping grace-
fully around the roulette wheel against the direction of the
numbers, seemed to be playing a game.

"Click click click . . ."

Only that ball. Certainly not the people who were watching it, suspended in the torment of the ball's caprice. That
whim to which all these hands had brought votive offerings,
the piles of gold there on the yellow squares of the table. The
same hands were now trembling in the anguish of waiting;
unconsciously they toyed with more gold, the money for the
next bet, as all eyes seemed to plead: O gracious ivory ball,
our cruel goddess, look down upon us and, if it may please
you, alight!

I had happened there, at Monte Carlo, by chance.

It was after one of the usual scenes with my mother-in-law
and my wife, those fights which, in the weakness and oppression following my recent double tragedy, now filled me with
intolerable disgust. I was unable to stand my own boredom,
my contempt for this miserable way of life with no hope of
improvement, deprived of the comfort of my dear little child,
with no compensation, however slight, for the bitterness, the
squalor, the horrible desolation into which I had fallen. Then,
acting almost on the spur of the moment, I fled from the town,
on foot, with Berto's five hundred lire in my pocket.

As I walked along, I decided first to go to Marseilles, taking
the train from the station of the next town, towards which I

was going. From Marseilles I would embark at random, with a third-class ticket, perhaps for America.

After all, could anything worse befall me than what I had suffered and was still suffering at home? No doubt, I was only heading for new chains, but they surely wouldn't seem heavier than the ones I had just ripped from my ankles. And in addition I would see other countries, other peoples, another life, and I would at least escape from the depression that was stifling, crushing me.

But then, by the time I reached Nice, I felt my spirits fail. My youthful impetuousness had long since been destroyed: ennui had sapped my strength, and my mourning had unmanned me. What discouraged me most was my scarcity of funds. With such a little sum, I would have to venture forth into the darkness of fate, travel so far, to a life of which I knew nothing, for which I was completely unprepared.

So I got off the train at Nice. Still not quite determined to go back home, I was wandering around the city when I happened to stop in front of a large store on the Avenue de la Gare. Over the entrance was a sign with bold, gilt lettering:

DÉPÔT DE ROULETTES DE PRÉCISION.

In the window roulette wheels of every dimension were displayed, as well as other gambling equipment, and various publications with the picture of a roulette wheel on the cover.

It's a well-known fact that unhappy people often become superstitious, and though they may mock the hopeful credulity of others, their own superstition at times inspires the same hopes in them—hopes that remain unfulfilled, of course.

I remember that after reading the title of one of those pamphlets, *Méthode pour gagner à la roulette*, I turned away from the store with a contemptuous smile of commiseration. But, when I had taken a few steps, I turned back (only out of curiosity, mind you!) and went into the shop. With the same contemptuous smile, I bought the pamphlet.

I had no idea what it was about, of how the game was played. I started reading the pamphlet, but I still understood very little.

—Perhaps, I thought, it's because my French isn't very good.—

No one had ever taught me the language; I'd learned a little on my own, skimming some books in the library. But I wasn't at all sure of how French was pronounced, and I was afraid that people would laugh if I spoke.

At first, this fear made me hesitate to go. But then I reminded myself how, a few hours earlier, I had set out with the idea of going all the way to America, without any notion of English or Spanish. So after all, with my smattering of French and with the pamphlet to guide me, I could at least venture as far as Monte Carlo, only a step away.

—My mother-in-law and my wife, I said to myself in the train, know nothing about the little sum I have left in my wallet. I'll go and squander it there, to remove any temptation. I only hope I can keep enough to pay my return fare. And if not . . . —

I had heard there was no shortage of trees, good sturdy ones, in the garden around the casino. All things considered, I might hang myself quite economically from one of them with my belt; I would even cut a romantic figure. People would say: "I wonder what enormous amounts that poor man must have lost!"

To tell you the truth, the casino was a disappointment. The entrance isn't bad, I admit; obviously they meant to raise a kind of temple to Luck, with those eight marble columns. A large central door and two smaller doors at either side. The word *Tirez* was written on them: so far so good. I could also translate the *Poussez* on the central door; it clearly meant the opposite. I pushed and went inside.

The worst possible taste! Irritating, too. They could at least give all the people who go there to lose so much money the satisfaction of being fleeced in a place less sumptuous but more beautiful. Every large city now takes pride in having a fine slaughterhouse for poor dumb animals, which—lacking any education—cannot appreciate their surroundings. Of course, it's also true that most of the people who come here have little interest in the taste of the rooms' decoration. The people on the sofas all around the walls, for instance, are often in no condition to judge the questionable elegance of the upholstery.

Usually, those sofas are occupied by poor wretches whose passion for gambling has affected their brains in a singular way: they sit there studying the so-called balance of probability, and they seriously ponder the coups they are going to try, a whole architecture of gambling, based on the various ups and downs of the numbers. They want, in short, to extract a logic from chance, which is like saying, blood from stones; and they are convinced they'll succeed, today or at the latest, tomorrow.

But you mustn't let anything here surprise you.

"Ah, the 12! The 12!" a gentleman from Lugano said to me, a huge man whose appearance inspired the most consoling reflections on the human race's capacity for resistance. "The 12 is the king of numbers, and he's mine! He never betrays me. Oh, he amuses himself by spiting me sometimes, even often. But then, at the end, he always rewards me for my faithfulness."

That huge man was in love with the number 12 and could talk of nothing else. He told me how, the day before, his number had refused to come up even once; but he hadn't given in. Every time, he had obstinately bet on 12. He had stayed at the table to the very end, to the moment when the croupiers announce: *"Messieurs, aux trois derniers!"*

Well, at the first of those last three spins, nothing happened. And nothing happened at the second. Then, the third and last time, bang! out came the 12.

"He spoke to me!" the man concluded, his eyes glistening with tears of joy. "He spoke to me!"

Of course, having lost all day long, he had only a few coppers left for that last bet, so he didn't recoup anything. But what did he care? His number, the number 12, had spoken to him!

Listening to the man's words, I was reminded of four verses by poor old Tweezer, whose notebook of puns and crackbrained poems had turned up when we were leaving our old home and is now in the library. I recited the lines to that man:

> I awaited Dame Fortune, day after day.
> At last she heard my sighs. Her
> Fickle steps advanced my way—
> But then she proved a miser.

The man took his head in both hands and pressed his face painfully, for a long time. I looked at him, first surprised, then alarmed.

"What's wrong?"

"Why, nothing. I'm laughing," he answered.

That was the way he laughed. His head pained him so much that he couldn't bear the tremor of his laughter.

Now go and fall in love with number 12, if you dare!

Before trying my luck (though I hadn't the slightest illusions about it), I wanted to stand there for a while and watch the others, to discover how the game went.

It didn't seem at all complicated, as my booklet had led me to believe.

In the center of the table, on the numbered green cloth, the wheel was set. All around the table were the gamblers: men and women, old and young, from every country and walk of life, some sitting, some standing, as they hastily and nervously arranged the little or big piles of louises or crowns or bank notes on the yellow numbers in the squares. Those who couldn't get close—or who chose to stand back—would tell the croupier the numbers and the colors they wanted to bet on, and the croupier would promptly arrange their stakes in the proper places, using his rake with splendid dexterity. A silence fell, a strange, anguished silence, alive with restrained violence, broken from time to time by the sleepy, monotonous voices of the croupiers: "*Messieurs, faites vos jeux!*"

And farther on, at other tables, other equally monotonous voices would be saying: "*Le jeu est fait! Rien ne va plus!*"

And finally the croupier would drop the ball into the wheel: Click, click, click . . .

And every eye turned to the ball, with a variety of expressions: anxiety, defiance, anguish, terror. Some of the people who had remained standing, behind the others lucky enough to find chairs, now pushed forward to keep their eyes on their money, before the croupier's rake reached out and seized it.

Finally, the ball dropped into a slot, and the croupier repeated in his usual voice the formula, announcing the number that had come up and its color.

I risked my first bet—a few crowns—at the table to your left in the first room. I bet, at random, on number 25, then I too stood there watching the treacherous ball. But I was smiling, thanks to a curious tickling sensation at the pit of my stomach.

The ball dropped into its slot, and the croupier announced: "*Vingt-cinq! Rouge, impair et passe!*"

I'd won! I was reaching out for my now-multiplied pile when I noticed a tall gentleman, his heavy, pointed shoulders supporting a small head with gold spectacles over a pug nose, a sloping forehead, long, lank hair gray-blond like his mustache and goatee. Unceremoniously he pushed me aside and picked up my money.

In my poor and halting French, I tried to explain to him that he had made a mistake—unintentionally, of course!

He was a German, and his French was worse than mine, but he spoke it with a lion's courage. He turned on me, saying that the mistake was mine, and the money was his.

I looked around, stunned. Nobody breathed a word, not

even my neighbor, who had seen me place my few coins on 25. I looked at the croupiers: impassive, immobile as statues.

—So that's how it is!—I said to myself, and I quietly picked up the other sum that I had put on the table before me. I went off.

—That's a method *pour gagner à la roulette*, I thought, which is not included in my booklet. Who knows? Perhaps, after all, it's the only method!—

But Luck, for some secret motive of her own, chose to contradict me, in solemn and memorable terms.

I went over to another table, where the stakes were high, and stood there for a long while examining the people around me. Most of them were gentlemen in tail coats, but there were a number of ladies, more than one of whom looked dubious to me. There was a very blond little man, with large, blue, bloodshot eyes with almost white lashes; at first his appearance aroused my suspicions. He was also wearing a tail coat, but it was obvious that he wasn't used to evening dress. I wanted to see him put to the test. He placed a large bet. He lost. He remained calm. He bet again, heavily this time. Now here was a man who wouldn't try to steal my poor stake. Even though I had been stung at my first attempt, I was ashamed of my own suspicion. With all these people boldly throwing away gold and silver by the handful as if it were sand, should I then fear for my own pittance?

Among the others, I noticed a pale, waxen young man with a huge monocle in his left eye. He affected an air of sleepy indifference, sprawled in his chair. He drew his louises from the pocket of his trousers and set the money on any number at random. Then, not watching, toying with his nascent mustache, he waited for the ball to drop. When it did, he asked his neighbor whether or not he had lost.

While I watched him, he lost every time.

His neighbor was a thin and very elegant gentleman of about forty, but his neck was too long and frail, and he was almost chinless, with black, darting eyes and handsome,

abundant raven hair combed straight back. He obviously enjoyed telling the young man he had lost. As for himself, he
occasionally won.

I took my place next to a heavy-set man whose skin was so
dark that his eyelids and the circles under his eyes looked as if
they had been smoked. His hair was iron-gray, but his goatee
still almost entirely black and curly. He was the picture of
vigor and health, and yet, as if the course of the little ball
brought on asthma, at every spin he began to gasp and hack
helplessly. People turned to look at him, but he rarely noticed
them. If he did, he would stop for a moment and glance
around with a nervous smile, then start coughing again, unable to do anything about it until the ball had dropped into
its slot.

Little by little, as I watched the others, I too was slowly
seized with the gambling fever. My first tries went badly. Then
I began to feel myself in a strange, brilliant state of intoxication. I acted almost automatically, in sudden, unconscious
fits of inspiration. Every time, I bet after all the others. There!
Then I was immediately alert, certain that I would win. And I
won. At first I placed small bets, then gradually I bet more,
and still more, not even counting the sums. This kind of lucid
intoxication grew in me, and even a few losses couldn't spoil it,
because I seemed to have foreseen even those. Indeed, occasionally I said to myself: There, this time I'll lose, I *must* lose.
I was electrified. Suddenly I was inspired to risk everything at
once, win or lose. I won. My ears were buzzing, I was bathed
in a cold sweat. I thought that one of the croupiers, apparently surprised at my tenacious good luck, was observing me.
In my agitation I felt a kind of challenge in that man's gaze,
and again I bet everything, all I had brought with me and all
I had won, without thinking twice. My hand returned to the
same number as before, 35. I was about to draw the money
back again, but no, I left it there, as if obeying an order.

I shut my eyes; I must have been very pale. The silence was
intense, and I felt that it was all for me, as if everyone else

were suspended in my terrible anxiety. The ball spun, an eternity, with a slowness that made my unbearable torture even worse. Finally it dropped.

I waited until the croupier in his usual voice (which seemed very far away to me) announced: "*Trente-cinq, noir, impair et passe!*"

I took the money and I had to move away, staggering like a drunken man. I sank down on a sofa, exhausted, resting my head against the back in a sudden, irresistible need to sleep, to refresh myself with a little rest. And I was almost giving way when I felt a weight, a material weight on me; it quickly brought me round. How much money had I won? I opened my eyes, but had to close them again at once, because my head spun. The heat in the room was suffocating. What? Was it evening already? I had glimpsed the lighted chandeliers. And how long had I been gambling? Very slowly I stood up. I went out.

In the vestibule it was still daylight. The cool air heartened me.

A number of people were strolling there. Some were alone, lost in thought. Others, in twos and threes, were chatting and smoking.

I observed them all. New to the place and ill at ease, I would have liked to seem at least a little at home there, and I studied the ones who looked most nonchalant. But then, when I least expected it, one of these habitués would suddenly turn pale, his eyes would glaze over, and in silence he would throw away his cigarette and run back into the gambling room, amid the laughter of his companions. Why did they laugh? I also smiled, instinctively, looking on idiotically.

"A *toi, mon chéri!*" I heard a low, slightly hoarse feminine voice say to me.

I turned and saw one of those women who had been sitting around my table earlier; smiling, she held out a rose to me, keeping another for herself. She had just bought them at a flower counter, there in the foyer.

Did I look so clumsy, so gullible?

I was seized with violent annoyance. Without thanking her, I refused the flower and started to move away from her, but she laughingly took my arm and—assuming a very familiar tone with me in front of the others—she began to speak in a low, pressing voice. I gathered that she wanted me to go with her, since she had just watched my strokes of luck. Following my instructions, she proposed to place bets for us both.

I shook her off indignantly, and left her standing there.

A little later, when I went back into the gambling room, I saw her in conversation with a dark, squat, bearded man with rather shifty eyes, a Spaniard from the look of him. She had given him the rose previously offered to me. As the two of them started, I realized that they were talking about me; I was on my guard.

I went into another room and approached the first table, with no thought of betting. A few moments later, the squat man—now without the woman—also came to the table, pretending to be unaware of me.

I began to glare at him steadily, to show him I was aware of everything and he needn't try to pull any tricks with me.

But this man didn't look in the least like a thief. I saw him gamble, heavily. He lost three times in a row. He blinked constantly, perhaps because of the effort it was costing him to conceal his emotion. After his third loss, he looked at me and smiled.

I left him there and went back to the other room, to the table where I had won before.

The croupiers had changed. The woman was there, where she had been before. I hung back, to avoid being noticed, and I saw that she was gambling modestly and not betting every time. I stepped forward; she glimpsed me. She was about to place a bet, but she held back, obviously waiting for me, so that she could put her money on the same number. But she waited in vain. When the croupier said, "*Le jeu est fait! Rien ne va plus!*", I looked at her. She wagged her finger at me, playfully threatening. For a while I didn't gamble, then aroused at the spectacle of the other gamblers, and sensing that my previous inspiration was rising in me again, I forgot all about her and began to bet once more.

What was the mysterious prompting that guided me infallibly through the unpredictable shifts of the numbers and colors? Was this simply a miracle of unconscious guesswork? If so, how can you explain certain mad, yes mad, fits of obstinacy which, when I think about them, still make me shiver, since I was staking everything, my whole life perhaps, on those spins which were outright challenges to fate? No, no, I felt profoundly an almost diabolical force within me, and thanks to it, I could charm and master Chance, bind it to my whim. I wasn't the only one who felt this, the same conviction spread rapidly to the others, and by now nearly all of them were following my extremely risky play. I don't know how many times red came up, as I kept obstinately betting on it. If I put my money on zero, zero came up. Even the young man who pulled the louises out of his trouser pocket was stirred and excited; the dark heavy-set man was coughing louder than ever. The excitement around the table increased from moment to moment: everyone was trembling with impatience, making brief nervous gestures, in a barely controlled hysteria, anguished and terrible. The croupiers themselves had lost their rigid impassivity.

Suddenly, at a particularly wild bet, I felt a kind of dizziness. I sensed the terrible responsibility that was weighing on me. I had been virtually fasting since morning, and I was shuddering from head to toe in my violent emotion. I couldn't stand it any longer, and after that last win, I stumbled away. I felt someone grasp my arm. Highly excited, his eyes darting flames, the bearded Spaniard wanted to hold me in there at all costs: it was quarter past eleven, he said, the croupiers were announcing the *trois derniers*. We would break the bank!

He spoke to me in a highly comical, bastard Italian, since in my dazed state, I had insisted on answering him in my own language.

"No, no, that's enough. I can't stand any more! My dear sir, let me go."

He let me go, but he came after me. He climbed with me into the train going back to Nice, and he insisted that I dine with him and take a room in his hotel.

At first I wasn't displeased by the almost timorous admiration this man seemed so happy to display towards me, as if I were a wizard. Human vanity at times doesn't reject even offensive tributes and accepts bitter, poisonous incense from base, unworthy censers. I was like a general who had won a desperate, hard-fought battle, but by accident, without knowing why. I was gradually coming back to my senses and, as I realized this, my annoyance at this man's company increased.

Still, despite all my efforts, when I got off at Nice, I couldn't shake him. I had to have dinner with him. Then he confessed he had been the one to send that suspect woman to me there in the foyer of the casino: for three days he had been furnishing her with wings to fly, or at least to skim the ground, wings made of bank notes. In other words, he gave her a few hundred lire so that she could try her luck. She must have won a good sum that evening, following my game, since she hadn't put in an appearance at the exit.

"*Que puedo?* What to do? The *pobrecita* find herself a better man. *Yo soy* . . . old man. And, *agradecido Dios, ántes,* . . . I finish with her!"

He told me that he had been in Nice for a week, and going every morning to Monte Carlo where, until that evening, he had had an incredible run of bad luck. He wanted to know how I managed to win. I surely must understand the secret of the game or possess some infallible rule.

I laughed and told him that until that very morning, I had never seen a roulette wheel, nor even a picture of one; I had had no notion of the game, no suspicion that I would ever play it and win in that way. Now I was more stunned and dazzled than he.

He wasn't convinced. In fact, deftly changing the subject (no doubt he believed he was dealing with an out and out rascal) and speaking with wondrous ease that half-Spanish and half-God-knows-what language of his, he ended up by making me the same offer that he had sent me, earlier in the day, through the prostitute at the casino.

"No, no, really," I said, trying to placate his touchiness with a smile. "Can you seriously go on believing there are rules for that kind of gambling, or that it contains some secret? It's all luck! I had some luck today, but tomorrow I might not have any, or I may have more—I hope I do!"

"Then *porqué* . . ." he asked. "Why today you don't *aproveciarse* your luck?"

"*Apro*—?"

"Yes, how you say? Take advantage."

"My dear sir, I was gambling according to my limited means!"

"*Bien!*" he said. "*Podo yo* . . . for you. You bring luck. I bring the money."

"And then perhaps we might lose!" I concluded, still smiling. "No, no . . . See here, if you really think I'm so lucky— and I may be at gambling, but I'm not lucky at anything else, I can tell you—then we'll do this: with no agreement between us, and no responsibility on my side, since I refuse to accept any, you can bet your large sums where I place my small ones, as you did today, and if all goes well . . ."

He didn't allow me to finish. He burst into strange laughter, meant to sound malicious, and he said: "Ah no, *mi Señor.* No! Today yes, but tomorrow no, *seguro!* You bet big with my money, *bien!* But if no, then I not bet. *Gracias!*"

I looked at him, trying to understand what he meant; in his words and in his laughter there was no doubt some offensive suspicion of me. I was upset and I demanded an explanation.

He stopped laughing, but on his face there remained the fading print of that laughter.

"*Digo no* . . . I not do it," he repeated. "*No digo mas!*"

I slammed my hand down on the table and insisted, in an angry voice: "That won't do! You must speak, explain what you meant by your words and by that idiotic laughter of yours! I don't understand!"

I saw him grow pale, almost shrink as I spoke; obviously he was about to apologize. I stood up, indignant, shrugging.

"Humph! I have only contempt for you and your suspicions, which I can't even imagine!"

I paid my bill and left.

I once knew a venerable man, worthy of the greatest respect because of his exceptional gifts and intelligence. But he wasn't respected at all, simply because of a pair of trousers which he insisted on wearing. They were white I believe, with checks, and clung too tightly to his scrawny legs. The clothes we wear, their cut and color, can make people have the strangest opinions of us.

But I was all the more annoyed now, since I didn't believe I was badly dressed. I wasn't in evening clothes, of course, but I was in black, in very respectable mourning. And besides if that German pig was able to take me for a fool in these same clothes, grabbing my money with the greatest of ease, how was it that this Spaniard now took me for a thief?

—Perhaps it's on account of my beard, I thought as I went away, or because my hair's too short . . . —

Meanwhile I was looking for some sort of hotel so that I could shut myself in a room and see how much I had won. I felt stuffed with money; it was all over me, in the pockets of my jacket, of my trousers, of my waistcoat: gold, silver, bank notes. There must be an enormous amount!

I heard a clock strike two. The streets were deserted. A carriage went by, and I climbed in.

Starting with almost nothing I had made about eleven

thousand lire! I hadn't seen such money for a long time, and at first it seemed a huge sum. But then, when I thought of the life I had once led, I felt a great depression. What? Had two years in the library with their supplement of other disasters impoverished my spirit to this degree?

I started stinging myself with this new venom, as I looked at the money on the bed:

—Go now, virtuous, modest librarian, go back to your home and use this treasure to placate the widow Pescatore. She'll think you've stolen it and will therefore immediately acquire great respect for you. Or else go to America as you first planned, if the widow's esteem doesn't seem a fit reward for your great achievement. You could go there now, with this sum. Eleven thousand lire! What wealth!—

I gathered up the money, threw it into the bureau drawer, and went to bed. But I couldn't fall asleep. What was I to do, after all? Return to Monte Carlo and give back those unusual winnings? Or be content with them and enjoy the money modestly? But how? Was I now able to enjoy anything with the family I had created for myself? I would dress my wife a little less miserably, though she no longer bothered to try to please me. She even seemed to do everything to appear unattractive in my sight, letting whole days go by without combing her hair, uncorseted, in slippers, her clothes falling off her.

Did she feel perhaps that, for a husband like me, it wasn't worth the effort to pretty herself up? For that matter, after the grave risk she had run in childbirth, she had never really regained her physical health. And, as far as her spirit was concerned, she became more bitter every day, not only against me, but against everyone. Rancor and the lack of any real affection had fostered a dull laziness in her. She hadn't even grown fond of our little girl, whose birth—along with the twin who died after a few days—had represented a terrible defeat for Romilda, in the face of Oliva's handsome plump little boy, born a month later with no trouble after a very happy pregnancy.

All the disgust and frictions that come when Need, like a scrawny black cat, nests in the ashes of a spent hearth, had made living together odious to us both. Could I, with eleven thousand lire, restore peace in our home and resuscitate that love wickedly killed at birth by the widow Pescatore? What folly! Well, what was I to do then? Leave for America? But why should I go so far in search of Fortune, when the goddess apparently had meant me to stop here in Nice in front of that shop which sold gambling equipment? Now I had to prove I was worthy of her, of her favors, if—as it seemed—she wanted to grant them to me. Forward! All or nothing! If worst came to worst, I would merely be where I had been before. What was eleven thousand lire, after all?

So the next day I went back to Monte Carlo. I went back for the next twelve days in a row. I no longer had the time or the capacity to be amazed by the favors—more fabulous than unusual—of Fortune! I was out of my mind, literally mad! I am not amazed by it even now, since unhappily I know what Fortune was preparing for me, by first favoring me in that way. In nine days of desperate gambling I amassed a really enormous sum. After the ninth day, I began to lose, and the losses were precipitous. The miraculous talent failed me, as if it no longer found nourishment in my exhausted nervous energy. I didn't know how—or rather I was physically unable—to stop in time. I did stop, I saved myself, not through any virtue of mine, but because of a violent, horrible sight, one apparently not infrequent in that place.

I was going into the gambling rooms on the morning of the twelfth day when the gentleman from Lugano, the one in love with the number 12, overtook me. Breathless and distraught, he announced more with gestures than with words that somebody had killed himself just now, there, in the garden. I immediately thought it was my Spaniard, and I felt remorse. I was sure he had helped me win. On the first day after our argument, he had refused to bet where I did, and he had lost every time. In the days after that, seeing how persistently I won, he had tried to follow my game, but then I didn't want him to, and as if guided by the hand of Fortune, present but invisible, I had started moving from one table to another. For the last two days I hadn't seen him, since I had started losing, in fact; perhaps I was losing because he no longer pursued me.

I was absolutely sure, as I ran towards the indicated spot, that I would find him there, lying on the ground, dead. But instead I found the pale young man who had affected an air of sleepy indifference as he pulled louises from his pocket and bet them without even looking at the table.

He seemed smaller, there in the middle of the *allée*. His feet were neatly together, as if he had stretched out beforehand, so as not to be hurt when he fell. One arm lay along his body, the other was outstretched, the hand clenched and one finger, the index finger, still in the position of firing. Near that hand was his revolver, and not far away, his hat. At first I thought that the bullet must have come out of his left eye, causing all that blood to trickle over his face. But no, the blood, now clotted, had spattered there, some from his nostrils and some from his ears. More blood had flowed abundantly from the little hole in his right temple, and this had formed a pool over the yellow sand of the path. A dozen wasps were buzzing around. Some greedily lighted on his eye. Among all the people there looking on, no one had thought of driving them away. I took a handkerchief from my pocket and spread it over that poor, horribly disfigured face. No one thanked me; I had spoiled the best part of the spectacle.

I ran off. I went back to Nice and left the city that same day.

I had about eighty-two thousand lire with me.

I could have imagined all sorts of things then, but not that something similar was going to happen to me, on the evening of that very day.

VII. I Change Trains

I was thinking:
—I'll buy back Hen Coop farm and retire to the country.
I'll become a miller. A man's well off when he's close to the
earth, and when he's beneath it, better off still.

—Every trade, after all, contains some consolation. Even the
gravedigger's. The miller can console himself with the racket
of the millstones and the dust that hangs in the air and
clothes him in flour.

—I'm sure they don't even open a sack there in the mill
nowadays. But as soon as it's mine again:

—"Signor Mattia, the crossbar! Signor Mattia, the axle's
broken! Signor Mattia, the teeth of the little wheel!"

—Just as when my poor mother was still alive, and Malagna
was our business manager.

—And while I run the mill, our farmer will steal the produce
of the land from me; if I start to keep an eye on him, then the
miller will steal my share of the flour. And the miller on one
side and the farmer on the other will make a seesaw, with me
in the middle, enjoying myself.

—It would probably be best for me to open my mother-in-
law's respected chest of drawers, take one of Francesco Antonio Pescatore's old suits which his widow preserves with
camphor and pepper like holy relics. Then I could dress up
the widow Marianna in the suit and send her out to be the
miller and keep a watch on the farmer.

—The country air would certainly do my wife good. Perhaps
some of the trees will lose their leaves at the sight of her, and
the birds will fall silent; I only hope that the spring doesn't

go dry. And I will stay on as librarian, all alone, at Santa Maria Liberale.—

These were my thoughts, as the train sped on. I couldn't close my eyes; the body of that young man would appear to me at once with terrible clarity there on the path, so neat and small, under the huge, still trees in the cool morning. So I had to comfort myself with another nightmare, less bloody (in the literal sense, at least): the vision of my mother-in-law and my wife. And I took pleasure in imagining the scene of my arrival, after thirteen days of mysterious disappearance.

I was certain (I could almost see them) that when I came in, they would both affect the most contemptuous indifference. A bare glance, as if to say: What? Back again? We thought you'd broken your neck.

They would be silent, and so would I.

But after a little while, the widow Pescatore would no doubt start spitting bile, harping on the job I had probably lost.

In fact, I had carried off the key to the library with me. At the news of my disappearance, they had certainly broken in the door, on orders from the police. Then failing to find my dead body inside, with no other trace or news of me, the people at City Hall may have waited three or four or five days, a week perhaps, expecting I would return. And then they would have given my job to some other local idler.

So, the widow would say, how could I just sit there like that? I'd thrown myself into the street again, with my own hands. Well, I could stay there! Two poor women were under no obligation to keep a no-good like me, a jailbird who ran off all of a sudden, God only knows for what foul purpose, etc., etc.

And I would keep my mouth shut.

Gradually Marianna Pescatore's bile would increase, at my spiteful silence; it would mount and boil and explode. And I would still keep quiet!

Then, at one point, I would take my wallet from my breast pocket and begin to count out my thousand-lire notes on to the table: there, there, there . . .

Marianna Pescatore's eyes would widen, her jaw would fall open, and so would my wife's.

Then:

"Where did you steal that money?"

— . . . seventy-seven, seventy-eight, seventy-nine, eighty, eighty-one; five hundred, six hundred, seven hundred; ten, twenty, twenty-five . . . Eighty-one thousand seven hundred and twenty-five lire and forty centesimi in my pocket . . .

I would then quietly gather up the bills, replace them in my wallet and stand up.

"So you don't want me around the house any more? Very well. Thanks very much. I'm leaving, and good-by to all!"

I laughed as I thought of the scene.

My traveling companions looked at me and also smiled to themselves.

Then, to achieve a more serious mien, I made myself think about my creditors, among whom I'd have to share out those bank notes. I wouldn't be able to hide them. And besides, if they were hidden, what use would they be to me?

That pack of hounds would never allow me to enjoy my gains. To make back their money at the mill and with the farm's produce, the creditors would have to wait God only knows how long, since they would also have to pay the receiver, and he was probably consuming everything as greedily and thoroughly as the millstones ground the wheat. Now perhaps, by offering them cash, I could probably come to good terms with them. I began to calculate:

—So much to that old horsefly Recchioni, and so much to Filippo Brisigo and I only hope the money goes to pay for his funeral, so he won't suck blood from any more poor wretches. So much to Cichin Lunaro, the Turinese; and so much to the widow Lippani . . . And who else is there? Ah, that's just the

beginning. There's Della Piana, and Bossi, and Margot-
tini . . . And there go all my winnings!—

When you came to think about it, I'd won all that money
at Monte Carlo for them! That two-day losing streak now
made me furious! I'd have been rich again . . . really rich!

Now I heaved huge sighs which disturbed my fellow
travelers more than my smiles had earlier. But I could find no
peace. Evening was beginning to fall; the air seemed made of
ashes, and the gloom of the journey was unbearable.

At the first station inside Italy I bought a newspaper, in the
hope that it would put me to sleep. I unfolded it and by the
light of the electric bulb, I began to read. So I was consoled
to learn that the Château of Valençay, at auction for the
second time, had been sold to M. le Comte de Castellane for
the sum of two million three hundred thousand francs. The
property around the château amounted to two thousand eight
hundred hectares, the largest estate in France.

—More or less like the Hen Coop . . .

I read that in Potsdam the Emperor of Germany had received the Moroccan ambassador at noon, and that the
Secretary of State, Baron von Richtofen, had been present.
The mission, then presented to the Empress, had remained
for luncheon—and I imagine they stowed away quite a lot
too!

The Czar and Czarina of Russia had also been receiving;
at Peterhof a special mission from Tibet presented Their
Imperial Majesties with some gifts from the Lama.

—Gifts from the Lama?, I asked myself, shutting my eyes
pensively. What can they be?—

Poppies—because I then fell asleep. But ineffectual poppies,
for I soon woke up as the train jolted, stopping at another
station.

I looked at the clock. It was a quarter past eight. In another
hour or so, then, I'd be home.

The newspaper was still in my hand. I turned it over, hoping that the second page would contain some gift better than the Lama's. My eyes fell on the headline:

SUICIDE

like that, in heavy black type.

I immediately thought that it might be the young man in Monte Carlo and I hastened to read it. But I stopped in surprise at the first line, in very small print: *By telegraph from Miragno.*

—Miragno? Who can have committed suicide in my town?—

I read on: *Yesterday, Saturday the 28th, in the waters of a millrace, a body was found in an advanced state of putrefaction . . .*

Suddenly my eyes clouded over, as I thought I glimpsed in the next line the name of my farm. Since I was having difficulty reading that fine print with only one eye, I stood up, to be nearer the light.

. . . putrefaction. The mill is located on a farm property known as the Hen Coop, about a mile from our city. When the city officials, as well as other people, had hurried to the spot, the body was recovered from the millrace and a guard mounted, until the legal formalities could be carried out. Later the corpse was identified as that of our . . .

My heart leaped into my throat. Half out of my mind, I stared at my fellow travelers, all asleep.

Hurried to the spot . . . recovered from the millrace . . . guard mounted . . . was identified as that of our librarian . . .

—Me?—

Hurried to the spot . . . later . . . as that of our librarian Mattia Pascal, who disappeared several days ago. His suicide was attributed to financial reverses.

—Me?—*Disappeared . . . identified . . . Mattia Pascal . . .*

My heart pounding, I reread those few lines with fierce haste, again and again—I don't know how many times. In a first impulse, all my vital energies arose violently to protest, as if that piece of news, so irritating in its laconic impassivity, could be true even for me. But even if it weren't true for me, it was still true for the others, and the certainty of my death, which those others had felt since yesterday, was like a permanent, crushing, unbearable tyranny . . . I looked at the other travelers again, as if they too, before my very eyes, were sleeping in that certitude. And I was tempted to shake them from their painful, uncomfortable positions, shake them awake and shout that it wasn't true.

—How was such a thing possible?—

And I reread once again the astounding news.

I couldn't wait. I wanted the train to stop, or to race wildly ahead. Its monotonous progress, like a stubborn, deaf, grave robot, increased. I kept clenching and unclenching my fists, digging my nails into my palms. I opened the paper, then folded it over to reread the news item which I knew already by heart, word for word.

—*Identified!* How could they possibly have identified me? . . . *In an advanced state of putrefaction* . . . Ugh!—

For a moment I saw myself there, in the greenish water of the millrace, soaked, swollen, horrible, floating . . . In instinctive horror, I folded my arms across my chest and touched myself with my hands, clasping my body:

—No, not me . . . not me . . . But who can it have been? He must have looked like me, of course . . . Perhaps he also had a beard, like mine . . . my same build . . . And they identified me! . . . *disappeared several days ago* . . . Of course! But I'd like to know who was in such a hurry to identify me. Can that poor wretch have been so like me? Dressed like me? In every detail? But perhaps it was the widow, yes, Marianna Pescatore surely. Oh, she fished me out at once, she recognized me at once! Why, to her it seemed too good to be true! Naturally! "Yes, it's him. It's my son-in-law! Ah, *poor Mattia . . . my poor, poor boy!*" And she no doubt started crying. Perhaps she knelt down by the body of that poor man, who was unable to give her a kick and shout: *"Get away from me! I never saw you before in my life!"*—

I was shaking with rage. Finally the train stopped at another station. I opened the door and jumped down, with a confused notion that I should do something at once: send an urgent telegram to deny that report.

My leap from the train saved me, as if it had shaken that stupid idea from my head. In a flash I glimpsed . . . of course! my liberation, the freedom of a new life!

I had eighty-two thousand lire with me, and now I wouldn't have to give the money to anyone! I was dead, dead! I had no debts now, no wife, no mother-in-law. Nobody! Free! Free! Free! What more could I ask for?

As I was thinking these things, I must have remained in a very peculiar attitude there on the station platform. I had left the door of the carriage open. I saw a number of people around me, shouting at me—I don't know what. Finally one man shook me and, shouting still louder, thrust me towards the car:

"The train's leaving!"

"Let it go, let it leave, my dear sir!" I shouted back at him. "I'm changing trains!"

Now a sudden suspicion had assailed me: the thought that the news item had already been proved false, that the error at Miragno had been discovered, that the relatives of the real dead man had come forth to rectify the mistaken identification.

Before rejoicing as I had been doing, I had to make certain, I had to have more detailed and precise news. But how?

I searched my pockets for the newspaper. I'd forgotten it in the train. I turned and looked at the deserted track, which stretched off, shining in the silent night; and I felt lost, in a void, at this miserable little whistle stop. A still stronger suspicion then assailed me: had I dreamed it all?

No, no:

By telegraph from Miragno. Yesterday, Saturday the 28th . . .

There: I could repeat the whole dispatch from memory. There was no doubt about it! And yet, it was too brief; it wasn't enough to satisfy me.

I looked at the station and read the name: ALENGA.

Would I find other newspapers in the town? I recalled that it was Sunday. That morning therefore *Il Foglietto* had appeared in Miragno, the only paper printed there. I had to get myself a copy at all costs. There I'd find all the details that I needed. But how could I hope to find *Il Foglietto* here in Alenga? Well, I'd wire the newspaper office under a false name. I knew the editor, Miro Colzi—Skylark as everyone at Miragno called him—ever since he had published, as a young man, his first and last volume of verse with this tender title.

But wouldn't a request from Alenga for copies of his paper be a great event for Skylark? Surely the most interesting item that week, and therefore the leading article of the issue, would be my suicide. Wouldn't I risk arousing his suspicions by my strange request?

—Nonsense! I thought, Skylark would never suspect I haven't really drowned myself. He'll assume the request is due to some other important article in today's number. For months he's been attacking City Hall because of the sewers and the gas system. He'll think somebody here is interested in that campaign.—

I went into the station.

Luckily, the driver of the only carriage—who also delivered the mail—was in there gossiping with the station clerks. The village was about three quarters of an hour by carriage from the station, and it was uphill all the way.

I got into that decrepit, rickety old buggy, which had no headlights, and off we drove into the darkness.

I had many things to ponder, and yet the violent reaction I had felt at the news so closely concerning me now revived in me the same black, unfamiliar loneliness; and for a moment I felt myself plunged into the void again, as I had felt earlier at the sight of the empty tracks. I seemed frighteningly cut off from life, my own survivor, lost now, waiting to live beyond death, but still unable to glimpse the way ahead.

To think about something else I asked the driver if there was a news agent in Alenga.

"How's that? No, sir!"

"Don't they sell papers in Alenga?"

"Ah, yes, sir! The druggist sells them. Grottanelli's the name."

"Is there a hotel?"

"There's Palmentino's inn."

He had climbed down from the box to lighten the load of the old jade, who was snorting with her nostrils on the ground. I could barely discern him. At one point he lighted his pipe and then I saw him, in occasional flashes, and I thought: if he only knew the man he is carrying . . .

But I immediately asked myself the same question:

—Who is he carrying? I don't know either. Who am I now? I must think about it. A name, I must find at least a name at once, to sign the telegram and to avoid embarrassment if they ask me to sign the book at the inn. For the present if I can think of a name, that'll be enough. Now let's see. What is my name?

I would never have imagined that the choice of a name and surname would arouse such frenzy in me and cost me such an effort. Especially the surname! I combined syllables at random, without thinking, and certain odd names emerged, like: *Strozzani, Parbetta, Mazzoni, Bartusi*—they immediately got on my nerves. I couldn't find any rightness, any sense in them . . . Come now, a name, any name! Mazzoni, for example. Why not? Giuseppe Mazzoni . . . There! that's done! But a moment later, I shrugged: of course, Giuseppe Mazzini . . . —And my frenzy began again.

I reached the village, still with no name chosen. Fortunately the druggist there was also postmaster and telegraph operator, stationer, news agent, and I don't know what else, since these functions satisfied my needs. I bought a copy of each of the few newspapers he took: papers from Genoa, *Il Caffaro* and *Il Secolo XIX*. I asked him then if I could have *Il Foglietto* of Miragno.

This Grottanelli had an owl's face with two very round eyes, like glass, over which he lowered almost painfully, his cartilaginous eyelids.

"*Il Foglietto?* I never heard of it."

"It's a little provincial sheet, a weekly," I explained. "I'd like to have it. Today's issue, that is."

"*Il Foglietto?* I never heard of it," he repeated carefully.

"Never mind! I don't care whether you've heard of it or not. I'll pay for a money order to the paper. I'd like to have ten or twenty copies, tomorrow, or as soon as possible. Can this be done?"

He didn't answer. His eyes staring dully, he repeated once again: "*Il Foglietto?* I never heard of it." Finally he decided to allow me to dictate the telegram, giving his pharmacy as the return address.

And the next day, after a sleepless night, disturbed by a storm of churning thoughts, in Palmentino's inn, I received fifteen copies of *Il Foglietto*.

In the two Genoa papers, which I had hurriedly read the night before as soon as I was alone, I hadn't found a word. My hands were trembling now, while I unfolded *Il Foglietto*. On the first page: nothing. I looked at the two central pages, and a funereal black line immediately sprang to my eyes. It was at the top of page three, and under it, in large letters, there was my name. Like this:

MATTIA PASCAL

There had been no news of him for several days: days of terrible concern and unspeakable anguish for his grieving family. The anguish was shared by many of our fellow citizens, who loved and respected him

for his goodness of spirit, his amiable character, and
for that natural modesty which—with his other gifts
—permitted him to bear with resignation the blows
of Fate, which in recent times had reduced him to
a humble condition after years of carefree ease.

After the first day of his inexplicable absence, his
alarmed family repaired to the Boccamazza Library,
where in his zeal, he spent most of the day, enriching
his already lively mind with profound reading. The
door was found locked. At that locked door, the first
fearful, dire suspicion arose, a suspicion which was
for a time dispelled by the hope that he had merely
left our city for some personal reason. This hope
lasted several days, but gradually grew weaker.

And, alas! the sorrowful truth was to be all too
grim!

The recent loss of his beloved mother and, at the
same time, of his infant daughter, after the disastrous decline of his family fortunes, had profoundly
disturbed the spirit of our poor friend. As a result,
about three months ago, he had already made a first
attempt to put an end to his existence, there in the
very millrace whose surroundings reminded him of
the past glories of his family and its happier days. As
the poet says:

> There is no greater pain
> Than to recall a happy time
> In wretchedness . . .

Sobbing, his eyes filled with tears, an old miller,
faithful and devoted to the family of his former mas-
ters, told us this story, standing by the soaked, disfigured corpse. Night had fallen, a lugubrious
darkness, and a red lantern had been set there on the
ground near the body, which was being guarded by

two Royal Carabinièri. Old Filippo Bruni (whose noble character may serve as an example to all right-thinking folk) spoke and wept with us. On that first sad night he had succeeded in preventing the unhappy young man from carrying out his violent intention, but that second time, there was no Filippo Bruni present, ready to save him. And Mattia Pascal lay perhaps for a whole night and half of the next day in the waters of that millrace.

We shall not attempt to describe the heartbreaking scene that took place on that spot when, towards evening day before yesterday, the inconsolable widow stood before the unrecognizable remains of her beloved companion, who had gone to join their little daughter.

The entire city shares her grief, and displayed its sorrow by accompanying the body to its last resting place, where brief, but heartfelt words of farewell were spoken by our City Councilor, Cavalier Pomino.

To the poor family, in its days of profound mourning, to the victim's brother Roberto, far from Miragno, we extend our most profound condolences, and with our heart sorely torn, we say for the last time to our good Mattia: Vale, *beloved friend,* vale!

M.C.

Even without those two initials, I would have recognized Skylark as the author of the obituary.

But first of all I must confess that even though I had been expecting it, the sight of my name printed there under that black line did not cheer me up in the least. Instead, it made my heart beat faster, and after a few words, I had to stop reading. The "terrible concern and unspeakable anguish" of my family did not make me laugh, nor did the love and respect of my fellow citizens for my virtues, nor my zeal in my duties. The memory of that sad night at the mill, after the death of Mamma and my baby, which now served as proof—the conclusive evidence—of my suicide, surprised me at first, as an unforeseen and sinister intervention of chance; then it filled me with remorse and dejection.

No, no, I hadn't killed myself because of the death of Mamma and of my little girl, even though I may have been thinking of it that night! I had run away in despair, true enough; but here I was now, coming back from a gambling hell, where Fortune had strangely smiled on me, and was smiling on me still. Instead, another man had killed himself in my place. A stranger, no doubt, and I was robbing him of the mourning of his relatives and friends far away. I was condemning him—oh supreme mockery!—to undergo tears that didn't belong to him, insincere mourning, and even the funeral encomium of the powdered Cavalier Pomino!

This was my first reaction on reading my obituary in *Il Foglietto*.

But then I thought that, after all, it wasn't my fault the man had died; and that if I announced my return, it would bring only me back to life, not him. I also thought that, by taking advantage of his death, I wasn't defrauding his family, but doing them a good turn; for them, indeed, I was the dead man, not he; and they could believe that he had merely vanished. They could go on hoping, hoping that one of these days he would reappear.

That left my wife and my mother-in-law. Was I really expected to believe in their suffering at my death, in all that "unspeakable anguish," that "heartrending grief" in Skylark's funereal masterpiece? For God's sake! If they had only opened slowly one eye of that dead man, they would have realized that he wasn't I. And even if we admit that they didn't want to do that, it still isn't so easy to mistake a complete stranger for your own husband.

Why had they been in such a hurry to identify me as that dead man? Did the widow Pescatore hope that Malagna, moved, perhaps not without remorse for my cruel suicide, would come to the aid of my poor widow? Well then, if they were satisfied, so was I!

—Dead? Drowned? Then bury the whole business and never another word about it!—

I got up, stretched, and heaved a deep sigh of relief.

VIII. *Adriano Meis*

My next, and immediate, step was to make a new man
of myself, not so much to deceive the others, who had chosen
to deceive themselves with a carelessness perhaps not deplorable in my case, but certainly not praiseworthy. No, this next
step was taken rather to obey Fortune and to fulfill my own
personal need.

There was little or nothing to boast of in that miserable
life they had insisted on ending there in the millrace. After all
the mistakes he had made, Mattia Pascal perhaps deserved
no better fate.

Now I wanted to remove every trace of him, not only ex-
ternally, but also within myself.

I was alone now, and no one on earth could be more alone
than I, with every tie dissolved, every obligation removed,
free, new, completely my own master, without the burden of
my past, and with the future before me, which I could shape
as I pleased.

Ah, it was like having wings! How light I felt!

The attitude past events had given me towards life had no
further reason to exist. I had to acquire a new attitude, without making the least use of the wretched experiences of
Mattia Pascal.

It was all up to me: I could and should be the molder of my
new destiny, to the extent that Fortune had chosen to permit.

—And above all, I said to myself, I will cherish this freedom
of mine. I'll walk with it along smooth, ever new paths; I'll
never force it into burdensome dress. Whenever the spectacle
of life takes on an unpleasant aspect, I'll close my eyes and

walk on. I'll try to pass most of my time with so-called in-animate things, seek out lovely views and charming, quiet spots. Little by little, I'll give myself a new training. With patient, loving study, I'll transform myself so that, finally, I can say not only that I lived two lives, but that I was two men.—

To begin with, a few hours before leaving Alenga, I had already gone to a barber to have my beard trimmed shorter. I wanted to have it completely shaved off then and there, and my mustache along with it; but the fear of arousing suspicion in that little town had restrained me.

The barber was also the village tailor, an old man, his kidneys almost bent double from his long habit of stooping, always in the same position. He wore his spectacles on the tip of his nose. He must have been more tailor than barber; he swooped down on my beard like a wolf on the fold, and already it was no longer mine. He was armed with a pair of huge scissors, good for cutting cloth, and he had to hold them with both hands. I didn't dare breathe. I shut my eyes and opened them again only when I felt him shake me slightly.

The good man, all in a sweat, was holding out a little mirror so that I could say he had done a good job!

That was asking too much!

"No, thank you . . ." I hedged. "Put it away. I wouldn't want to frighten it."

He stared at me and asked: "Frighten what?"

"Why, that little mirror. It's charming. It must be an antique . . ."

It was round, with a handle of inlaid bone: who knows what its history was and how it happened to end up there in this barber-tailor shop. But finally, to avoid displeasing the proprietor, who continued to stare at me in amazement, I held it up before my eyes.

A good job, indeed!

In that first devastation I glimpsed the monster who, in a little while, would emerge from the necessary, radical alteration of the features of Mattia Pascal! Another reason for hating him! The tiny chin, pointed and receding, which he had concealed for years under that huge beard, seemed almost a piece of treachery. Now I would have to expose it, the ridiculous little thing! And what a nose he had left to me! And that eye!

—Ah, that eye—I thought—off to one side in ecstasy; that will remain forever even in my new face! To conceal it, I can only wear a pair of dark glasses, which will help—I can imagine how!—give me a more likable appearance. I'll let my hair grow, and with this handsome, broad forehead, my spectacles, and my chin clean-shaven, I'll look like a German philosopher. With a frock coat and a broad-brimmed hat.—

There was no middle course. I had to be a philosopher perforce with a face like that. Well, so be it; I'd equip myself with a discreet, smiling philosophy in order to move in the midst of this poor human race which, no matter how hard I tried, I couldn't stop regarding as base and a little ridiculous.

My name was virtually presented to me in the train, a few hours after it had left Alenga for Turin.

I was traveling with two gentlemen who were having a lively argument about Christian iconography, a subject on which they both seemed highly erudite, at least to an ignoramus like me.

One of them, the younger, had a pale face oppressed by a thick, rough beard; he seemed to take particular delight in announcing the information—which he said came from ancient times—that Christ was very ugly. This opinion, according to him, was borne out by Saint Justinus Martyr, by Tertullian, and I forget who else.

He spoke in a huge, cavernous voice that was in strange contrast with his inspired manner.

Yes, yes, ugly, terribly ugly! And Cyrilus of Alexandria said so too. Indeed, Cyrilus of Alexandria even went so far as to say that Christ was the ugliest of men.

His companion was a dreadfully thin old man, quite serene

in his ascetic squalor, and yet with a wrinkle at the corners of his mouth that revealed a subtle irony. He sat almost on his spine, with his long neck stretched forward as if under a yoke. He insisted, on the other hand, that the most ancient reports were not to be trusted.

"Because in the first centuries, the Church was concerned entirely in consolidating the doctrine and the spirit of her Inspirer, and gave small thought, yes, small thought to His physical features."

At a certain point they began to talk about Veronica and about the two statues in the city of Paneas that were believed to be images of Christ curing the woman with an issue of blood.

"No, no!" the bearded young man exclaimed. "There can be no more doubt nowadays! Those two statues represent the Emperor Hadrian, with the city kneeling at his feet."

The old man calmly went on expounding his view, which must have been the contrary; because the other man, losing his self-control, kept looking at me and repeating: "Hadrian."

". . . *Beronike*, in Greek. And from *Beronike* then comes *Veronica* . . ."

"Hadrian!" (*to me*).

"Because the Beronike in the *Acta Pilati* . . ."

"Hadrian!"

He kept repeating *Hadrian!* like that, I don't know how many times, always with his eyes looking in my direction.

When they both got off at the same station and left me alone in the compartment, I leaned out of the window to watch them go; they were still arguing as they left the train.

At a certain point, however, the little old man lost his temper and started to run off.

"Who says so?" the young man asked him in a loud voice, standing still, as if challenging him.

Then the other man turned and shouted at him: "Camillo De Meis!"

He also seemed to be shouting that name at me, as meanwhile I mechanically repeated: "Hadrian . . ."

I promptly discarded that *de,* retained the *Meis,* and translated the emperor's name into Italian.

"Adriano Meis, yes . . . Adriano Meis has a fine ring . . ."

I also felt this name was well suited to the beardless face and the dark glasses, the long hair, and the broad-brimmed hat I would have to wear.

"Adriano Meis! Excellent! They've baptized me."

Now that I had cut off any memory of my previous existence, now that my spirit was firmly determined to begin a new life from this point, I was filled and uplifted by a fresh, infantile happiness. My consciousness seemed to have become virgin, transparent again, and my spirit was alert, ready to use everything to the best advantage in the construction of my new self. At the same time my soul was running riot, in the joy of this new freedom. I had never looked at mankind or at the world in this way; the air between them and me seemed suddenly free of mist; and the new relations that had to be established between us now seemed easy, light, since I now had to ask little of them to achieve my personal satisfaction. Oh, that delicious lightheartedness! Serene, indescribable bliss! Fortune had suddenly cut me free from all tangles, had severed me from ordinary life, had turned me into a bystander, looking on at the struggles of the others, and warned me secretly:

"You'll see . . . you'll see how strange it will look now, when you observe it from outside! Take that man back there, ruining his liver and enraging a poor old soul, simply by insisting that Christ was the ugliest of men . . ."

I smiled. I had a way of smiling at everything now: at the trees in the countryside, for example, which rushed towards me in odd attitudes in their illusory flight; at the villas scattered here and there, where I enjoyed imagining farmers with swollen cheeks, puffing at the fog, the olive tree's enemy, or with their fists raised against heaven, which was sending no rain; and I smiled at the little birds that scattered in fright as this black monster rushed noisily through the landscape; at the sway of the telegraph wires, over which news was sent to the papers, like the news of my suicide there at the old mill; I smiled at the poor wives of the stationmasters with rolled-up signal flags in their hands as they appeared, some pregnant, wearing their husband's cap on their heads.

But then, at one point, my gaze lighted on the little wedding band that encircled the ring finger of my left hand. This gave me a violent shock. I shut my eyes and clasped my left hand with my right, trying to pull off that little gold ring secretly, so as never to see it again. I remembered that it could be opened and on the inside there were two names engraved: *Mattia-Romilda*, and the date of the wedding. What could I do with it?

I opened my eyes and, for a long while, sat there, frowning and staring at the ring in the palm of my hand.

Everything around me had turned black.

Here was one link left of the chain that bound me to the past! The little ring, so light in itself, and yet so heavy! But the chain was already broken, and therefore, away with this link, too!

I started to throw it out of the window, but I caught myself in time. Now that chance had showered such exceptional favors on me, I could no longer trust everything to chance. I was obliged to believe anything possible; this for instance: that a little ring thrown into the open countryside might be found by a peasant and, going from hand to hand, with those two names engraved inside and that date, the ring might cause the truth to come out, the fact that the man drowned at the mill was not the librarian Mattia Pascal.

—No, no, I thought. A more secure place . . . But where?—

At that moment the train stopped at another station. I looked out, and immediately a solution occurred to me. I was at first a little reluctant to carry it out. I say this now to excuse myself to those readers fond of the handsome gesture, people who don't reflect and who don't like to remember that the human race is burdened by certain physical needs to which even a man bowed with grief is subjected. Caesar, Napoleon, and unjust as it may seem, even the most beautiful of women . . . But enough of this. On one side there was written the word WOMEN; on the other, MEN. And there I disposed of my wedding ring.

Then, not for pleasure so much as to try to give a certain substance to this new life of mine, till now suspended in a void, I set myself thinking about Adriano Meis, imagining a past for him, asking myself who was my father, where I had been born, etc. I did this calmly, with an effort to see everything clearly and fix it all in my mind, down to the smallest detail.

I was an only child. On this point, it seemed to me, there could be no argument.

It would be hard to be more singular than I . . . And yet . . . No! Who knows how many there are like me? In my same condition, my unknown brothers. You leave your hat and your jacket, with a letter in the pocket, near the railing of a bridge over a deep river; then instead of jumping off, you calmly go away, to America or some such place. A few days later an unrecognizable corpse is fished out of the river: why, it must belong to the man who left the letter on the bridge. And that's the end of that! True, I hadn't done this of my own free will; I hadn't left a letter, nor a jacket, nor a hat . . . But still I'm like the rest, with this added advantage: I can enjoy my freedom without remorse. Others chose to make me a present of it, and so . . .

And so, we'll say I'm an only child. Born . . . —wisest not to pin down a specific birthplace. How can that be avoided, though? You can't be born on a cloud, after all, with the moon as midwife, even though I did once read in the library that the ancients—along with many other jobs—assigned this task also to the moon, and pregnant women called upon her aid, giving her the name of Lucina.

No, not on a cloud; but for example, on an ocean liner. Yes, a man could be born there. Excellent! Born during a voyage. My parents were traveling because . . . because I have to be born on a ship! Now, Adriano, be serious about this! What plausible reason could there be for putting a pregnant woman, almost ready to give birth, on a ship . . . ? Had my parents gone to America perhaps? Why not? Plenty of people do . . . Even Mattia Pascal, poor man, wanted to go. So shall we say that this eighty-two thousand lire was earned by my father there, in America? Nonsense! With that kind of money in his pocket, he would have waited for his wife to have her baby comfortably on dry land. And besides, what foolishness! An emigrant doesn't earn eighty-two thousand lire all that easily in America. My father—what was his first name, by the way? Paolo? Yes, Paolo Meis. My father, Paolo Meis, had been deceived like so many others. He had drudged away for three years, or four, and then, discouraged, he had written a letter from Buenos Aires to my grandfather . . .

Ah yes, a grandfather. I really wish I had known a grand-father, a lovable little old man, for example, like the one who had just got off the train, the scholar who studied Christian iconography.

The imagination is capricious at times! What inexplicable necessity caused me, at that moment, to imagine that my father, Paolo Meis, had been a wastrel? Ah yes, he had caused poor grandfather so much suffering; he had married against the old man's will and had run off to America. Perhaps he too insisted that Christ was ugly. Everything must have seemed ugly to him there in America, with his wife about to have a baby. So when he received money from grandfather, he came away at once, even with my mother in that condition.

But why did I have to be born during the voyage, after all? Wouldn't it be even better for me to be born in America it-self, in Argentina, a few months before my parents came back to the old country? Of course. In fact, it was the thought of his innocent grandchild that had moved the old man to pity; for my sake alone he had pardoned his erring son. And so, as a mere infant I had crossed the ocean, in third class no doubt, and I had caught bronchitis during the voyage and only a miracle had saved my life. Splendid! Grandfather used to tell me about this often. But I was never to complain afterwards, as would have been normal, that I should have died then, when I was only a few months old. No, for after all, what griefs had I had to bear in my life? Only one really: the death of my poor grandfather, who had brought me up. My father, Paolo Meis, irresponsible, unable to bear any kind of yoke, had fled back to America after a few months, leaving his wife and me with the old man. And he had died out there, of yellow fever. When I was three, I lost my mother too; therefore I couldn't remember my parents at all, and knew only these bare facts about them. But there was another thing! I didn't even know the precise place of my birth. In Argentina, yes. But where? Grandfather didn't know, either because my father hadn't told him or because the old man had forgotten, and I naturally couldn't be expected to remember.

To summarize then:

(a) only child of Paolo Meis; (b) born in South America, in Argentina, exact locality not specified; (c) brought to Italy at the age of a few months (bronchitis); (d) no recollection and scarce information concerning parents; (e) brought up by grandfather.

Where? Oh, everywhere, more or less. First in Nice. Vague memories: *Place Masséna*, the *Promenade, Avenue de la Gare* . . . Then, in Turin.

That's where I was heading now, and I had all kinds of plans; I planned to choose a street and a house, where grandfather had left me till I was ten in the care of a family that I would make up when I was there on the spot, so that it would have all the local characteristics. I was planning to live, or better, to pursue with my imagination, the boyhood of Adriano Meis there, against a background of reality.

This pursuit, this imaginative construction of a life that had never really been lived but had been pieced together gradually from other lives and from places until it was made mine and felt mine—all this process brought me a new, strange joy, not without a certain sadness too, in the first days of my wanderings. It was my occupation. I lived not only in the present, but also for my past, that is, for the years that Adriano Meis had not lived.

I retained nothing or very little of what I had first imagined. It's true that nothing can be invented without some kind of roots, deep or shallow, in reality; and even the strangest things can be true, indeed no one's fantasy is capable of conceiving certain follies, certain improbable adventures which explode in the riotous midst of real life. And yet how different living, breathing reality seems from the inventions we draw from it! How many things, substantial, minute, unimaginable, our invented product needs before it can become again that very reality from which it was born. How many threads bind our invention to the complicated tangle of life, threads we have severed to make our creation a thing apart!

Now what was I if not an invented man? A walking invention who wanted and, for that matter, was forced to remain apart, even when thrust into reality.

Witnessing the lives of others, observing them minutely, I saw their infinite ties, and at the same time, I saw all my own snapped threads. Could I take these threads and knot them to reality again? Who knows where they would have drawn me; perhaps they would have been immediately transformed into the reins of runaway horses, hurtling towards the abyss with the poor chariot of my imperative invention. No. Those threads should be tied only to my fantasy.

I followed little boys between five and ten along streets and in parks, and I studied their movements, their games. I collected their expressions until, little by little, I had composed the childhood of Adriano Meis. I succeeded so well that it finally acquired an almost real consistency in my mind.

I didn't want to imagine a new mother. I would have felt I was profaning the vivid, painful memory of my real mother. But a grandfather, yes, I wanted to create that grandfather of my early daydreams.

Ah, how many grampas, how many little old men I followed and studied, in Turin, in Milan, in Venice and Florence, putting a little of each into the composition of my own grandfather. I took the bone snuffbox and the checked handkerchief of one of them, the cane of another; a third furnished me with spectacles and a chin whiskers; a fourth, with his walk and the way he blew his nose; and a fifth supplied his manner of talking and his laugh. The result was a little old man, refined and somewhat crusty, a lover of the arts, a broadminded Granddad who decided I wasn't to follow a regular course of study, because he preferred to teach me himself in conversation, taking me from city to city, through museums and galleries.

As I visited Milan, Padua, Venice, Ravenna, Florence, Perugia, this imagined grandfather was with me always like a shadow, and more than once he spoke to me, through the mouth of some aged guide.

But I also wanted to live for myself, in the present. From time to time I would be gripped by the thought of this unique, boundless freedom of mine and I would feel a sudden happiness, so strong I was almost lost in a blissful daze; I felt freedom fill my breast with a long, broad breath which uplifted my whole spirit. Alone! Alone! Alone! My own master! Having to account for nothing, to no one! For instance, I could go wherever I pleased. To Venice? Yes, Venice! Florence? Florence! This happiness accompanied me everywhere. Ah, I remember one sunset in Turin, in the first months of that new life, near a bridge over the Po where a dam checks the rush of the water and makes it churn there angrily. The air was marvelously pellucid; all the objects in shadow seemed enameled in that transparency. And as I watched, I felt so drunk with freedom that I was almost afraid I'd go mad, that I couldn't bear it for very long.

I had already achieved my external transformation from head to foot: clean-shaven, with a pair of light-blue spectacles, my hair long and artistically disheveled. I really looked like another person! I would stop sometimes at a mirror to converse with myself and I would burst out laughing.

—Adriano Meis! Happy man! Too bad you have to be got up like that . . . But, after all, what do you care? This is fine! If it weren't for that eye, *his*, that imbecile Mattia's, you wouldn't be downright ugly, even in the somewhat aggressive oddity of your appearance. You make women laugh a bit, that's true. But that's not your fault after all. If that Mattia hadn't worn his hair so short, you wouldn't be forced to wear yours so long; and I know that it isn't because of your personal preference that you now go around clean-shaven like a priest. Can't be helped. And when women laugh . . . laugh along with them; that's the best you can do.—

For that matter, I was living with myself and by myself almost exclusively. I occasionally exchanged a few words with hotel clerks, with waiters or fellow guests, but never out of any desire to strike up a conversation. Indeed, my reluctance made me realize that I had no taste for lying. In any case, the others also showed little or no desire to talk to me, perhaps because of my appearance: they took me for a foreigner. I remember when I was visiting Venice I couldn't convince an old gondolier that I wasn't a German or an Austrian. I had been born, true enough, in Argentina, but of Italian parents. My real "foreign-ness", if you want to call it that, was of another kind, and I was the only one who knew it. I was no longer anything; no official records registered me, except the one in Miragno, but then as a dead man and under another name.

I wasn't upset by this, and yet I didn't care to pass for an

Austrian. I had never had any occasion to turn my thoughts to the word "fatherland." I had had too many other things to worry about in the past! But now, in my idleness, I was becoming accustomed to pondering many things I would never have believed could interest me even for a moment. To tell the truth, I fell into this habit unintentionally and often I ended up by shrugging my shoulders, annoyed. Still I had to busy myself with something when I felt tired of wandering and looking at things. To escape from my irritating, futile reflections, I sometimes filled whole sheets of paper with my new signature, trying to write in a different hand, holding the pen in a different way from before. But at a certain point I tore up the paper and threw the pen away. I could have been an illiterate if I'd wanted! To whom did I have to write? I no longer wrote letters or received any.

This thought—like many others, too—plunged me into the past. I saw my house again, the library, the streets of Miragno, the beach; and I asked myself: Will Romilda still be wearing black? Perhaps she is, for appearances' sake. And what can she be doing?—And I imagined her, as I had seen her about the house so many, many times; and I also imagined the widow Pescatore, no doubt cursing my memory.

—I'm sure that neither of the two of them, I thought, has been even once to visit the grave of that poor man, and yet he died so cruelly. I wonder where they buried me? Aunt Scolastica may not have wanted to spend the money for me that she spent on Mamma. And Roberto even less. He probably said to himself: What made him do it? He could have gone on being librarian, living on two lire a day.—I probably lie like an outcast, in potter's field . . . Ah, best not to think of it! I'm only sorry for that poor man, who probably had relatives more humane than mine, kin who would have treated him better.—But, after all, what does he care now? He's got rid of his troubles!—

For some time I went on traveling. I decided to go outside of Italy, so I visited the beautiful Rhine country, as far as

Cologne, going down the river on a steamer. I stopped off at the most important cities: Mannheim, Worms, Mainz, Bingen, Coblenz . . . I would have liked to go farther north than Cologne, beyond Germany, to Norway; but then I decided that I had to limit my freedom. My money had to last the rest of my life, and it wasn't a large sum. I might live for another thirty years and always in this same situation, outside laws, with no documents to prove, in the first place, my actual existence. So it was impossible for me to find any kind of employment. And if I didn't want to get myself into a mess, I would have to live on a small, fixed amount. When I had done some figuring, I realized I shouldn't spend more than two hundred lire per month—not very much, but for over two years I had lived on far less, and not alone. So I would adapt myself.

At heart I was already a little tired of that wandering around, always silent and alone. I was instinctively beginning to feel the need of company. I realized this on a sad November day in Milan, when I had only recently come back from my brief trip in Germany.

It was cold and threatening to rain, as evening fell. Under a street lamp I saw an old match peddler whose box of wares, hanging from his neck on a strap, prevented him from wrapping himself up in the wornout cloak that was on his shoulders. From his fists, clenched under his chin, a string fell to his feet. I bent down to look and there, between his tattered shoes, I discovered a tiny puppy, only a few days old, trembling with the cold and whining constantly, huddled on the ground. Poor little animal! I asked the old man if he'd sell it to me. He said he would and added that he'd sell it cheap, too, even though the puppy was worth a great deal, ah yes! the little creature would grow up into a handsome dog, a big animal!

"Twenty-five lire . . ."

The poor little puppy continued to tremble, taking no pride in this high evaluation; he surely knew that this price didn't reflect his own future merits but the stupidity that his master thought he had read in my face.

Meanwhile I had had time to realize that, in buying that dog, I would indeed be acquiring a discreet and faithful friend, who would love me and respect me without having to ask who I really was and where I came from or if my papers were in order; but I would also have to pay a dog tax . . . I who no longer paid any taxes! This struck me as a first step towards compromising my freedom, a slight breach I would be making in it.

"Twenty-five lire!? Good-by!" I said to the old peddler.

I pulled my hat down over my eyes and, as a fine drizzle began to fall, I walked away, thinking, however, for the first time that this boundless freedom of mine was no doubt beautiful but that it was also something of a tyrant, since it wouldn't permit me even to buy a little puppy.

IX. A Bit of Fog

Diverted by my travels, intoxicated by my new freedom,
I hardly noticed whether that first winter was severe or rainy
or foggy. Now the second winter took me by surprise; I was,
as I said before, a bit weary of wandering and determined to
restrain myself from now on. I realized that . . . yes, there
was a bit of fog, and it was cold; I also realized that, though
my spirit tried to ignore the weather, I suffered from it nevertheless.

"I suppose . . ." I scolded myself, "that it should never be
cloudy, just so that you can enjoy your freedom in peace!"

I had amused myself enough, running hither and yon; in
that year Adriano Meis had lived his carefree youth; now he
had to become a man, consider his position, accustom himself
to quiet, modest living. Oh, that would be easy for him, free
as he was, and with no obligations!

Or so I thought at the time, and I began to wonder what
city would be the best permanent home for me, since I
couldn't go on living like a bird without a nest—not if I was
to establish an ordered existence for myself. But where? In a
large city or a small one? I couldn't make up my mind.

I shut my eyes and, in my thoughts, returned to those cities
I had already visited; I went from one to the other, lingering
in each until I could recapture in detail that certain street,
that square, whatever place I remembered most vividly. And
I would say then:

"Yes, I've been there, too. Ah, how much life eludes me,
how much life is stirring, bustling here or there, in all its
variety. And in how many places have I said: *Here* I could

settle down! *Here* I'd be happy to live! And I envied the in-habitants living there quietly, with their habits, their daily tasks, never knowing the painful sense of precariousness that keeps the traveler's spirit in a state of suspense."

This painful precariousness still gripped me and prevented me from loving the bed where I lay down to sleep, the various objects that surrounded me.

Every object is transformed within us according to the images it evokes, the sensations that cluster around it. To be sure, an object may please us for itself alone, for the pleasant feelings that a harmonious sight inspires in us; but far more often the pleasure that an object affords us does not derive from the object in itself. Our fantasy embellishes it, surround-ing it, making it resplendent with images dear to us. Then we no longer see it for what it is, but animated by the images it arouses in us or by the things we associate with it. In short, what we love about the object is what we put in it of our-selves, the harmony established between it and us, the soul that it acquires only through us, a soul composed of our memories.

Now how could any of this happen to me while I was living in a hotel room?

A house, a real house all my own—could I ever have one? My funds were very scarce . . . Perhaps a humble little place, only a few rooms? Easy now: I would have to see, consider all sorts of things carefully first. Of course, I could only be free, really free, like this, with a suitcase in my hand, here today, there tomorrow. If I stayed in one place, became the owner of a house, ah: then taxes followed immediately and official lists. Wouldn't they register my name at the city hall? Certainly they would! How? A false name? Ah, but then—who knows?—perhaps there would be secret investigations of me on the part of the police . . . Complications, in other words, trouble . . . No, no, I saw that I could no longer have a house of my own, objects of my own. I would take lodgings with some family, however, a furnished room. Why should I torment myself over such a minor problem?

It was winter's fault; winter inspired these melancholy reflections; Christmas was near and made a man long for the warmth of a friendly nook, the peace and privacy of a home.

It wasn't my own home that I was yearning for, to be sure. The old house, my father's, the only house I could recall with regret, had long since been destroyed, and not by my new condition. So I could console myself, knowing I would hardly be happier if I were to spend this Christmas holiday (I shuddered) with my wife and mother-in-law at Miragno.

To laugh, to amuse myself, I pictured myself at the door of my house, with a fine Christmas cake under my arm.

". . . May I come in? Is this where the widow Romilda Pascal, née Pescatore lives? And the widow Marianna Pescatore?"

"Yes, sir. But who are you?"

"You might say I'm the deceased husband of Signora Pascal, that poor gentleman who died by drowning a few years ago. Yes, I've come straight from the other world to spend the holidays with my family, thanks to the permission of my superiors! But I must leave again at once!"

If she saw me again suddenly like that, would the widow Pescatore die of fright? What? Her? Not likely! She would kill me off a second time, in the space of a day or two.

My good fortune—and I had to convince myself of this— my good fortune lay precisely there: in my liberation from my wife, my mother-in-law, my debts, the humiliations of my first life. Now I was free of everything. Wasn't that enough for me? Why, I had a whole life ahead of me. For the moment . . . there were probably many people lonely like me!

"Yes, but those others . . ." It was the bad weather, that cursed fog, that made me pensive. ". . . are either foreigners, or else they have a home elsewhere, and one of these days they can go back to it. Or if they don't have a home now, as you don't, they can have one tomorrow, and in the meanwhile they can enjoy the hospitality of some friend. But, to look the truth in the face, you will always be a foreigner everywhere: that's the difference. A foreigner to life, Adriano Meis."

I shrugged my shoulders, annoyed, and cried: "Very well then! All the less bother! You say I have no friends? I can make some . . ."

In the restaurant where I ate at that time, a man who sat next to me had already indicated his readiness to strike up a friendship with me. He was about forty: rather bald, dark, with gold spectacles which refused to stay on his nose, perhaps because of their heavy golden chain. Ah, he was such a nice little man! Just think: when he stood up and put his hat on his head, he immediately seemed a different person: he looked like a boy. His physical defect was his legs; they were too short; they didn't even reach the floor when he was seated. It would be incorrect to say that he rose from his chair, he climbed down from it really. He tried to compensate for this failing by wearing high heels. What's wrong with that? Yes, those heels *did* make too much noise; but they made his little birdlike steps so charmingly imperious.

And he was very smart, even ingenious—perhaps a tiny bit shrewish and mercurial—with ideas of his own, unconventional ones. He was a Cavalier, too.

He had given me his calling card: *Cavalier Tito Lenzi.*

While we're on the subject of calling cards, I almost made myself unhappy because of the poor figure I cut, unable to give him one of my own. I still hadn't had any cards made; I was somehow reluctant to have my new name printed. What pettiness! We can live without calling cards, can't we? You just speak your name aloud, and that's that.

And so I did. But, to be truthful, my real name . . . No, no more of that!

What a fine talker Cavalier Tito Lenzi was! He even knew Latin; he could quote Cicero as if it were nothing at all!

"Conscience? Why, the conscience is of no use, my dear sir! It can never suffice, as a guide. That might be possible, but only if the conscience were a lofty castle, so to speak, and not the village square. That is to say, if we could imagine ourselves in isolation, and if our conscience weren't by nature open to others. In the conscience, as I see it, there is an essential—oh yes, essential—relationship between myself, who am thinking, and the other beings, of whom I think. And therefore the conscience isn't a self-sufficient absolute—do I make myself clear? When the sentiments, the tendencies, the tastes of these others, of whom I think and you think, are not reflected in me or in you, we can never be content or calm or happy. And therefore all of us struggle to have our sentiments, our thoughts, our inclinations reflected in the conscience of others. And if this process doesn't take place because, as it were, the air at that moment refuses to carry the seeds and make them flower . . . the seeds of your idea into the mind of another, why then, my dear sir, you cannot say that your own conscience is sufficient. Sufficient for what? To allow you to live alone? To become sterile in the shadows? Ah, come, come. Mind you, I hate bombast, I hate rhetoric, that gossipy old liar, that flirt with spectacles on. Rhetoric throws out her chest and declares this fine sentence: '*I have my conscience and that's enough for me.*' Indeed! Cicero had already said: '*Mea mihi conscientia pluris est quam hominum sermo.*' But Cicero—let's be quite frank—eloquence, oh yes, eloquence, but . . . God save us, my dear sir! More boring than a child learning the violin!"

I could have kissed him. But alas, the dear little man chose not to go on with these subtle, intellectual discussions of which I have just given you a sample; he began to become more personal, and then, though I had thought our friendship was easy and already well-launched, I immediately felt some embarrassment, I felt a force within me, obliging me to draw back. As long as he did the talking and the conversation flitted over vague subjects, all was well; but now Cavalier Tito Lenzi wanted me to talk.

"You're not from Milan, are you?"

"No . . ."

"Just passing through?"

"Yes . . ."

"Nice city, Milan, eh?"

"Yes, quite nice . . ."

I sounded like a trained parrot. And the more pressing his questions became, the farther away I moved with my answers. Soon I was in America. But when the little man learned that I had been born in Argentina, he sprang from his chair and came over to shake my hand warmly: "Ah, I congratulate you, my dear sir! I envy you! America . . . I've been there."

He'd been there? Run!

"In that case," I hastened to say, "I'm the one who must congratulate you for having been there. Because I can almost say I've never been there, though I am a native. I left when I was only a few months old, so my feet have never really touched American soil."

"What a shame!" Cavalier Tito Lenzi exclaimed sadly. "But I suppose you have relatives back there!"

"No, none . . ."

"So you came to Italy with your whole family, and settled down here? Where do you live?"

I shrugged.

"Oh . . ." I sighed, on pins and needles. "Here for a while, and there . . . I haven't any family, and . . . I move about!"

"How pleasant! You're a lucky man! To travel . . . So you've no one at all?"

"No one . . ."

"How pleasant! You're lucky, indeed. I envy you!"

"You have a family, I take it?" I asked him in turn, to change the subject from myself.

"Ah no, alas!" he then sighed, frowning. "I'm all alone, and always have been!"

"Like me then . . ."

"But I'm bored, my dear sir! Bored!" the man snapped. "For me, solitude . . . ah yes, I'm tired of it. I've many friends, but believe me, when you've reached a certain age, it isn't so enjoyable to go home and find no one there. Hm! There are those who understand, my friend, and those who don't. Those who understand, in fact, say: 'I mustn't do this, I mustn't do that,' so as not to commit some stupidity or other! Splendid! But at a certain point we realize that all life is stupidity; so tell me yourself what it means never to have done anything foolish. At the very least it means you have never lived."

"But you . . ." I tried to comfort him. "You are still in time fortunately . . ."

"To behave stupidly? Ah, but I already have. A great many times, believe me!" he answered, with a gesture and a fatuous smile. "I've traveled, I've moved about as you have and . . . adventures, love affairs . . . some quite curious and exciting . . . yes, many have befallen me. Why, for example, in Vienna one evening . . ."

I was dumfounded. What? Amorous adventures? Him? Three or four or five in Austria, in France, in Italy . . . even in Russia? And what adventures they were! Each more daring than the last . . . Here, to give you a sample, is a bit of dialogue between him and a married woman:

LENZI:—Ah yes, dear lady, if you stop and think . . . Betray your husband? . . . Heaven forfend! Faithfulness, honesty, dignity . . . three big and holy words . . . all with capital letters. And then, Honor! another huge word . . . But believe me, dear lady, in practice it's quite another matter. A matter of small importance! Ask other ladies, your friends, who have ventured . . .

MARRIED WOMAN:—I have, and all of them experienced a great disappointment!

LENZI:—Naturally! That's quite understandable! Because those horrible words restrained them, held them back, and the ladies took a year, or six months at least, to make up their minds. Then the disappointment stems precisely from the disproportion between the act itself and the amount of thought that preceded it. You must make up your mind at once, dear lady: I want to, I shall! It's so simple!

All you had to do was look at him, consider for a moment his absurd, tiny little figure, to realize that he was lying; no other proof was needed.

My amazement was followed by my deep depression and embarrassment for him, since he wasn't aware of the wretched effect that these cock-and-bull stories of his were bound to produce. I was depressed also because I saw this man lying with such enjoyment and nonchalance, though he had no need to, whereas I, who couldn't avoid lying, had to force myself, and every time I did, I suffered and felt my spirit writhing within me.

Depression and irritation. I wanted to grasp his arm and shout at him: Tell me, Cavalier, why? Why?

If, however, my depression and irritation were natural enough, I realized, on sober reflection, that such a question would have been foolish, to say the least. In fact, if that little man so bestirred himself to make me believe in these adventures of his, the reason was precisely that he had no need to lie. But I . . . I was forced to by necessity. What for him could be an amusement, almost the exercise of a privilege, was for me the opposite, a painful duty, a punishment.

And what was the logical conclusion of this line of thought? Alas, that since my situation inevitably sentenced me to lie, I could never have another friend, a real friend. No house then, and no friends . . . Friendship means confiding, and how could I ever confide in anyone the secret of my life, without name or past, a life which had sprung up like a mushroom from the suicide of Mattia Pascal? I could have only casual acquaintances, I could allow myself only brief exchanges of alien words with my fellow men.

Well, those were the inconveniences of my good fortune.

So it had to be! Was I going to lose heart over it?

"I'll live by myself and with myself, as I've lived until now!"

Yes, but you see . . . to tell the truth, I was afraid that I would no longer be satisfied or happy alone with my own company. And then, as I touched my face and found it clean-shaven, as I ran my hand over the long hair or touched the spectacles on my nose, I felt a strange emotion; I seemed no longer to be I, it was as if I weren't touching myself.

Let's be fair: I had got myself up like that for others, not for myself. Now did I have to go on living with myself in that masquerade? If everything I had imagined and constructed concerning Adriano Meis was of no use for other people, to whom was it useful? Me? But I could believe it, if at all, only when others believed it, too.

Now if this Adriano Meis lacked the courage to tell lies, to plunge into the midst of life; if he drew back and returned to his hotel, tired of seeing himself alone in the Milan streets on those sad winter days; if he shut himself up in the company of the deceased Mattia Pascal, then I could foresee that things would begin to go badly for me, that little or no pleasure lay ahead, and that my fine stroke of luck, when you came right down to it . . .

But perhaps the truth was this: that in my unlimited freedom, I found it difficult in some way to begin to live. When I was about to come to a decision, I felt myself restrained, I seemed to see all kinds of obstacles and shadows and hindrances.

So again, I drove myself out into the streets, I observed everything, I stopped for any trifle, and reflected at length on the most insignificant things. When I was tired, I would go into a café, read a newspaper or two, look at the people coming and going, until finally I would go out as well. But life—observed in this way, as if by an outside spectator—seemed shapeless and aimless; I felt lost in the jostling crowds. And the din, the constant ferment of the city dazed me.

—Oh why . . . I asked myself desperately, . . . does mankind toil so to make the apparatus of its living more and more complicated? Why this clatter of machines? And what will man do when machines do everything for him? Will he then realize that what is called progress has nothing to do with happiness? Even if we admire all the inventions that science sincerely believes will enrich our lives (instead they make it poorer, because their price is so high), what joy do they bring us, after all?—

In an electric tram the day before, I had come upon a poor man, one of those men who can't help communicating to others anything that goes through his mind.

"What a splendid invention!" he said to me. "With two pennies, in the space of a few minutes, I can cover half of Milan."

He saw only the two pennies of the fare, that poor man, and he never thought that his miserable little salary was consumed every month, and wasn't enough for him to live on, dazzled as he was by that noisy life, with the electric tram, electric light, etc., etc.

And yet, I thought, science has the illusion that it is making our existence easier and more comfortable. But even admitting that it's easier, with all these difficult, complicated machines, I still ask: What worse turn could they do a man condemned to futile activity than to make it easy and almost mechanical for him?

I went back to my hotel.

There, in a corridor, at one of the windows a cage hung with a canary in it. Since I couldn't converse with others, and I didn't know what else to do, I began to converse with him, with the canary. I imitated his sounds with my lips, and he really thought someone was speaking to him. He listened and perhaps in that tweet-tweet of mine, he heard welcome news of nests, of trees and freedom . . . He flitted about the cage, turning and jumping, looking at me sideways and shaking his head, then he answered me, questioned me, and listened again.

Poor little bird! He did move me, though I didn't know what I had said to him . . .

And yet, when you think about it, doesn't something similar happen among us humans? Don't we also believe that nature speaks to us? And don't we think we find a meaning in her mysterious voices, an answer— according to our desires— to the anxious questions that we ask her? And nature, in her infinite greatness, perhaps hasn't the faintest idea of us and our vain illusion.

You see the kind of conclusions that can come from a jest prompted by idleness, when a man is condemned to live alone with himself! I was almost ready to hit myself! Was I on the brink of becoming a philosopher seriously?

No, no, my behavior wasn't logical. I couldn't go on like this any longer. I had to overcome all my reluctance; I had to make up my mind at all costs.

In short: I had to live, live, live!

X. Holy Water Stoup and Ash Tray

A *few days later I was in Rome, to settle down there.*
Why Rome and not somewhere else? I see the real reason
only now, after all that has happened to me, but I won't tell
it here. I don't want to spoil my story with reflections which,
at this point, would be out of place. I chose Rome first of all
because I liked it more than any other city, and also because
it seemed more suited to receive with indifference, among all
the other foreigners, a foreigner like myself.

The choice of a home, or rather of a decent room on a
quiet street with some discreet family, cost me considerable
effort. Finally I found it in Via Ripetta, in sight of the river.
To tell the truth, my first impression of the family that was
to house me was not very favorable; and when I went back to
my hotel I wondered for a long time if it wouldn't be better
for me to go on hunting.

On the fifth floor, there were two name plates on the door:
PALEARI on one side, and PAPIANO on the other. Under the
latter there was also a calling card, held by two tacks, on which
I read *Silvia Caporale.*

The door was opened by an old man of about sixty (Paleari? Papiano?) in heavy underwear and bare feet in a pair of
grimy slippers. His pink, plump, hairless torso was naked, his
hands soapy, and on his head there was a glistening turban of
foam.

"Oh, forgive me!" he cried. "I thought it was the maid . . .
You must excuse my appearance . . . Adriana! Terenzio!
Come this minute! There's a gentleman . . . Please wait a
moment . . . Come in . . . What can I do for you?"

"Is there a furnished room for rent here?"

"Why, yes sir! Ah, here's my daughter. You can speak with her. Hurry, Adriana, the room!"

A tiny little miss appeared, all confused. She was blond and pale, her light blue eyes were sweet and sad like all her other features. Adriana—the same name as mine! *Think of that!* I said to myself: *as if I'd chosen on purpose!*

"Where's Terenzio?" the man with the foam turban asked.

"Why, Papa, you know perfectly well he's in Naples. He's been there since yesterday. Leave us now! If you could see yourself," the young girl answered, mortified, in a tender voice which, despite her slight irritation, expressed the gentleness of her disposition.

The man withdrew, repeating: *Of course, of course*, shuffling off in his slippers, and continuing to soap his bald head and his huge gray beard.

I couldn't help smiling, but in a kindly way, not wanting to mortify the daughter further. She half-shut her eyes, as if to avoid seeing my smile.

At first I thought she was hardly more than a child, but as I examined her expression more carefully, I realized that she was already a young woman and therefore obliged to wear that house dress which made her seem a little clumsy, unsuited as it was to her tiny body and her delicate features. She was in half mourning.

Speaking in a very low voice and avoiding my eyes (who knows what her first impression of me was!) she led me along a dark hall to the room that I was to rent. When she opened the door, I felt my chest expand at the air and the light that came in through the two broad windows overlooking the river. In the remote distance you could see Monte Mario, then the Ponte Margherita and the whole new Prati quarter as far as Castel Sant'Angelo. The windows looked down on the old Ripetta bridge and the new one which was being built near it, farther on, the Ponte Umberto, then all the old houses of Tordinona which followed the broad curve of the river. In the background, in the same direction, there were the green heights of the Janiculum, the high fountain of San Pietro in Montorio, and the equestrian statue of Garibaldi.

Because of that spacious view I took the room, which was furnished with attractive simplicity, with light wallpaper, white and blue.

"This little terrace here," the girl in the house dress said, "also belongs to us, at least for the moment. We're told that it's going to be torn down, though, because it's an obstruction."

"A what?"

"Obstruction. Isn't that the word? They're going to build a new street along the river, but not for a long time yet."

Hearing her speak softly and with such seriousness, dressed in that way, I smiled and said: "Oh really?"

She took offense. She lowered her eyes and bit her lip slightly. Then, to make her speak again, I then said very gravely: "I beg your pardon, Signorina, but . . . there aren't any children in the house, are there?"

She shook her head, without opening her mouth. Perhaps she sensed still a touch of irony in my question, though I hadn't meant any. I had said *children*, not *little girls*. Again I hastened to make amends: "And . . . another thing, Signorina. You don't rent out any other rooms, do you?"

"This is the best we have," she answered, without looking at me. "If it doesn't satisfy you . . ."

"No, no . . . I was merely asking, to know whether . . ."

"We rent another one," she said, looking up with an air of forced indifference. "On the other side of the house, over the street . . . A single lady lives there; she's been with us two years now. She gives piano lessons . . . not in the house."

As she said this, she gave me the faintest hint of a smile, a sad smile, and added: "There is my father, myself, and my brother-in-law . . ."

"Paleari?"

"No, Papa's name is Paleari. My brother-in-law is Terenzio

Papiano. But he is about to leave, with his brother, who is also here with us for the moment. My sister died . . . six months ago."

To change the subject, I asked her the price of the room, and we came to an immediate agreement. I asked her if I should leave a deposit also.

"As you wish," she said. "If you would like to leave your name, in any case . . ."

I touched my jacket with a nervous smile and said: "I'm afraid . . . I'm afraid I don't have my card with me . . . My name is Adriano . . . Yes, I know, I heard you also called Adriana, Signorina. Perhaps this displeases you . . ."

"Oh no. Why should it?" she said, evidently noticing my odd embarrassment and laughing this time like a real child.

I laughed too and added: "Then, if it doesn't displease you, my name is Adriano Meis: there! Could I move in this very evening? Or perhaps it would be better if I came back to-morrow morning . . ."

She answered, "As you please," but I went away with the impression that I would have given her great pleasure if I had never come back at all. I had dared be disrespectful to her grown-up house dress.

A few days later, however, I could see for myself that the poor girl really did have to wear that dress, which she would probably have been quite glad to remove. The entire burden of the housekeeping was on her shoulders, and if she hadn't been there, the situation would have been disastrous!

Her father, Anselmo Paleari, the old man who had appeared to me in a foam turban, had a brain also made more or less of foam. The first day I moved into the house, he presented himself to me not only—as he said—to apologize again for the improper way he had appeared the first time, but also to have the pleasure of making my acquaintance, since I had the appearance of a scholar, or perhaps, of an artist.

"Am I wrong?"

"I'm afraid you are. Artist—no, not at all! Scholar . . . hm, barely . . . I like to read an occasional book."

"Oh, you have some good ones," he said, examining the backs of the few volumes I had already lined up on the shelf over the desk. "One of these days I'll show you mine, eh? I have some good ones, too. Hmph!"

And he shrugged his shoulders, standing there, absent-minded, his eyes staring, obviously unaware of everything, of where he was or with whom. He repeated his "Hmph" a few more times, the corners of his mouth pulled down, then he turned his back and left, without even saying good-by.

Then and there I felt somewhat amazed, but later, when he took me to his room and showed me his books as he had promised, I understood not only that moment of absent-mindedness but many other things as well. The titles of the books were of this sort: *La Mort et l'audelà*, *L'homme et ses corps*, *Les sept principes de l'homme*, *Karma*, *La clef de la Théosophie*, *ABC de la Théosophie*, *La doctrine secrète*, *Le Plan Astral*, etc., etc.

Signor Anselmo Paleari was a member of the theosophical school.

He had been prematurely retired from his position as chief clerk in an office of I forget what Ministry, and this retirement had ruined him not only financially, but also, since he was now free, master of his time, it had plunged him entirely into his fantastic studies and his fuddled meditations, separating him more than ever from real life. At least half of his pension must have been spent on those books. He had already created a little library of them, but the theosophical doctrine apparently did not completely satisfy him. A spirit of criticism must also have been gnawing at him, because along with those theosophical books, he also had a rich collection of philosophical essays and studies, ancient and modern, and volumes of scientific enquiry. In recent times he had also dedicated himself to spiritualistic experiments.

In his lodger, the piano teacher Signorina Silvia Caporale,

he had discovered exceptional mediumistic talents, not yet fully developed, of course, but which would surely develop with time and practice until she would prove superior to all the most celebrated mediums.

For my part, I don't mind saying that never have I seen a pair of eyes sadder than those of Signorina Silvia Caporale, in a face as vulgar and ugly as a carnival mask. They were very black, intense, oval, and gave the impression that behind them there there was a lead counterweight as in certain automatic dolls. Signorina Silvia Caporale was past forty and she also had a handsome mustache under her lump of a nose, which was always enflamed.

Later I learned that this poor woman was lovesick and drank. She knew she was ugly and now old, and she drank out of desperation. Certain evenings she came home in a really deplorable state: her hat all askew, her lumpy nose as red as a beet, and her eyes half-shut, sadder than ever.

She would throw herself on the bed, and immediately all the wine she had drunk would come out of her, transformed into an infinite stream of tears. Then our poor little godmother in the house dress would have to sit up with her and console her late into the night; Adriana had pity on her, and this pity overcame any disgust. She knew that the woman was alone in the world and very unhappy, with a rage in her body that made her hate her life, to which she had already twice tried to put an end. Slowly, Adriana would make her promise to be good, and never do it again; and then, oh yes, the next day we would see the Signorina appear, all furbelowed, affecting certain monkeylike poses, suddenly transformed into an innocent and spoiled child.

She earned a few lire now and then, helping some aspiring singer rehearse her numbers for a café chantant, but she spent the money at once either for drink or for frippery, and she never paid for her room or for the simple meals that she ate there with the family. But she couldn't be sent away. How would Signor Anselmo Paleari carry on his spiritualistic experiments without her?

Beyond that, however, there was another reason. Signorina Caporale, at her mother's death two years earlier, had given up her old home and, on coming to live with the Palearis, had entrusted about six thousand lire, proceeds from the sale of her furniture, to Terenzio Papiano for some business affair which he had proposed to her. It was a completely safe, profitable venture. But the six thousand lire had vanished.

When Signorina Caporale confessed all this to me herself, in tears, I could excuse Signor Anselmo Paleari to some extent for his folly in exposing his own daughter to contact with a woman of this kind.

Of course, for little Adriana, so instinctively good and even too kind, there was no reason to fear; in fact, what secretly made her suffer more than anything else were those mysterious practices of her father, who called up spirits through Signorina Caporale.

Little Adriana was religious. I realized that one of my first days there because of a blue-glass holy water stoup which hung on the wall over the night table next to the bed. I had lain down with a still-lighted cigarette in my mouth and had begun to read one of those books of Paleari's; absently, I had then put the burnt-out end in that stoup. The next day, the stoup had been removed. On the night table instead there was an ash tray.

I asked her if she had removed it from the wall, and with a slight blush, she answered: "Forgive me, I thought that you had greater need of an ash tray."

"Why, was there holy water in the stoup?"

"Yes. We have the church of San Rocco just opposite . . ."

And she went out. So the tiny little godmother wanted me to be holy, did she? She must, if she had taken holy water from the font at San Rocco for my stoup. For mine and, certainly, for her own. Her father probably didn't use one. And in the holy water font of Signorina Caporale, if she had one, there was no doubt altar wine.

Thanks to the curious emptiness in which I had been suspended for such a long time, the slightest event now made me sink into long meditations. The matter of the holy water stoup reminded me that since my boyhood days I hadn't observed any religious practices, nor had I entered any church to pray, after the departure of Tweezer, who used to take me to church with Berto, on Mamma's orders. I had never felt the necessity to ask myself if I really had any faith. And Mattia Pascal had died a sinful death without the comforts of religion.

Suddenly I saw that I was in a singular situation. For all the people who had known me, I had solved—for better or worse—the most annoying and disturbing problem that a living person can face: the problem of death. Who knows how many people at Miragno were saying: "He's lucky, after all! He's solved the problem at least."

But, in the meanwhile, I had really solved nothing. Now I found myself with Anselmo Paleari's books in my hands, and these books taught me that the dead—the really dead—were in my very same condition, the "husks" of the Kamaloka, suicides especially, whom Mr. Leadbeater, author of the *Plan Astral* (*premier degré du monde invisible, d'après la théosophie*), depicts as ravaged by all human appetites but unable to satisfy them, since these spirits are without their carnal body, but are unaware that they have lost it.

"Just think of that," I said to myself, "I might almost believe that I really did drown there in the millrace, and that I am merely deceiving myself with the notion that I'm still alive."

It's well known that certain kinds of madness are contagious. Paleari's, though I rebelled against it at first, ended up by infecting me. Not that I really believed I was dead, though it would have done no harm if I had: the hard thing is dying; once you're dead, I don't believe you can harbor the sorry desire of returning to life. No, I suddenly realized that I would have to die again: that was the trouble! I'd completely forgotten. After my suicide in the millrace, I naturally had seen nothing but life ahead of me. And now, here was Signor Anselmo Paleari constantly putting the shadow of death across my path.

That dear man could talk about nothing else! He talked about it, however, with such fervor, and in his impetuous talk, he came out with images and expressions so singular that, as I listened, I lost all desire to be rid of him or to go and live elsewhere. Besides, though Signor Paleari's faith and doctrine sometimes seemed puerile to me, they were at least comforting; since I now realized that one of these days I would have to die properly, I wasn't sorry to hear death spoken of in this way.

"Is it logical or isn't it?" he asked me one day, after reading aloud a passage from a book by Finot, filled with a philosophy so sentimentally macabre that it was like the dream of a drug-addicted gravedigger; it concerned, of all things, the life of the worms born from the decay of the human body. "Is it logical, or isn't it? Matter, yes, let's admit that everything is matter. But there are all sorts of forms, types, qualities. There is stone and there is the intangible air, for heaven's sake! In my body alone, there is the fingernail, the tooth, the hair; there's even the delicate eye tissue, after all. Now, my dear sir, who can contradict that? But what we call the soul may also be matter. You'll agree, I hope, that it isn't matter like the fingernail or the tooth or the hair; it may be matter like air, or what have you. You admit the existence of air, don't you? Well, why not the soul then? Is this logical or isn't it? Matter, matter, my dear sir. Follow my line of reasoning, and just see where it leads you if you admit my premises. Let's take Nature. We now consider man as the heir of a countless series of generations, don't we? The product of a slow natural process. But you, my dear Signor Meis, believe that man is also an animal, a cruel animal and, all things considered, a far from praiseworthy one. I concede this. But then I say: all right, man—in the scale of living creatures—doesn't represent a very high stage. From the worms to the human being let's say there are eight—no, seven—no, five steps. But, good heavens! Nature has toiled thousands and thousands and thousands of centuries to climb up those five steps, from the worm to man; Nature has had to evolve—am I right?—this matter to reach the form and the substance of that fifth step, to create this animal that steals and kills and lies, but is also capable of writing the *Divine Comedy* or of making sacrifices, Signor Meis, as my mother and your mother did. Does it then, all of a sudden, return to zero? Is that logical? My nose, my foot may become worms, but my soul, mind you, even though it's also matter—who's saying it isn't?—my soul isn't the same as my nose or my foot. Isn't that logical?"

"I beg your pardon, Signor Paleari," I objected. "Suppose a great man goes out for a walk, he falls, strikes his head, and becomes an idiot. What about his soul?"

Signor Anselmo sat staring for a moment, as if a boulder had suddenly fallen at his feet.

"His soul?"

"Yes. You . . . or I, who am certainly not a great man, but still . . . well, a rational man . . . I walk, I fall, I strike my head and become an idiot. What about my soul?"

Paleari clasped his hands and, with an expression of benevolent sympathy, answered: "For heaven's sake, Signor Meis, why would you want to fall and strike your head?"

"It's just a hypothesis . . ."

"No, no, my friend; go out for your walk and never fear. Instead, let's take the case of old people, who don't have to fall and strike their heads in order to become simple-minded. Well, what does it mean? You want to prove, with this argument, that when the body weakens so does the soul, and that when one is extinct so is the other. Am I right? But, my dear Signor Meis. Think for a moment of the contrary: think of bodies that were extremely weak and yet contained the light of the soul to the very brightest degree: Giacomo Leopardi! or many, many old people: His Holiness Leo XIII, for example! What then? Imagine a piano and a musician. At a certain stage, after much playing, the piano is out of tune, one key doesn't strike, two or three strings break. Well, of course, with an instrument in that shape, even the best of musicians would play badly. And if the piano were silent, would the musician cease to exist?"

"The piano would stand for the brain, and the musician for the soul, I suppose?"

"It's an old metaphor, Signor Meis! Now if the brain is damaged, the soul inevitably seems simple-minded, or mad, or whatever. What I mean is this: if the musician breaks his instrument, whether on purpose or by accident, he will pay for it; whoever damages a thing has to pay . . . everything is paid for in life. But this is another question. You know that mankind, all mankind, for as far back as we can trace it, has always aspired to a future life, a next world? Does this mean nothing to you? This is a fact, a cold fact, actual proof."

"They say that the instinct of self-preservation . . ."

"No, no, my friend, I don't give a fig for this wretched skin that covers me! It's a burden I bear because I know I have to bear it. But, by God, if they can prove to me that after I've borne it for another five or six or ten years, I won't have paid my toll, or done my duty, if they prove that everything ends there, why, I'd throw this body away today, this very moment. So where's your instinct of self-preservation then? The only reason I preserve myself is that I feel it won't end like that! The individual man is one thing, they say, and mankind is another. The individual ends, the species continues its evolution. That's a fine way of reasoning! Just look here a moment! As if I weren't mankind, and you, and all of us, one by one. And doesn't each of us feel the same thing, that it would be the height of absurdity, it would be atrocious if everything were to consist in this, this miserable breath of air which is our life on earth, fifty or sixty years of boredom and suffering and toil—for what? For nothing! For mankind? But mankind itself must come to an end one day. Just think a moment: this life, all this progress, this evolution, what's the reason for it? Nothing! And nothing, pure nothingness, they say doesn't exist . . . The healing of the planet? Isn't that what you said the other day? Very well. Healing. But it depends in what sense. The evil of science, Signor Meis, lies precisely there: it concerns itself only with life."

"Ah," I sighed, with a smile. "Since we have to live . . ."

"But we also have to die!" Paleari replied.

"I understand . . . but why think about it so much?"

"Why? Because we can't understand life, if we don't explain death in some way. The motive, the direction of our actions, the thread to lead us out of the maze, dear Signor Meis, the light must come from beyond, from death."

"From all that darkness?"

"Darkness? It may seem dark to you! But try lighting a little lamp of faith, with the pure oil of the soul. If the lamp fails, then we wander about here, in this life, like so many blind men, in spite of all the electric light we've invented. For life, the electric light does very well; but, my dear sir, we also need that other light to illuminate our death for us. Mind you, some evenings I try to light a little lantern of my own, with red glass: we must try every possible way to see somehow. At present my son-in-law Terenzio is in Naples. He'll be back in a few months, and then I'll invite you to be present at one of our modest little sessions, if you like. And perhaps that lantern . . . who knows? . . . No, I don't want to tell you any more about it for the moment."

As you can see for yourself, the company of Anselmo Paleari wasn't very pleasant. But, if you stop and think about it, could I—without running risks, without being forced to lie—hope for anything else, for the companionship of someone not removed from life? I was reminded again of Cavalier Tito Lenzi. Signor Paleari, at least, didn't want to know anything about me; he was satisfied simply with the attention I paid to his talk. Almost every morning, after his habitual ablutions, he would accompany me on my walks. We would go to the Janiculum or the Aventine, or to Monte Mario, sometimes as far as the Ponte Nomentano, always talking about death.

—This is what I've gained by not really dying, I thought. Some gain!—

Sometimes I tried to draw him on to other subjects, but apparently Signor Paleari had no eyes for the life around him. He walked almost always with his hat in his hand; at times, he would raise it as if to greet some shade and exclaim: "Nonsense!"

Only once did he, unexpectedly, ask me a direct question: "Why are you living in Rome, Signor Meis?"

I shrugged and answered: "Because I like it here . . ."

"And yet it's a sad city," he observed, shaking his head. "Many people are surprised that no enterprise ever succeeds here, that no living idea takes root. But these people are surprised because they refuse to admit that Rome is dead."

"Rome is dead, too?" I exclaimed, upset.

"It's been dead a long time, Signor Meis! And any effort to bring it back to life would be futile, I believe. Shut in the dream of its majestic past, the city refuses to consider the wretched life that insists on teeming around it. When a city has lived a life like Rome's, of such outstanding, even unique character, it can't then become a modern city, that is to say, a city like all the others. Rome lies there, her great heart shattered, below the Capitoline. Do these new houses belong to Rome? Look here, Signor Meis. My daughter Adriana told me about the holy water stoup that was in your room. You remember? Adriana took it from your room, but then, the other day, she dropped it and it broke. Only the little bowl remained and now it's in my room, on my desk, assigned to the same purpose for which you used it accidently one evening. Well, Signor Meis, the destiny of Rome is exactly the same. The popes—in their own fashion, mind you—turned the city into a holy water font; and we Italians, in our way, have made it an ash tray. We've come here from every village and country to scatter over it the ashes from our cigar, a symbol of the frivolity of our wretched life and of the bitter, poisonous pleasure it gives us."

XI. At Evening, Looking at the River

Thanks to the respect and the affection shown me by the master of the house, I more and more became one of the family; and at the same time, my situation became more and more difficult, the secret embarrassment I had already experienced was now often a piercing remorse, as I saw myself an intruder in their midst, with a false name, altered features, a fictitious and almost non-existent identity. And I determined to withdraw back as far as I could, constantly reminding myself that I shouldn't move too close to the lives of others, that I had to flee all intimacy and be content to live as I had before, completely outside life.

"Free!" I said again, but I was already beginning to perceive the meaning of this freedom of mine and to measure its boundaries.

For example, my freedom meant standing there at evening, leaning out of a window to look at the river as it flowed, black and silent, between its new banks, under the bridges whose lamps were reflected in the water, writhing like serpents of fire. I would follow the course of that water in my mind, from its remote source in the Apennines, through the various countryside, now through the city, then again into the country to its mouth. In my thoughts I would conjure up the gloomy, restless sea into which these waters, after their long journey, would enter and be lost. And from time to time I would open my mouth and yawn.

"Freedom! . . . Freedom! . . ." I murmured. "But, after all, wouldn't it be the same elsewhere?"

Sometimes, in the evening, I would see our little godmother

on the small terrace next to my room, in her house dress, busily watering the pots of flowers.— There is life! I thought.— And with my eyes I followed the gentle girl in her sweet duty, waiting patiently for her to look up towards my window. But in vain. She knew that I was there, but when she was alone she pretended not to be aware of me. Why? Was her reserve merely shyness, or was the sweet girl still offended, by my cruel, obstinate lack of consideration for her, the result of an effort of my will?

Now, when she set down the watering can, she would lean on the railing of the terrace, also gazing at the river, perhaps to show me by her attitude that she didn't bother her head about me, since she had far more serious things of her own to ponder, and that she needed solitude.

I smiled to myself at this thought; but then, seeing her leave the terrace, I thought that my opinion might also be wrong, the fruit of the instinctive annoyance that anyone feels when he sees others ignoring him. But then:—For that matter, I asked myself, why shouldn't she ignore me? Why should she speak to me, if there's no need? Here I represent the tragedy of her life, her father's madness; perhaps I represent a humiliation for her. Perhaps she still yearns for the days when her father was working and there was no need to rent out rooms and have strangers in the house. And a stranger like me, especially! Perhaps I frighten her, poor child, with this eye of mine and these spectacles . . . —

The sound of a carriage on the nearby wooden bridge roused me from these reflections. I sighed impatiently, and withdrew from the window. I looked at the bed, at my books, and hesitated briefly at the choice. But finally I shrugged, clamped my old hat on my head and went out, hoping that outside I could shake off this furious boredom.

Following the inspiration of the moment, I would go either to the most crowded streets or to the loneliest spots. I remember one night, in St. Peter's Square, I felt I was in a dream, an almost distant dream, which came to me in that

past world, gathered there in the arms of the majestic colon-
nade, in the silence that the constant sound of the two foun-
tains seemed only to increase. I went over to one of them, and
then that water seemed alive to me, and all the rest seemed
ghostly and profoundly melancholy in the motionless solem-
nity.

Going home, along the Via Borgo Nuovo, at one point I
encountered a drunk who, as he passed me and saw my pensive look, bent down and stuck his head forward a little, to
look at my face from below. Then he shook my arm slightly
and said: "Be happy!"

I stopped abruptly, surprised; I looked him up and down.

"Be happy!" he repeated, accompanying this exhortation
with a movement of his hand which seemed to mean: What
are you brooding over? Don't bother about anything!

And he went stumbling off, one hand against the wall to
hold himself up.

At that hour, in that deserted street, near the great church,
my mind still filled with the thoughts that it had inspired, the
apparition of this drunken man and his strange, affectionate,
and philosophically compassionate advice stunned me. I stood
there for I don't know how long, watching him lurch away;
then I felt my daze break, in a burst of mad laughter.

"Happy! Yes, my friend. But I can't go into a tavern, the
way you do, to look in the bottom of a glass for the happiness
you advise. I wouldn't be able to find it there, alas. And I
can't find it anywhere else, either! I go to a café, among worthy
people, who smoke and chat about politics. Happy all of them,
joyous indeed! But according to a little imperialist lawyer
who frequents that café, we could be happy on a single condition: if we were governed by a benevolent absolute monarch.
You don't know these things, poor drunken philosopher; they
never even cross your mind. But the real cause of all our sufferings, of this sadness of ours—do you know what it is? Democracy, my dear man. Yes, democracy; that is, the govern-
ment of the majority. Because when power is in the hands of

a single man, this man knows he is one and must make many happy; but when the many govern, they think only of making themselves happy, and the result is the most absurd and hateful of tyrannies. Of course! Why do you think I suffer? I'm suffering because of a tyranny masked as freedom . . . Ah well, time to go home!"

But that was to be the night of encounters.

A little later, as I was walking along Tordinona almost in darkness, I heard a loud cry, above other, stifled cries, in one of the narrow alleyways that run into that street. Suddenly I saw a tangle of squabbling people in front of me. Four wretches armed with knotty clubs were attacking a woman from a brothel.

I mention this adventure not to glorify my courage, but to tell instead of my fear as a result of what happened. There were four of those rogues, but I had a sound cane with an iron tip. It's true that a pair of them came at me with knives, but I defended myself as best I could, swinging my cane in a circle, and ducking this way and that so as not to be caught in the middle. In the end I managed to bring the iron tip of the cane squarely down on the head of the most insistent of the four; I saw him stagger, then run off. The other three, fearing that the woman's screams would bring people to the scene, followed the first. I discovered that I had been somehow wounded on the forehead. I shouted at the woman, who hadn't stopped calling for help, and told her to be quiet. But seeing my face streaked with blood, she couldn't control herself and, all disheveled and weeping, she wanted to help me, and bandage me, taking from around her neck a silk scarf that had been torn in the fighting.

"No, no thank you," I said, rejecting her help with disgust. "It's nothing . . . Go, go now . . . don't let them see you."

And I went to bathe my forehead at the fountain which is below the steps of the nearby bridge. But while I was there, up came two breathless policemen who wanted to know what had happened. The woman, a Neapolitan, promptly started

narrating the horrible event, and produced the most affectionate and admiring phrases in her dialect on my behalf. I had a
hard time ridding myself of those two eager policemen, who
absolutely wanted me to go with them to the station and
make a report. Fine! That's all I would need! To be involved
with the police, to appear in the newspapers almost as a
hero . . . I! who must remain in the shadow, unknown to
everyone . . .

A hero . . . a hero who couldn't be heroic . . . unless it
meant actually dying . . . But then, I was already dead!

"Excuse my asking, Signor Meis, but are you a widower?"
This question was asked me point-blank one evening on
the terrace by Signorina Caporale, who was there with Adriana. They had invited me to sit with them for a while.

At first I was irked. I answered: "No. Why do you ask?"

"Because you're always rubbing your ring finger with your
thumb, as if you were twisting a ring around your finger . . .
Isn't that so, Adriana?"

You see what women bother to observe! Certain women,
that is; because Adriana declared that she had never noticed
it.

"You haven't watched yourself!" Signorina Caporale cried.

I had to admit that, though I had never noticed it myself, it
was quite possible that I had such a habit.

"As a matter of fact," I felt called upon to add, "for a long
time I did wear a little ring there. I had to have a goldsmith
cut it off, because it was too tight and it hurt me."

"Poor little ring!" the older woman moaned, writhing,
since she was in a kittenish mood that evening. "It was that
tight, was it? It didn't want to let go of your finger, eh? Perhaps it was the souvenir of a . . ."

"Silvia!" little Adriana interrupted her, in a tone of reproach.

"What's wrong?" the other woman said. "I was going to

say a first love . . . Come, talk to us, Signor Meis. Aren't you ever going to do any talking?"

"There . . ." I said, "I was thinking of the conclusion that you drew from my habit of rubbing my finger. An arbitrary conclusion, my dear lady. Because, to my knowledge, widowers don't remove their wedding rings. If anything, it's the wife who weighs on the man's mind, not the ring, after the wife has gone. Indeed, just as veterans like to display their medals, so I believe widowers like to wear their wedding ring."

"Yes, yes," the Signorina exclaimed. "You're very good at changing the subject!"

"Change it? Not at all! I wanted to go into it more thoroughly."

"Really? I never pry. I was just saying that I had the impression . . . nothing more."

"The impression that I'm a widower?"

"Yes. Don't you agree, Adriana, that Signor Meis acts like a widower?"

Adriana started to glance up at me, but then lowered her eyes at once; in her shyness, she could never return another's gaze. She smiled briefly, her usual sweet, sad smile, and said:

"You expect me to know how widowers act? How strange you are!"

A thought, a memory must have come into her mind at that moment. It upset her, and she turned to look at the river below. The other woman certainly understood, because she also sighed and turned to look at the river.

A fourth person, invisible, had forced himself on us. Finally I realized this too, and as I looked at Adriana's mourning, I imagined that Terenzio Papiano, the brother-in-law still in Naples, mustn't have acted like a proper widower and that instead, according to Signorina Caporale, this was how I behaved.

I must confess I was pleased when the conversation came to such a bad end. The sorrow caused Adriana by the thought of her dead sister and of the widower Papiano was, for Signorina Caporale, the punishment for her indiscretion.

Except that, if we want to be fair, what I considered indiscretion was after all only a completely forgivable natural curiosity which my strange silence was bound to inspire. And since solitude was now unbearable to me, and I couldn't resist the temptation to approach others, they had a right to know something about me. And I had to resign myself to satisfying them, as best I could, that is to say by lying and inventing; there was no other way out! The others weren't to blame; I was. And now my guilt was aggravated by lies. But if I didn't want to lie, if it made me suffer, I would have to go away, back to my lonely, silent wandering.

I noticed that even Adriana, who never asked me a question that wasn't completely tactful, still was all ears whenever I answered the questions of Signorina Caporale, whose questions—to tell the truth—often went beyond the limits of natural, pardonable curiosity.

For example, one evening there on the terrace, where we now had become accustomed to gather after I came home from supper, the Signorina asked me such a question, laughing and defending herself against Adriana, who cried at her in agitation: "No, Silvia! I forbid you! Don't you dare!"

Signorina Caporale's question was this: "Forgive me, Signor Meis, but Adriana wants to know why you don't grow at least a mustache . . ."

"That's not true!" Adriana shouted. "Don't believe it, Signor Meis! She was the one who . . . I . . ."

She suddenly burst into tears, our dear little godmother. And Signorina Caporale promptly tried to comfort her by saying:

"No, no, dear . . . Come . . . What harm is there? There's nothing wrong with . . ."

Adriana pushed her away with one elbow: "What's wrong is that you lied, and you make me angry! We were talking about actors in the theatre, who are all . . . like that, clean-shaven, and then you said: '*Just like Signor Meis. I wonder why he doesn't at least grow a mustache*' . . . and I only repeated: '*I wonder!*' . . ."

"Well," the other woman went on, "if a person says *I wonder*, it means that the person wants to know!"

"But you said it first!" Adriana protested, highly annoyed.

"May I answer?" I asked, to restore calm.

"No, excuse me, Signor Meis. Good evening!" Adriana said, and she got up to leave.

But Signorina Caporale grasped her arm: "Come, don't be such a silly little thing! It's all in fun . . . Signor Adriano is a kind man. He excuses us. Isn't that so, Signor Adriano? You tell her . . . why don't you grow at least a mustache."

This time Adriana laughed, her eyes still filled with tears.

"Because it's a deep, dark mystery," I answered, comically changing my tone of voice. "I'm in a conspiracy!"

"We don't believe you!" the Signorina cried, in the same tone; but then she added: "Still and all, there's no denying you're a secretive type. What were you doing, for example, at the post office this afternoon?"

"At the post office? Me?"

"Yes, sir. Do you deny it? I saw you with my own eyes. It was around four o'clock . . . I happened to be crossing Piazza San Silvestro . . ."

"You must be mistaken, Signorina. I wasn't there."

"I see, I see," she answered, disbelieving. "Secret correspondence . . . Am I right or not, Adriana? This gentleman never receives any letters here at the house. The maid told me. So there."

Annoyed, Adriana writhed in her chair.

"I don't receive any here at the house, or at the post office either," I answered. "All too true, alas. Nobody writes me, Signorina, for the simple reason that I no longer have anybody who can write me."

"Not even a friend? Is that possible? Nobody?"

"Nobody at all. Just myself and my shadow on this earth.

I've dragged my shadow about, here and there, constantly, never stopping this long before in any one place, never long enough to form a lasting friendship."

"Lucky you!" the piano teacher exclaimed with a sigh. "To have traveled all your life! Tell us about your travels at least, since you don't want to talk about anything else."

Little by little, I passed the shoals of the first embarrassing questions, thrusting others away with the oar of falsehood, my lever and my support, gripping as if with both hands the questions that pressed me hardest, to turn them prudently away; and finally, the fragile bark of my fiction could reach the open sea and hoist the sails of fantasy.

And now, after a year or more of forced silence, I experienced a great pleasure in talking, on and on, every evening there on the little terrace, telling of what I had seen, of observations I had made, incidents that had happened to me here and there. I surprised even myself at the number of impressions I had received while traveling, impressions that my silence had buried within me, and that now, as I spoke, came springing to life, on my lips. This private wonder gave an extraordinary color to my tales; and as the two listening women showed their delight, I slowly began to long for a happiness I had never really enjoyed, and this regret also gave flavor to my narrative.

After a few evenings, Signorina Caporale's attitude towards me altered radically. Her mournful eyes were charged with such intense languor that they more than ever suggested an inner counterweight of lead, and accentuated the comic contrast between those eyes and her carnival mask of a face. There was no doubt about it: Signorina Caporale had fallen in love with me!

After my first, ridiculous surprise, I realized that in all those evenings I had never been talking for her sake, but for the other girl who always sat there in silence, listening. Evidently Adriana, too, had sensed that I was speaking for her alone, because we came to a kind of tacit agreement to enjoy to-

gether the comic and unexpected effect of my talk on the
highly sensitive sentiments of the forty-year-old piano teacher.

Still, even with this surprise, no thought less than pure ever
entered my mind concerning Adriana; her innocent goodness,
suffused with melancholy, couldn't inspire anything of the
kind. But at that first secret understanding I felt as much joy
as her delicate shyness could allow. She would give me a fleeting glance, like a sudden flash of tenderness and grace; a smile
of commiseration for the ridiculous folly of that poor woman.
Or an occasional benevolent reproach with her eyes and a
brief nod, if I started to press our innocent jest too far, giving
hopeful string to the soaring kite of the Signorina, which either
flew high in the heavens or dipped at some violent or unexpected earthward tug from me.

"You would have to be heartless," the Signorina said to me
once, "if what you say is true, about your going through life
untouched . . . I can't believe it."

"Untouched? How?"

"Yes . . . I mean without feeling any passions . . ."

"Ah, never, Signorina Caporale, never!"

"In the first place, you've never condescended to tell us
where you got that little ring that you made a goldsmith cut
off because it was too tight . . ."

"And it was hurting my finger! Didn't I tell you about it?
Of course I did! It was a present from my grandfather, Signorina."

"Liar!"

"Have it your way, but I can even tell you that my grandfather gave me that little ring in Florence, when we were
coming out of the Uffizi Gallery. And you know why? Because, though I was only twelve, I had mistaken a Perugino
for a Raphael. That's right. And as a prize for my mistake, I
was given the ring, which grandfather had bought at some
stall on the Ponte Vecchio. Because the old man, for some
reason of his own, firmly believed that the painting by Peru-

gino should have been attributed to Raphael. There's your mystery explained! You can easily imagine the difference between the slender hand of a twelve-year-old boy and this great paw of mine. You see? Now I'm all like this, like this clumsy hand that wears no pretty rings. Perhaps I do have a heart, but I'm also capable of fair thinking. I look at myself in the mirror, with these spectacles—aren't they pathetic?—and I feel hopeless. 'My dear Adriano', I say to myself, 'How can you expect any woman to fall in love with you?' "

"What an idea!" the Signorina cried. "Do you consider that fair thinking? No, no, it's terribly unfair towards us women. A woman, dear Signor Meis, is more generous than a man, and she isn't so prone to consider only external beauty."

"Let's say then that women are braver than men, Signorina. Because I admit that to love a man like me, a woman would have to have a good deal of courage, in addition to being generous."

"Come now! You just enjoy talking like that, making yourself out to be uglier than you are."

"That's true. And you know why? To keep anyone from feeling compassion for me. You see, if I tried to fix myself up in some way, people would say, 'Look at that poor man; he thinks that mustache makes him look less ugly.' Not I. If I'm ugly, then I'll *be* ugly, wholeheartedly, without asking for compassion. What do you say to that?"

Signorina Caporale heaved a deep sigh.

"I say that you're wrong," she continued. "If you tried growing a little beard, for example, you'd soon realize you're not the monster you say you are."

"And what about my eye?" I asked her.

"Well, since you mention it so frankly," she answered, "I've been wanting to say something to you for some time. Why don't you have an operation? It's very simple nowadays, and you could be rid of that little defect in no time."

"You see, Signorina?" I concluded. "Women may indeed be more generous than men, but I'd like to point out that, little by little, you've advised me to make myself a new face."

Why had I insisted so on this subject? Did I really want Signorina Caporale to blurt out, in Adriana's presence, that she could love me—indeed, *did* love me—as I was, clean-shaven and with that misplaced eye? No. I had talked this much and asked the Signorina all these detailed questions because I had realized the pleasure that Adriana felt, perhaps unconsciously, when the other woman gave me such victoriously reassuring answers.

So I understood that, despite my odd appearance, Adriana *could have* loved me. I didn't say this even to myself, but from that evening on, the bed I slept in seemed softer, and the objects that surrounded me seemed more attractive, the air I breathed seemed lighter, the sky bluer, and the sun brighter. I chose to believe that this change still came from the fact that Mattia Pascal had ended up there in the mill-race, and because I, Adriano Meis, after having wandered vaguely for a while in new, boundless freedom, had finally regained my balance, achieved the ideal I had set for myself, to make a new man of myself, to live another life which now, at last, I felt within me to the full.

And my spirit became gay again, as in my first youth; I had rid myself of the poison of experience. Even Signor Anselmo Paleari no longer seemed so boring: the shadow, the gloom, the fogginess of his philosophy had all disappeared in the sunlight of my new joy. Poor Signor Anselmo! He didn't realize that, of the two things he said all of us should ponder while on earth, I was thinking only of one. But perhaps—why not?— he also must have thought of living, in his own happier days. The poor piano teacher was more deserving of sympathy; not even her wine succeeded in making her *be happy*, as that unforgettable drunk had said in the Via Borgo Nuovo. She wanted to live, poor thing, and she thought that men were selfish, valuing only external beauty. Did she then feel beautiful inside, in her soul? Ah, who knows the sacrifices she would have been capable of, if she had found a "generous" man? Perhaps she might never have drunk another drop of wine.

—If we admit, I thought, that to err is human, then doesn't justice become superhuman cruelty?—

And I determined to stop being cruel to poor Signorina Caporale. I was determined, but alas, I was cruel through no fault of mine. In fact, the less I wanted to be, the more cruel I was. My affability was new fuel to her all too easy fire. And so when I spoke, the woman turned pale, while Adriana blushed. I don't really know what I said, but I felt that every word, its sound, its tone never went so far as to upset the person to whom I was really speaking, never broke the secret harmony that already—I don't know how—had been established between us.

Our spirits have their own private way of understanding one another, of becoming intimate, while our external persons are still trapped in the commerce of ordinary words, in the slavery of social rules. Souls have their own needs and their own ambitions, which the body ignores when it sees that it's impossible to satisfy them or achieve them. And every now and then when two people communicate only with their souls, if they are suddenly alone somewhere, they are full of anguish and feel almost a violent repulsion at the thought of the slightest physical contact, an uneasiness that drives them apart, but ceases immediately when a third person appears. Then, the anguish past, the two souls seek each other again with relief and again exchange smiles at a distance.

How often I experienced this with Adriana! But I thought her embarrassment was the effect of her natural shyness, and I thought mine came from the remorse aroused by my deceit, the whole fiction of my existence, which I had to keep up in the face of the purity and the simplicity of that sweet and gentle creature.

Now I saw her with different eyes. But hadn't she also really been transformed in the past month? Didn't her timid glances now glow with a more vivid inner brightness? Didn't her smiles seem less sad, as she went about her daily task of being our wise little godmother, the task that at first had seemed to me merely a role she was childishly playing?

Yes, perhaps she too instinctively felt my same need, the need for the illusion of a new life, though she didn't know what it could be. This vague desire, like an aura from the soul, had gradually opened for her, as for me, a window on to the future, where a ray of intoxicating warmth came to us. But we didn't know how to move closer to that window, either to shut it or to look out and see what was on the other side.

Poor Signorina Caporale felt the effects of this bliss of ours, delicate though it was.

"You know something, Signorina?" I said to her one evening. "I've almost decided to take your advice."

"What advice?" she asked.

"To have an oculist operate on me."

The Signorina clapped her hands in delight.

"Oh, wonderful! Doctor Ambrosini! Go to him. He's the best; he operated on poor Mamma's cataract. You see, Adriana? You see? The mirror spoke. What did I tell you?"

Adriana smiled, and so did I.

"No, it wasn't my mirror, Signorina," I said. "I begin to feel it's necessary. For a while now the eye has been hurting me. It's never been of great use to me, but I still wouldn't want to lose it altogether."

That wasn't true. Signorina Caporale was right. It was the mirror; my mirror had spoken to me and said that, if a fairly simple operation could remove from my face that repulsive feature so associated with Mattia Pascal, then Adriano Meis would be able to do without his blue spectacles and even allow himself a mustache. In short, he could adjust his body to the changed state of his spirit.

A few days later, a scene that I watched in the night from behind one of my shutters suddenly dismayed me.

The scene took place on the little terrace next to my room,

where I had sat until about ten with Adriana and the Signorina. After retiring to my room, I had idly begun to read one of Signor Anselmo's favorite books, *Reincarnation*. At a certain point I thought I heard voices on the terrace; I listened more carefully, in case it was Adriana. No. Two people were talking in low, tense voices; I heard a man, but it wasn't Signor Paleari. Still he and I were the only men in the house. My curiosity aroused, I went to the window to look through the blinds. In the darkness I thought I could make out Signorina Caporale. But who was the man talking with her? Had Terenzio Papiano arrived unexpectedly from Naples?

From something the Signorina said in a slightly louder voice, I realized that they were talking about me. I moved closer to the window and listened more intently. The man was obviously irritated by some news that the piano teacher must have given him about me; and now, she was trying to mitigate his reaction.

"Rich?" he asked at one point.

The Signorina answered: "I don't know . . . He seems to be. He certainly lives on an income, without doing any work . . ."

"Always about the house?"

"No, no. Besides you'll see tomorrow . . ."

When she said this, she called him *tu*. So Papiano (there was no doubt that he was the man) was Signorina Caporale's lover . . . Then why had she appeared so interested in me all these past weeks?

My curiosity was now more aroused than ever; but as if to spite me, the two began to speak very softly. Since my ears were no help then, I tried putting my eyes to work. And there, I saw the Signorina put her hand on Papiano's shoulder. A little later, he brushed it away rudely.

"How could I prevent it?" she said, raising her voice slightly in a tone of intense exasperation. "Who am I? What do I represent in this house?"

"Call Adriana here," the man ordered her, imperiously.

Hearing Adriana's name spoken in that tone, I clenched my fists and felt my blood boil in my veins.

"She's asleep," the Signorina said.

He answered her grimly, menacing: "Go wake her up! Right away!"

I don't know how I kept myself from flinging open the blinds in a fury.

The effort I made to restrain myself like that made me suddenly aware of my situation. The very words that poor woman out there had just said with such exasperation now rose to my own lips: "Who am I? What do I represent in this house?"

I drew back from the window. But then I immediately thought of a justification. It was my business, after all: those two were talking about me, and that man wanted also to talk about me with Adriana. I was obliged to listen, to discover the man's feelings on the subject of myself.

I readily accepted this excuse for my indelicacy in spying and eavesdropping, though I sensed I was only putting self-protection first, to avoid admitting the much more profound interest that was aroused in me at that moment.

I went back to peering through the slats of the blinds.

Signorina Caporale was no longer on the terrace. The man, left alone, had gone to look at the river, resting his elbows on the railing, his head in his hands.

Filled with furious anxiety, bending over, clasping my knees, I waited for Adriana to appear on the terrace. The long wait didn't tire me; on the contrary, it gradually calmed me and gave me an increasing sense of satisfaction. I supposed that, in her room, Adriana had refused to give in to the bullying of that villain. Perhaps the Signorina was pleading with her. And meanwhile, there on the terrace, the man was consumed with annoyance. I hoped the piano teacher would soon come back to say that Adriana chose not to get up. But no: there she was!

Papiano went over to her at once.

"Go to bed!" he said to the Signorina, no longer calling her *tu*. "Leave me alone to speak with my sister-in-law."

The woman obeyed, and then Papiano started to close the outside blinds between the dining room and the terrace.

"No, no!" Adriana said, holding her arm against the blind.

"But I have to talk to you!" her brother-in-law growled, in a grim tone, forcing himself to speak softly.

"Then talk as we are. What do you have to say to me?" Adriana went on. "You could have waited till tomorrow."

"No, now!" he said, grasping her arm and drawing her to him.

"Really!" Adriana cried, struggling proudly.

I couldn't stand it any longer. I opened my blinds.

"Oh, Signor Meis," she called at once. "Would you mind stepping out here for a moment?"

"Here I am, Signorina!" I quickly answered.

My heart pounded in my breast with joy and gratitude, and with one leap I was in the hall. But there, near the door of my room, I found almost coiled up on a trunk a thin, very blond young man with a long, almost transparent face. He opened his blue, languid, dazed eyes a crack, and I stopped for a moment to look at him in surprise. Then I realized this must be Papiano's brother, and I ran out on the terrace.

"Signor Meis, I'd like to introduce . . ." Adriana said, "my brother-in-law, Terenzio Papiano, who has just come this minute from Naples."

"Charmed! Delighted!" the man exclaimed, taking off his hat, bowing low, and shaking my hand warmly. "I'm sorry I've had to be away from Rome all this time, but I'm sure that my little sister-in-law here has taken good care of you. Hasn't she? If you need anything, don't hesitate to say so. For instance, if you want a larger writing desk . . . or something else, speak right up . . . We like to have our guests happy; it's an honor to have you with us."

"Thank you, thank you," I said. "But I have everything I need. Thank you."

"Not at all. It's our duty! And consider me, too, at your disposal, if I can be of help to you in any way at all . . . Adriana, child, you were asleep . . . Go on back to bed, if you want . . ."

"Oh, now that I'm up . . ." Adriana said, with her sad smile.

And she went over to the railing to look at the river.

I sensed that she didn't want to leave me alone with this man. What was she afraid of? She stayed there, as if lost in thought, while the man, still holding his hat, spoke to me of Naples. He had had to stay longer there than he planned, in order to copy a number of documents from the private archives of the most excellent Duchessa Teresa Ravaschieri Fieschi: *Mamma Duchessa* as everyone called her, or *Mamma Charity* as he would have preferred to call her. The documents were of exceptional importance and would throw new light on the end of the Kingdom of the Two Sicilies and especially on the figure of Gaetano Filangieri, Prince of Satriano. The Marchese Giglio—Don Ignazio Giglio d'Auletta—who employed Papiano as secretary, meant to describe the prince in a detailed and forthright biography. At least as far as the Marchese's devotion and loyalty to the Bourbons would allow him to be forthright.

Papiano went on and on. He certainly enjoyed his own loquaciousness, and as he spoke, he modulated his voice like an experienced amateur actor; he inserted a little laugh here, made an expressive gesture there. My head was ringing like an anvil, and I merely nodded from time to time, glancing towards Adriana, who continued to look at the river.

"Ah yes, alas," Papiano concluded, in a baritone key, "a Bourbon sympathizer and a priest lover, that's the Marchese Giglio d'Auletta. Whereas myself, I . . . (I have to say this in a low voice, even here in my own home) salute the statue of Garibaldi there on the Janiculum every morning as I leave the house. Have you noticed? You get a good view of it from here. And I constantly feel like shouting: 'Hurrah for the twentieth of September!' but I have to work as that reactionary's secretary. A worthy man, mind you, but a Bourbon sympathizer and black! . . . Yes, my dear sir . . . We have to earn our bread, eh? I swear that many a time I feel like spitting on it, if you'll pardon the expression. It sticks in my throat. It chokes me . . . But what can I do? Bread! . . . Bread!"

He shrugged his shoulders twice, held up his arms, then slapped his hips.

"Come, come, Adriana, my child," he said then, running over to her and putting both his hands on her waist. "To bed! It's late . . . the gentleman is no doubt sleepy."

At the door of my room, Adriana clasped my hand warmly, as she had never done before. When I was alone, for a long time I kept my hand clenched, as if to hold on to her hand's pressure. All that night I lay awake, thinking, in the grip of mad longings. The ceremonious hypocrisy, the insinuating, garrulous servility, the malevolence of the man would certainly have made it unbearable for me to stay in the house where he undoubtedly wanted to act as tyrant, exploiting the kindliness of his father-in-law. Who knows what wiles he would adopt? He had already given me a sample, changing his manner abruptly when I appeared. But why did he so disapprove of my staying in the house? Why wasn't I simply a lodger like anyone else? What had Signorina Caporale said to him about me? Could he really be jealous of her? Or was he jealous of someone else? That suspicious, arrogant manner of his, the way he sent the piano teacher off so that he could be alone with Adriana, to whom he had then spoken so violently; her rebellion; her refusal to let him close the blinds; the agitation that had always seized her in the past at any mention of her absent brother-in-law—all these things confirmed my hateful suspicions that the man was planning something that involved her.

But why was I racking my brain like this? Couldn't I, after all, leave the house if the man bothered me even for a moment? What was keeping me here? Nothing. Then with tender satisfaction, I remembered how she had called me from the terrace, as if to seek my protection, and how she had clasped my hand so tightly afterwards . . .

I had left the shutters and the curtain open. At a certain point the moon, as it sank, lingered in the frame of my window, as if to spy on me. Catching me still awake in my bed, it seemed to say: "I know what it is, my dear. I knew long ago. But you don't, do you?"

XII. Papiano and My Eye

"*The tragedy of Orestes in a marionette theatre!*" Signor
Anselmo Paleari came into my room and announced. "Automatic marionettes, the very latest invention. This evening at
eight-thirty in Via dei Prefetti, number 54. That's worth going
to, Signor Meis."

"The tragedy of Orestes?"

"Yes. *D'après Sophocle*, the poster says. It must be *Elektra*.
Now listen to the curious idea that's occurred to me: if at the
climax of the play, just when the marionette who is playing
Orestes is about to avenge his father's death and kill his
mother and Aegisthus, suppose there were a little hole torn in
the paper sky of the scenery. What would happen? Answer me
that."

"I don't know," I said with a shrug.

"But it's easy, Signor Meis! Orestes would be terribly upset
by that hole in the sky?"

"For what reason?"

"Let me go on. Orestes would still feel his desire for vengeance, he would still want passionately to achieve it, but his
eyes, at that point, would go straight to that hole, from which
every kind of evil influence would then crowd the stage, and
Orestes would feel suddenly helpless. In other words, Orestes
would become Hamlet. There's the whole difference between
ancient tragedy and modern, Signor Meis—believe me—a hole
torn in a paper sky."

And he went shuffling out.

From the nebulous heights of his abstractions, Signor Anselmo often allowed his thoughts to come hurtling down in this way, like avalanches. The reason, the logic, the appropriateness of them remained up there, among the clouds, so that it was difficult for the listener to understand him.

Still the thought of the puppet-Orestes, disturbed by a hole in the sky, lingered for a long time in my mind. —Lucky marionettes, I sighed, over whose wooden heads the false sky has no holes! No anguish or perplexity, no hesitations, obstacles, shadows, pity—nothing! And they can go right on with their play and enjoy it, they can love, they can respect themselves never suffering from dizziness or fainting fits, because for their stature and their actions that sky is a proportionate roof.

—And the prototype of those marionettes, my dear Signor Anselmo, I went on thinking, is here in your house: your unworthy son-in-law, Papiano. Who is more content than he with the paper sky, so low over his head, comfortable and serene dwelling of that God who is proverbially broadminded and is ready to close his eyes and raise his hand in absolution, that God who repeats sleepily at every little fraud: *"Help yourself, and I will help you."* And your Papiano helps himself in every sense. For him life is a game of skill. How he enjoys plunging into every kind of intrigue: quick and bold and talkative!—

Papiano was about forty, tall of stature and robust of limb; he was slightly bald with a big mustache, graying a bit under the nose, a handsome, big nose with flaring nostrils. His eyes were gray and sharp, as restless as his hands. For example, at times while he was talking with me, he would realize—I don't know how—that behind him Adriana was having difficulty in cleaning or straightening some object in the room. He would promptly say, *"Pardon!"*

Then he would run to her and take the object from her hands: "No, my dear, not like that. Watch!"

He would clean it himself and put it back in its place, then return to me. Or else he would sense that his brother, who suffered from epileptic fits, was going into a spell, and he would run to give him little slaps on the cheeks, or tweak his nose: "Scipione! Scipione!"

Or he would blow his breath into the boy's face, to bring him round.

No doubt, I would have enjoyed all this enormously, if I hadn't had my terrible Achilles' heel!

From the very beginning, Papiano obviously knew about it or—at least—sensed it. He began a siege, all full of ceremony and polite gestures like so many hooks, meant to draw words out of me. It seemed to me that everything he said, even his most superficial question, concealed a trap. I didn't want to appear distrustful for fear of increasing his suspicions; but my irritation at his servile and assiduous attentions prevented me from dissembling my reactions.

My irritation also came from two private, secret causes. One was this: here I was, having committed no evil act, having done no one harm, yet forced to be on my guard, frightened, suspicious, as if I had lost the right to live in peace. And the other cause? I was unwilling to confess it even when I was alone, and that was why it was so terribly irritating. It was all very well for me to say to myself:—Idiot! Leave the house! Be rid of that tiresome Papiano once and for all!—

I didn't leave; I wasn't able to leave any more.

My inner struggle not to admit consciously my feelings for Adriana prevented me meanwhile from reflecting on the effects of this new emotion on my abnormal existence. There I was, bewildered, distraught, dissatisfied with myself, in constant turmoil, and yet always with a smile on my face.

The plotting I had overheard that evening from behind my blinds had never become any clearer to me. It was as if Papiano's bad first impression, based on information received about me from Signorina Caporale, had been erased the moment I was introduced to him. He was tormenting me, of course, but he seemed to do it automatically. He certainly had no secret plan to make me go away. On the contrary! What was afoot then? Adriana, after his return, had become sad and elusive as in the early days. Signorina Silvia Caporale no longer called Papiano *tu* in the presence of others; but he, with his swaggering manner, addressed her in the familiar form quite openly. He even went so far as to call her *Rhea Silvia*; I couldn't really interpret these joking ways of his, these liberties. True enough, the poor woman's disorderly life didn't entitle her to any great respect, but neither did she deserve to be treated like that by a man who was not related to her in any way.

One evening (there was a full moon, and it was as bright as day) I saw her from my window, sad and alone, there on the terrace where we gathered rarely now, no longer with our former pleasure, since Papiano also joined us and did all the talking. Driven by my curiosity, I decided to go out and surprise her in that moment of dejection.

As usual, in the hall just outside my door, I found Papiano's brother coiled on the trunk in the same position as when I'd seen him the first time. Had he decided to settle there? Or was he mounting guard over me, at his brother's orders?

On the terrace, Signorina Caporale was crying. First she refused to tell me anything, complaining simply of a bad headache. Then, as if suddenly coming to a decision, she turned to look me in the face, holding out her hand and asking: "Are you my friend?"

"If you'll give me the honor . . ." I answered, with a bow.

"Thank you. But for heaven's sake, don't say that merely out of politeness. If you knew how badly I need a friend, a real friend, at this moment! You should understand; you're alone in the world, like me . . . But you're a man . . . If you knew . . . If you only knew . . ."

She bit the handkerchief she was holding in her hand, trying to fight back her tears; unable to do this, she suddenly ripped the handkerchief several times, angrily.

"To be a woman, ugly, and old," she cried. "Three incurable misfortunes. Why do I go on living?"

"Calm yourself, please," I begged her, grieved. "What makes you talk like this, Signorina?"

I couldn't think of anything else to say.

"Because . . ." she blurted, then suddenly checked herself.

"Tell me," I urged her, "if you need a friend . . ."

She raised her torn handkerchief to her eyes, and . . .

"What I need is to die!" she moaned, with such profound and intense sorrow that I immediately felt a knot of anguish in my throat.

I'll never forget how sadly that withered, graceless mouth was twisted as she uttered those words, nor the trembling chin with its few, curling little black hairs.

"But not even death wants me," she went on. "It's nothing . . . forgive me, Signor Meis! What help could you give me? None. Words, at most . . . yes, a little sympathy. I'm an orphan, and I have to stay here and be treated like . . . perhaps you've noticed. And they haven't the right, really, you know? They're not giving me charity, after all . . ."

And here Signorina Caporale told me about the six thousand lire Papiano had taken from her, as I mentioned before.

Though the unhappiness of the poor woman interested me, this wasn't what I wanted to learn from her. Taking advantage (I admit) of her emotional state, caused partly perhaps by a few extra glasses of wine, I ventured a question: "Forgive me, Signorina, but why did you give him that money?"

"Why?" She clenched her fists. "Two treacheries, each blacker than the other. I gave it to him to show him I realized clearly what he wanted of me. You understand? While his wife was still alive, he . . ."

"I understand."

"Just imagine," she continued heatedly. "Poor Rita . . ."

"His wife?"

"Yes, Rita, Adriana's sister . . . for two years she lingered between life and death . . . You can imagine how I . . . But anyway, here they all know how I behaved; Adriana knows, and that's why she loves me. Yes, she does, poor little thing.

But now what's become of me? You know, for his sake I had to sell my piano, which was . . . everything to me. You understand? Not just because of my work; with my piano I could talk. As a girl, at the conservatory, I used to compose; I wrote some music after I'd taken my diploma, then I let it all go. But when I had my piano, I used to compose still, just for myself, improvising . . . I would unburden myself, lose myself so completely that at times I think I must have fallen to the floor in a faint. I don't myself know what came out of my soul then; my instrument and I were one, my fingers weren't just touching a keyboard: I was making my soul weep and cry out. I can only say this: one evening (my mother and I lived on a second floor) people gathered in the street below, and when I stopped, applauded me for a long time. I was almost frightened by it."

"Excuse me, Signorina," I said, trying to comfort her somehow. "Couldn't you hire a piano? I would so much like to hear you play, and if you would . . ."

"No," she interrupted me. "What could I play now? It's all over for me. I bang out stupid little songs, that's all. It's finished . . ."

"But Signor Terenzio Papiano," I again ventured, "promised to give you back that money, didn't he?"

"Him!" she said immediately in a burst of rage. "You think I ever asked him for the money back? Oh yes, he promises to give it to me now, if I help him . . . That's right: he wants me, of all people, to help him. He had the nerve to suggest it to me, calm as could be . . ."

"Help him? In what?"

"In a new wickedness of his. You understand? I see that you do understand."

"Adri— I mean, Signorina Adriana?" I stammered.

"Exactly. He wants me to help persuade her. Me! Me! You realize?"

"To marry him?"

"Of course. And you know why? She has—or ought to have

—a dowry of fourteen or fifteen thousand, the poor child. Her sister's dowry which he was supposed to give back at once to Signor Anselmo, because Rita died without leaving any children. I don't know what kind of fraud he's involved in now. He's asked for a year's time before giving it back. But he hopes that . . . hush! Here's Adriana!"

Closed in herself, more elusive than ever, Adriana approached us; she put her arm around Signorina Caporale's waist and greeted me with a slight nod. After what I had heard, I felt a violent annoyance at seeing her so subdued, almost the slave of that trickster's tyranny. A little later, like a shadow, Papiano's brother also appeared on the terrace.

"Look at him," Signorina Caporale said in a low voice to Adriana.

The girl half-shut her eyes and smiled bitterly. Then she shook her head and left the terrace, saying to me: "Excuse me, Signor Meis. Good evening."

"The spy," Signorina Caporale whispered to me, with a wink.

"But what is Signorina Adriana afraid of?" I blurted out, in my mounting irritation. "Doesn't she realize that, with her meekness, she encourages that man to become more overbearing, more of a tyrant? Listen, Signorina, I'll confess to you that I envy greatly all those who can enjoy life and take an interest in it; I admire them. Between the person resigned to being a slave and the man who assumes, even with brute force, the role of master, my sympathies are with the latter."

Signorina Caporale noticed the excitement in my words, and with a defiant air she said: "Then why don't you try rebelling, for a start?"

"Me?"

"Yes, you, you," she insisted, looking me in the eye, as if to incite me.

"What have I got to do with it?" I answered. "I could only rebel in one way: by leaving the house."

"Well," the Signorina concluded maliciously, "perhaps that is just what Adriana doesn't want."

"She doesn't want me to leave?"

She waved her tattered handkerchief in the air for a moment, then wound it around her finger, sighing; "Who knows?"

I shrugged.

"I'm off to have my supper!" I exclaimed, and abruptly left her there on the terrace.

To begin my rebellion that every evening, as I walked along the hall, I stopped at the trunk where Scipione Papiano was again huddled.

"I beg your pardon," I said. "Can't you find some other place to sit, where you'd be more comfortable? You're in my way here."

He looked at me stupidly, with his languid eyes, not in the least upset.

"Do you understand?" I insisted, shaking him by the arm.

But I might as well have spoken to the wall. Then the door at the end of the hall opened and Adriana appeared.

"Signorina, if you please," I said to her. "Try to make this poor boy realize that he could go and find somewhere else to sit."

"He's not well," Adriana tried to excuse him.

"All the more reason!" I answered. "This isn't the place for him; he can't get any air . . . and besides, sitting on a trunk . . . Shall I speak to his brother?"

"No, no," she hastened to answer. "I'll speak to him, don't worry."

"After all," I added. "I'm not yet king, so I don't need a sentry outside my door."

From that evening on, I lost my self-control. I began openly to try to force my way past Adriana's shyness. I shut my eyes and abandoned myself to my feelings, without any more reflection.

Poor, dear little godmother! At first she was torn between

fear and hope. She didn't dare entrust herself to hope, since she guessed that spite was driving me. But I sensed that her fear was also part of her hope, secret and almost unconscious until then, the hope that she wouldn't lose me. So as I now nourished this hope with my new boldness she couldn't completely give way to her fear, either.

This delicate bewilderment of hers, this sincere hesitation prevented me from facing myself at once, and drove me deeper and deeper into my tacit duel with Papiano.

At first I expected him to confront me promptly, dropping his usual airs and politeness. But no. He removed his brother from guard duty on the trunk, as I had asked; and he even took to joking about Adriana's embarrassed, confused manner when I was present.

"You must forgive her, Signor Meis; my little sister-in-law is as shy and modest as a nun!"

This unexpected submission, this nonchalance worried me. What was he up to now?

One evening I saw him come home with a stranger. The man entered the house, hammering his cane on the floor as if he wanted to hear himself walking, since on his feet he wore canvas shoes that made no noise.

"Now where is this dear relative of mine?" he started shouting, in a terrible Turin accent, without removing his little bowler, which was pulled down to his eyes like a sunshade. His eyes were befogged by the wine he had drunk. In his mouth was a pipe, which he also failed to remove; it seemed to be cooking his nose, even redder than Signorina Caporale's. "Now where is this dear relative of mine?"

"There he is," Papiano said, pointing to me; then he said: "Signor Adriano, a pleasant surprise for you! Here is Signor Francesco Meis, from Turin. Your relative."

"My relative?" I exclaimed, with a start.

The other man shut his eyes, raised his bearlike paw and held it out, waiting for me to shake it.

I left him there, in that attitude, and examined him for a while. Then I asked: "What kind of farce is this?"

"Why? What do you mean?" Terenzio Papiano said. "Signor Francesco Meis assures me that he is your . . ."

"Cousin," the other man added, without opening his eyes. "All us Meises are related."

"But I haven't had the honor of knowing you!" I protested.

"That's a fine one!" he cried. "That's exactly why I've come here to pay you a visit!"

"Meis? From Turin?" I asked, pretending to rack my brain. "But I don't come from Turin."

"What?" Papiano intervened. "Didn't you tell me that you lived in Turin until you were ten?"

"Of course he did!" the other man went on, annoyed that anyone should doubt what for him was completely certain. "Cousin! Cousin! This gentleman here . . . what's his name?"

"Terenzio Papiano . . . at your service."

"Terenziano . . . he told me that your Papa went to America. So what can that mean? It must mean that you're the son of Uncle Antonio, who went to America. And that makes us cousins."

"But my father's name was Paolo."

"Antonio!"

"Paolo! Paolo! Paolo! You think you know better than I do?"

He shrugged and cracked a smile. "I always thought it was Antonio," he said, scratching his chin with its gray beard, a four-day growth at least. "I don't want to contradict you. If you say it's Paolo, then Paolo it is. I don't remember too well, seeing as how I never met him personally."

Poor man! He was in a position to know better than I did the name of that uncle of his who had gone to America; but he gave in, since he wanted to be my relative at all costs. He told me that his father, whose name was Francesco the same as his, was the brother of Antonio . . . or rather, Paolo, my father, who had left Turin when my supposed cousin was just a nipper of seven. The older Francesco, a poor clerk, had always lived away from his family, a bit here, a bit there. And therefore his son now knew very little about his relations, paternal or maternal. But, in spite of all that, he was certain, yes, absolutely certain he was my cousin.

What about our grandfather? Had he known our grandfather at least? I asked him. Well, he had met him once, he couldn't remember whether in Pavia or Piacenza.

"Ah, really? So you actually met him? What was he like?"

He was . . . well, Francesco didn't remember, to be frank. "Ah, that was thirty years ago . . ."

He seemed to be in good faith; apparently he was a poor wretch who had drowned his soul in drink, to lighten the burden of his poverty and boredom. He nodded his head, with closed eyes, agreeing to everything I said. I began to enjoy the situation. I'm sure that if I had said we were children together, had grown up together, and that I had pulled his hair time and again, he would have nodded his agreement in that same way. There was only one thing I had to accept: we were cousins. He was firm on that score; it was established, and that was that.

At a certain point, however, I glanced at Papiano and saw him smugly grinning; I no longer felt like joking. I sent the poor, half-drunken man away, saying "Good-by, cousin" to him. Then I looked Papiano straight in the eye, and asked him, to make it clear that he had met his match: "Now tell me where you dug up that rare character?"

"Please forgive me, Signor Adriano!" the rogue began, and I had to admit that he was deft. "I realize that I unhappily . . ."

"No, no, you're always very happy!" I exclaimed.

"No, I mean . . . unhappily I didn't give you the pleasure I intended. Believe me, it was all pure chance. I had to go to the tax office this morning for the Marchese, my employer. While I was there, I heard someone call in a loud voice: *Signor Meis! Signor Meis!* I turned around at once, thinking that you were there, too, for some business matter, and that perhaps, who knows, I might be able to help you. Imagine! They were calling that rare character, as you so rightly describe him. And then . . . out of curiosity, I went over and asked him if his name was really Meis and where he came from, since I had the honor of having a Signor Meis in my home . . . That's how it happened! He assured me that you were certainly a relative of his, and he insisted on coming here to meet you . . ."

"This was at the tax office?"

"Yes, he works there, an assistant collector."

Was I to believe this? I decided to check. And it was true, but it was equally true that Papiano, his suspicions aroused, eluded me just as I wanted to confront him with his secret maneuverings. He slipped away from me, and continued to dig into my past, to attack me from behind like this. Knowing him well, I had reason to fear, alas, that with his sixth sense, he would sooner or later pick up my trail and woe to me if he did! He would surely follow it all the way back to the millrace.

So you can imagine my fright, a few days later, when, as I was in my room reading, I heard a voice from the hall, a voice still vivid in my memory, that seemed to come from the other world:

"*Agradecido Dios, ántes* . . . I remove it!"

The Spaniard? My little bearded, nervous Spaniard from Monte Carlo? The man who wanted to gamble in partnership with me, who made me so angry in Nice? . . . For God's sake! My trail! Papiano had succeeded in discovering it!

I sprang to my feet, clutching the table to keep from falling in my sudden anguish and confusion. Dazed, terrified, I pricked up my ears, with the idea of fleeing as soon as those two, Papiano and the Spaniard (it was the same one, beyond any doubt; I recognized that voice), had crossed the hall. Flee? Suppose Papiano, on coming home, had asked the maid if I were in? What would he then think about my flight?

But, on the other hand, if he already knew I wasn't Adriano Meis? Wait a minute! What information could that Spaniard have about me? He had seen me at Monte Carlo. Had I told him then my name was Mattia Pascal? Perhaps! I couldn't remember . . .

Without realizing it, I found myself in front of the mirror, as if someone had led me there by the hand. I looked at myself. Ah, that damned eye! On account of it, the man might recognize me. But how, how in the world had Papiano arrived at it, at my adventure in Monte Carlo? This is what amazed me more than anything else. And what was I to do now? Nothing. Wait for what had to happen.

Nothing happened. And yet, my fear wouldn't go away, not even that same evening, when Papiano explained the mystery, to me so inexplicable and terrible, of that visit, and proved he was far from being on the trail of my past. It was Chance, whose favors he had been enjoying for some time now, which had chosen to play another trick on me, producing that Spaniard, who perhaps hadn't the slightest recollection of me.

According to what Papiano told me about the man, I could hardly have avoided meeting him in Monte Carlo, because he was a professional gambler. The strange thing was that I should meet him now in Rome, or rather, that on coming to Rome, I should stumble into a house where he could also enter. Certainly, if I had had nothing to fear, this coincidence wouldn't have seemed so odd to me; don't we often unexpectedly run into people we've met elsewhere by chance? For that matter, the Spaniard had—or thought he had—good reason for coming to Rome and to Papiano's house. I was the one in the wrong; or Chance was, for having made me shave off my beard and change my name.

About twenty years earlier, the Marchese Giglio d'Auletta, whose secretary Papiano was, had married his only daughter to Don Antonio Pantogada, attaché at the Spanish Embassy to the Holy See. A short time after the marriage, Pantogada was discovered one evening in a gambling den along with some members of the Roman aristocracy; he was recalled to Madrid. There he did the same, or perhaps worse; and finally he was forced to resign from the diplomatic corps. From that time on, the Marchese d'Auletta hadn't known a moment's peace: constantly forced as he was to send money for the gambling debts of his incorrigible son-in-law. Four years ago, Pantogada's wife had died, leaving a little girl of about sixteen whom the Marchese had decided to take into his house, knowing all too well the hands she would be left in otherwise. But Pantogada at first refused to let the child go; finally, compelled by his pressing need for money, he gave in. Now he was forever torturing his father-in-law with threats to reclaim his daughter, and he had come to Rome that day with such an idea in mind. Or rather, with the idea of extorting more money from the poor Marchese, knowing that the grandfather would never, never abandon his beloved Pepita to Pantogada's clutches.

Papiano denounced Pantogada's blackmail with words of fire, and his gallant wrath was sincere. Still, while he was speaking, I couldn't help admiring the special apparatus of his conscience which could become honestly indignant about the misdeeds of others, while he himself was committing similar ones, quite calmly, against that good old man, his father-in-law Paleari.

But the Marchese Giglio this time decided not to give in. As a result, Pantogada would be staying on in Rome, and would certainly come to the house to call on Terenzio Papiano, with whom he was bound to get on splendidly. So I would inevitably run into the Spaniard one of these days. What could be done?

Unable to consult anyone else, I again consulted my mirror. In the glass the image of the late Mattia Pascal rose to the surface, as if from the depths of the millrace, with that eye, the only thing I still had of his. He spoke to me with these words: "What a nasty situation you've got yourself into, Adriano Meis! You're afraid of Papiano: admit it! And you want to blame me, always me! Just because I quarreled with that Spaniard in Nice. But I was right then, and you know it. Do you think that, for the present, it would suffice to remove the last trace of me from your face? Very well then, follow the advice of Signorina Caporale and call Doctor Ambrosini. He'll fix the eye up. Then . . . you'll see!"

XIII. The Little Lantern

Forty days in darkness.

A success . . . oh, the operation was a complete success. That eye would be just a tiny, tiny bit larger than the other. Nothing to think twice about. And then, meanwhile, forty days in the dark, there in my room.

I could discover for myself that, when he suffers, man forms a private idea of good and evil. I mean, of the good that others should do to him, which he demands as a right, as if he were entitled to some compensation for his suffering; and the evil that he can do to others, as if his sufferings, at the same time, permitted him anything. And if the others are not good to him, if they neglect their duty; he considers them guilty; whereas any evil he does to them, he easily excuses, as if it were his prerogative.

After several days of that blind prison, my desire, my need to be comforted in some way grew to a kind of rage. I knew, of course, that I was in a strange house, and that I should therefore be grateful to my hosts for the tender care they were taking of me. But it was never enough; it even irritated me, as if that care were given only out of spite. Naturally I guessed who was tending me. With these attentions, Adriana was showing me she was with me in thought, there constantly, in that room. Fine consolation! What good did this do me, if my own thoughts were following her all day, here and there through the house, in anguish? Only she could comfort me; she had to; she who could understand better than the others how my boredom was oppressing me, consuming me in the desire to see her or at least to hear her near me.

My anguish and my boredom were increased by my anger when I learned that Pantogada had left Rome almost at once. Would I have shut myself away for forty days in darkness, if I had known he was leaving so soon?

To console me, Signor Anselmo tried to prove, with a lengthy line of reasoning, that my darkness was imaginary.

"Imaginary? This darkness?" I shouted at him.

"Be patient for a moment, and I'll explain what I mean."

And then he explained. (Perhaps he was also preparing me for the spiritualistic experiments which, this time, were to be performed in my room to divert me.) As I say, he expounded a highly specious philosophical concept of his which you might call *lanternosophy*.

Every now and then the old man would break off and ask: "Are you asleep, Signor Meis?"

And I was tempted to answer: "Yes, thanks, I'm asleep, Signor Anselmo."

But since he meant well and was only trying to keep me company, I answered instead that I was very interested and begged him to go on.

Signor Anselmo did go on, first to declare that, alas, we human beings are not like the tree, which lives but does not feel. The earth, the sun, the air, the rain, and the wind, do not seem to the tree to be things different from itself: harmful or friendly things. But we, on the other hand, are born with a sad privilege: that of *feeling* ourselves alive. And from this a fine illusion results: we insistently mistake for external reality our inner feeling of life, which varies and changes according to the time, or chance, or circumstances.

And for Signor Anselmo this sense of life was like a little lantern that each of us carries with him, alight; a lantern that makes us see how lost we are on the face of the earth, and reveals good and evil to us. The lantern casts a broader or narrower circle of light around us, beyond which there is black shadow, the fearsome darkness which wouldn't exist if our lantern weren't lighted. And yet, as long as our lantern is

kept burning, we must believe in that shadow. When at the
end the light is blown out, will the perpetual night receive us
after the brief day of our illusion? Or won't we remain at the
disposal of Existence, which will merely have shattered our
trivial modes of reasoning?

"Are you asleep, Signor Meis?"

"Continue, continue, Signor Anselmo. I'm not asleep. I can
almost see it, that lantern of yours."

"Ah, good . . . But since your eye offendeth, let's not go too
deeply into philosophy, eh? Just for fun, we'll try to follow
those confused fireflies, our lanterns, into the darkness of
man's lot. First of all, I'd say that the lanterns are of many
different colors. What do you think? According to the glass
that is given us by Illusion, a great merchant she is, peddling
colored glass. But I also feel, Signor Meis, that in certain periods of history, as in certain seasons of the individual's life,
one color predominates, rather than another. Don't you think
so? In every age, men usually come to some agreement on the
opinions that give light and color to those big lanterns, our
opinions on abstract terms like *Truth, Virtue, Beauty, Honor,*
and what have you . . . For example, don't you think of the
big lantern of pagan *Virtue* as being red? Whereas Christian
virtue would be violet, a depressing color. The light of a common idea is fed by collective feeling; but if this feeling splits
into factions, the lantern of the abstract terms still remains,
of course, but the flame inside splutters and flickers and dies
down, as in all the so-called transitional periods. And history
is also full of fierce gusts of wind which suddenly blow out
those big lamps altogether. How wonderful! In the sudden
darkness, there is an indescribable scuffle of tiny individual
lanterns; some go this way, some that, some try to move
backwards, others in circles. Nobody can find the path; they
bump into one another or cluster together in groups of ten or
twenty, but they can't agree on anything, and they scatter
again in great confusion, in fury and anguish, like ants who
can't find the entrance to their anthill, trampled by the whims

of some cruel child. To my mind, Signor Meis, we are in one of these moments now. Darkness and confusion! All the big lanterns have been blown out. Which way are we to turn? Should we retrace our steps perhaps? Towards the surviving lamps, the lights that the great dead left burning on their tombs? I remember a lovely poem of Niccolò Tommaseo:

> My little lamp is fragile,
> It shines not like the sun.
> Its flame is not so agile
> As fires that leap and burn.
> But still it points towards Heaven
> From whence to me 'twas given.
>
> When I in earth am lying,
> Above me it will glow,
> The wind and the rain defying,
> Age it will never know.
> And proof against all dangers,
> At night, 'twill guide lost strangers.

"But then, Signor Meis, what if our lamp were lacking the holy oil that fed the poet's? Many people still go to the churches to find the proper fuel for their little lanterns. Most of them are poor old people, poor women to whom life has lied, and they go forward in the darkness of our existence with their feelings glowing like votive lights, which they carefully protect against the cold breath of the last disillusionments, so that the flame will keep burning at least so far, at least to the fatal brink. They hurry towards it, their eyes on the flame, thinking always: '*God sees me!*' so as not to hear the din of life around them, which rings in their ears like a string of blasphemous curses. '*God sees me . . .*' Because they see him, not only in himself, but in everything, even in their poverty, in their sufferings, which will be rewarded at the end.

"The faint, but steady light of those lanterns makes some

of us envious and upset. But others feel that, Jove-like, they are armed with thunderbolts tamed by science, and they carry electric light bulbs triumphantly, instead of those little lanterns, which inspire only contemptuous pity. Now I ask you this, Signor Meis: All this darkness, this enormous mystery about which philosophers at first speculated in vain and which even science doesn't deny, though now it rejects investigation of it—suppose this darkness were simply a deceit like another, a trick of our mind, a fantasy which isn't colored? Suppose we finally convinced ourselves that all this mystery doesn't exist outside us, but only within us? That it's a necessity, since we have our famous privilege of feeling life, our lantern in other words, as I've been saying? What if death, in short, which frightens us so much, didn't exist and were only —not the extinction of life—but the gust of air that blows out our lantern, our unhappy sense of living, a fearsome, painful sentiment, because it is limited, defined by that fictitious shadow beyond the brief circle of weak light that we poor, lost fireflies cast around us, where our life is trapped, as if excluded for a while from the universal, eternal life to which we think we should one day return, though in reality we are already there and will stay there forever, but without the sense of exile that torments us? The boundary is an illusion, relative only to our poor light, our individuality: in the reality of nature it doesn't exist. I don't know if you'll like the idea or not, but we have always lived and always will live with the universe. Even now, in our present form, we share in all the manifestations of the universe, but we don't know it, we don't see it, because, alas, this miserable light shows us only the little zone that it can reach . . . And even then, if it only showed us things as they are. But no, my dear sir! It colors things in its own way, and it shows us things that make us lament, though perhaps in another form of existence, we would laugh heartily over them, if we had mouths. Yes, Signor Meis, we would laugh at all the vain, stupid afflictions our lantern has caused us, at all the shadows, the strange, ambitious phantoms it cast before us, and at how we feared them!"

Now, since Signor Anselmo Paleari was so rightly critical of the little lantern that each of us carries with him, why did he want to light another one there in my room, a lantern with red glass for his spiritualistic experiments? Wasn't that first one enough?

I decided to ask him.

"It's a corrective!" he answered. "One lantern against the other. For that matter, this one goes out at some point, you know!"

"And does this seem to you the best way to see something?" I ventured to ask.

"If you'll forgive me for insisting," Signor Anselmo promptly replied, "the so-called light can also serve to make us see things mistakenly here, in our so-called life. To make us see beyond this, believe me, electric light is no help. In fact, it is harmful. You're quoting the silly opinions of certain scientists with narrow minds and even narrower hearts, who want to persuade people that experiments like ours in some way outrage science or nature. No, no! We want to discover other laws, other forces, other life in nature, but always in nature, outside our restricted normal experience. We want to break out beyond the narrow scope of our habitually limited senses. Now, I ask you, aren't scientists the first to say that environment and atmospheric conditions must be right if their experiments are to succeed? Can the photographer do without his darkroom? Well then? Besides there are all kinds of ways to check."

But as I could see for myself a few evenings later, Signor Anselmo used none of these. The experiments were all in the family! Could he ever suspect that Signorina Caporale and Papiano might enjoy deceiving him? Why should they? Where was the amusement in that? He was completely convinced, and he didn't need these experiments to strengthen his own faith. Perfect gentleman that he was, he never supposed that they might deceive him for some other end. As to the melancholy wretchedness and childishness of the results, theosophy itself was ready to give a plausible explanation. The superior beings on the *Mental Plane,* or those still higher, couldn't come down and communicate with us through a medium; so we had to be content with the coarser manifestations of the spirits of inferior beings on the *Astral Plane,* the plane nearest us.

Who could contradict him, after all?*

I knew that Adriana had always refused to take part in these experiments. Since I had been shut up in my room, in darkness, she had come in only rarely, and never alone, to ask how I felt. Every time that question seemed to be asked out of mere politeness, and so it was. She knew, she knew well how I felt! I thought I could even sense a hint of malicious irony in her voice. She didn't know the true reason of my sudden decision to submit to the operation, and she must therefore have believed that I suffered from vanity, that I was trying to make myself more handsome—or less ugly—with my eye fixed up in accordance with Signorina Caporale's advice.

"I'm fine, Signorina Adriana," I would answer. "I can't see a thing . . ."

"But you will see . . . You'll see even better afterwards," Papiano said.

Taking advantage of the darkness, I raised my fist in the air as if to plunge it into his face. He did these things on purpose surely, to make me lose what little patience I still had. He couldn't possibly be unaware of the irritation he inspired in me; I made it clear in every kind of way, yawning, sighing, but still—there he was. He continued to come into my room almost every evening (ah yes! *he* came) and to stay

---

* "Faith," wrote Maestro Alberto Fiorentino, "is the substance of things to be hoped, the argumentation and proof of things that are not visible."

(*Don Eligio Pellegrinotto's note.*)

there for hours on end, chattering incessantly. In that darkness his voice seemed to stifle me, it made me writhe in my chair as if I were sitting on thorns, my fingers clenched; I could have strangled him at times. Did he guess this? Did he sense it? At those very moments, his voice became even softer, almost caressing.

We always need to blame someone for our sufferings and our misfortunes. Papiano, basically, was doing everything to drive me away from that house. And if the voice of reason had been able to reach me in those days, I should have thanked Papiano from the bottom of my heart. But how could I hear that voice, how could I listen to reason, when it spoke to me through Papiano's mouth, when, for me, he was the opposite of reasonable, and the very embodiment of wrong? In fact, didn't he want to drive me away so that he could defraud Paleari and ruin Adriana? This was the only thing I could understand from all his talk then. Why did the voice of reason have to choose Papiano's—of all mouths—to speak to me? But perhaps it was I who, seeking an excuse, put the words in his mouth, so that what was right would sound wrong. For I was already caught in life's net, and my impatience wasn't because of the darkness, or because of the irritation Papiano aroused in me with his talk.

What did he talk to me about? About Pepita Pantogada, evening after evening.

Although I lived modestly, Papiano had got it into his head that I was very rich. And now, to distract my thoughts from Adriana, he was perhaps hoping to make me fall in love with the granddaughter of Marchese Giglio d'Auletta. He described her to me as a proud, wise girl, full of goodness and intelligence, frank and steady, yet vivacious and beautiful, too. Oh very beautiful, with her dark hair and her body which was slender and shapely at the same time. Fiery, with flashing eyes and lips that invited kisses. He needn't mention the dowry, of course. "Enormous!" The entire fortune of the Marchese, in fact. And the Marchese would no doubt be delighted to give the girl a husband promptly, not only to be rid of Pantogada, who was harassing him, but also because grandfather and granddaughter didn't get on too well; the Marchese was a weak man, completely absorbed in his dead world. But Pepita was strong, throbbing with life.

Couldn't he realize that the more he praised this Pepita, the more I disliked her, even before meeting her? And I would meet her, he said, a few evenings later, because he would persuade her to attend our next séance. I would also meet the Marchese Giglio d'Auletta, who was eager to know me, after all the things that Papiano had told him about me. But the Marchese no longer left his house, and he would never come to a séance anyway, because of his religious ideas.

"What?" I asked. "He won't come, but he allows his granddaughter to attend?"

"Because he knows that she will be in safe hands," Papiano said haughtily.

I didn't want to hear any more. Why did Adriana refuse to come to these experiments? Because of her religious scruples. Now, if the granddaughter of the Marchese Giglio could participate in these séances, with the consent of her devout grandfather, couldn't Adriana have come too? Armed with this logic, I tried to convince her, the night before the first gathering.

She had come into my room with her father, who said, as soon as he heard my proposal: "We're back where we were before, Signor Meis," he sighed. "When the Church has to face this problem, she pricks up her ass's ears and takes umbrage, as science does. And yet our experiments—as I've explained to my daughter time and again—aren't against religion any more than they're against science. In fact, as far as religion is concerned, they're a proof of the same truth that religion sustains."

"What if I were afraid?" Adriana objected.

"Of what?" her father replied. "Of the proof?"

"Or of the darkness?" I added. "We'd all be here with you, Signorina. Do you want to be the only one missing?"

"But I . . ." Adriana answered, embarrassed. "I don't believe in it, you see . . . I can't believe in it . . . and . . . Oh, I don't know!"

She couldn't go on. From the tone of her voice and from her embarrassment, I realized, however, that it wasn't only her religion which kept Adriana from attending the experiments. The fear she mentioned as an excuse could have other causes that Signor Anselmo didn't suspect. Or would she suffer if she had to watch the pathetic spectacle of her father childishly deceived by Papiano and Signorina Caporale?

I hadn't the heart to insist any further.

But, as if she had read the disappointment in my heart at her refusal, she blurted out, in the darkness, "Still . . ." and I seized upon it.

"Excellent! So we'll have you with us?"

"Just for tomorrow evening," she conceded, smiling.

Late the next day, Papiano came to prepare the room. He brought in a rectangular pine table, without drawers, unpainted, commonplace. He cleared a corner of the room and hung a sheet from a length of string. Then he brought in a guitar, a dog collar with rattles on it, and some other objects. These preparations were carried on by the light of the famous lantern with red glass. I need hardly say that, as he carried out the preparations, he never stopped talking.

"Now the sheet is necessary, you see . . . it serves as . . . well, you might say, it's the condenser for this mysterious power . . . It'll stir, Signor Meis, and swell out like a sail; sometimes it lights up . . . a strange light . . . starry, I'd almost call it. Mind you, we haven't managed to achieve any 'materializations' yet; but we've had lights. There'll be some this evening, if Signorina Silvia is in good form. She's in communication with a young man who studied with her at the Conservatory; he died, poor boy, of tuberculosis when he was eighteen. He came from . . . I don't know exactly, but I think it was Basel. But he and his family had settled for some time in Rome. A musical genius, he was; struck down by death before his talent could bear fruit. At least, that's what Signorina Caporale says. Even before she discovered that she was gifted as a medium, she used to communicate with the spirit of Max . . . Yes, his name was Max . . . ? Yes, Max Oliz, if I'm not mistaken. Sometimes when this spirit gripped her, why, she used to improvise on the piano until she fell to the floor in a faint. One evening people even gathered in the street below, and applauded her when she was finished . . ."

"And Signorina Caporale was almost frightened by it," I added, calmly.

"Ah, you know about it?" Papiano asked, taken aback.

"She told me herself. So the people were then applauding Max's music, played by the hands of Signorina Caporale?"

"That's it, all right. Too bad we don't have a piano in the house. We have to make do with a bit of a tune, a snatch of music on the guitar. Max gets angry sometimes, you know. He even tears the strings . . . But you'll hear, this evening. I think everything's in order now."

"Tell me, Signor Terenzio. Excuse my curiosity . . ." I asked, before he went out. "Do you believe in this? Really believe?"

"Well, the fact is," he answered promptly, as if he had foreseen the question. "To tell you the truth, I can't see my way clearly in this business."

"I should think not!"

"Oh, I don't mean because the experiments take place in the dark! The phenomena, the manifestations are real enough, no question about that. But we surely must believe our own senses . . ."

"Why? I should think just the opposite?"

"What? I don't understand."

"We deceive ourselves so easily. Especially when we enjoy believing a certain thing . . ."

"But I don't, you know. I don't enjoy it!" Papiano protested. "My father-in-law, who's made quite a profound study of all this—he believes in it. But, for that matter, I don't have the time to think about it . . . even if I wanted to. I'm kept so busy now with those damned Bourbons; the Marchese never gives me a moment's peace. I just pass an evening or so here, like this. For my part, I believe that as long as, by the grace of God, we're alive, we can't learn anything about death, so I see no point in worrying about it. Don't you agree? Instead, we should try to go on living as best we can. That's the way I look at it, Signor Meis. Well, see you later. Now I've got to run over to Via dei Pontefici and pick up Signorina Pantogada."

He came back about half an hour later, extremely cross: in addition to Signorina Pantogada and her housekeeper, a certain Spanish painter had come. He was introduced to me, through gritted teeth, as a friend of the Giglio household. His name was Manuel Bernaldez and he spoke correct Italian, though there was no making him pronounce the *s* in my last name. Every time he had to say it, it was as if he were afraid that *s* might hurt his tongue.

"Adriano *Mei*," he said, as if we had suddenly become fast friends.

—Adriano *Tui*, I was tempted to answer.

The women came in: Pepita, her housekeeper, Signorina Caporale, and Adriana.

"You, too? This is new!" Papiano said to her rudely.

He wasn't expecting this of me. Meanwhile, from the way he had introduced Bernaldez, I realized that the Marchese must have known nothing about the painter's coming to the séance, and that some intrigue with Pepita was afoot.

But the great Terenzio wouldn't give up his plan. As he arranged us around the table in the mystical circle, he placed himself next to Adriana and put Pepita beside me.

Wasn't I pleased? No. And neither was Pepita. Speaking exactly like her father, she rebelled immediately: "*Gracias, asi no puede ser!* Impossible. I must be between Señor Paleari and my duenna, my dear Señor Terencio!"

The reddish semidarkness made the forms of the people barely discernible, so that I couldn't see how far Señorita Pantogada's appearance corresponded to the portrait sketched for me by Papiano. Her behavior, her voice, and her immediate rebellion were, however, in complete agreement with the notion I had formed of her, after Papiano's description.

In refusing with such indignation the seat Papiano had assigned her beside me, the Señorita was, of course, insulting me; but I didn't take offense. I was delighted.

"Quite right!" Papiano exclaimed. "We can do this, then. Signora Candida can sit next to Signor Meis. Then you can sit next to her, Señorita Pepita. My father-in-law stays where he is; and so do the rest of us. Is that all right?"

No, no! That wasn't all right either: I didn't like it, nor did Signorina Caporale. It didn't please Adriana or—as was soon obvious—Pepita, who was much happier in a new seating arrangement worked out by, of all people, the highly inventive spirit of Max.

For the moment, however, I saw at my side a kind of ghost of a woman, with a little hill on her head (was it a hat? a kerchief? a wig? what the devil was it?). From beneath that huge encumbrance occasional sighs emerged, ending in a brief moan. Nobody had bothered to introduce me to Signora Candida. Now, in order to form the chain, we had to hold hands, and she was sighing. It didn't seem proper to her, after all! My God, what a cold hand she had!

With the other, she was holding the left hand of Signorina Caporale, who was sitting at the end of the table, her back to the sheet hanging in the corner. Papiano held her right hand. Next to Adriana, on the other side, the painter was sitting. And Signor Anselmo was at the other end of the table, opposite Signorina Caporale.

Papiano said: "First of all, someone must explain to Signor

Meis and to Señorita Pantogada, the language . . . what do you call it?"

"The tiptological language . . ." Signor Anselmo prompted.

"Please, explain to me, too," Signora Candida said, with sudden enthusiasm, wriggling in her chair.

"Of course! To Signora Candida, too, naturally."

"Well then," Signor Anselmo began to explain. "Two knocks mean *yes* . . ."

"Knocks?" Pepita interrupted. "What knocks?"

"Knocks," Papiano answered. ". . . against the table or on the chair or elsewhere, or even touching someone."

"Ah no-no-no-no-no!!" she exclaimed, springing to her feet. "I not like touching! *De chi?*"

"Why, by the spirit of Max, Señorita," Papiano explained. "I explained that to you on the way here. They don't hurt, never fear."

"They're tiptological," Signora Candida added, in a superior tone, commiserating.

"Now then," Signor Anselmo resumed, "two knocks are *yes*; three knocks mean *no*; four: *darkness*; five: *speak*; six: *light*. That's enough for the present. Now let us all concentrate, ladies and gentlemen."

Silence fell. We concentrated.

XIV. Max and His Exploits

Dread? No. Not a shadow of it. But a lively curiosity gripped me, and also a certain fear that Papiano was about to cut a very sorry figure. I ought to have been pleased, but I wasn't. Don't we all suffer, or feel at least a kind of chilly depression when we have to watch a play badly done by amateur actors?

—It's one of two things, I thought: either he's very clever, or else he's so determined to have Adriana beside him that he doesn't realize what he's doing, leaving Bernaldez, Pepita, me, and Adriana all dissatisfied and therefore ready to notice his trickery, since we have no pleasure to distract us. Adriana will be the first to notice, since she's nearest him; but she already suspects his deceit and is prepared for it. Since she can't be beside me, she's probably asking herself at this moment why she should stay on to watch a farce that is not only meaningless to her, but also disgusting and sacrilegious. And Bernaldez and Pepita, on the other hand, are probably asking themselves a similar question. Why doesn't Papiano realize this, now that his plan to put me beside Pepita has failed? Is he so confident in his own ability? We'll see.—

As I made these reflections, I wasn't giving a thought to Signorina Caporale. Suddenly she began to speak, as if she were dozing slightly.

"The chain," she said. "The chain is wrong . . ."

"Is Max already with us?" dear old Signor Anselmo asked eagerly.

The Signorina made us wait a good while for her answer.

"Yes," she said painfully, almost gasping. "But there are too many of us this evening . . ."

"That's true, all right," Papiano said hastily. "But the seating arrangement seems fine to me."

"Hush!" Paleari admonished him. "Let's hear what Max has to say."

"The chain," Signorina Caporale went on, "isn't properly balanced, he says. Here, on this side (*and she lifted my hand*), there are two women side by side. Signor Anselmo should exchange places with Señorita Pantogada."

"Of course!" Signor Anselmo cried, standing up. "Come, Señorita, sit here."

This time Pepita didn't complain. She was next to the painter.

"Now," the medium went on, "Signora Candida . . ."

Papiano interrupted her: "She must take Adriana's place— am I right? I'd thought of that myself. Splendid!"

I pressed Adriana's hand tight, so tight it almost hurt her, as soon as she came and took her place beside me. At the same time, Signorina Caporale was squeezing my other hand, as if to ask: "*Are you pleased now?*" "*Very pleased,*" I answered, with another squeeze, which also meant: "Go on now, and do whatever you like!"

"Silence!" Signor Anselmo commanded at this point.

Who had breathed a word? Who? Why, the table! Four knocks: *Darkness!*

I swear I didn't hear them.

But then, as soon as the little lantern had been put out, something happened which unexpectedly upset all my suppositions. Signorina Caporale let out a shrill scream; it made us all jump in our seats.

"Lights! Lights!"

What had happened?

A fist? Signorina Caporale had been struck in the mouth by a fist. Hard. Her gums were bleeding.

Pepita and Signora Candida sprang to their feet in fear.

Papiano also got up to turn the little lantern on again. Adriana immediately withdrew her hand from mine. His face red, because he was holding a match in his hand, Bernaldez was smiling, half-surprised and half-incredulous, as Signor Anselmo kept repeating in a highly alarmed voice: "A fist? What can be the explanation of it?"

That's what I was asking myself, alarmed. A blow? Then the two of them hadn't worked out the change of seats together. A blow? Signorina Caporale must have rebelled against Papiano. Now what?

Now, moving her chair back and pressing a handkerchief to her mouth, the Signorina was protesting: she would have no more to do with the séance.

And Pepita Pantogada was screaming: "*Gracias, señores, gracias!* Here there are blows given!"

"No, no, no!" Paleari cried. "Ladies and gentlemen, please: this is very strange, and quite new! We must ask for an explanation."

"Ask Max?" I said.

"Yes, Max. Can you have misinterpreted his suggestions about the chain, Signorina Silvia?"

"That's only too likely!" Bernaldez said, laughing.

"What do you think, Signor Meis?" Paleari asked; he had obviously taken a dislike to the painter.

"Yes, that certainly seems to be the case," I said.

But Signorina Caporale shook her head in firm denial.

"Well then?" Signor Anselmo went on. "How can it be explained? Max violent? It seems impossible. What do you say, Terenzio?"

Terenzio wasn't saying anything. He took refuge in the semidarkness and merely shrugged.

"Come," I said to Signorina Caporale. "Let's satisfy Signor Anselmo's wish, Signorina. Eh? Let's ask Max to explain, and if he proves to be in a . . . er . . . bad mood, then we'll drop it. Am I right, Signor Papiano?"

"Yes, yes," he answered. "Let's ask him by all means. I'm willing!"

"But *I'm* not!" Signorina Caporale retorted, turning towards him.

"Are you speaking to me?" Papiano said. "Why, if you prefer to let it go . . ."

"Yes, that would be best . . ." Adriana hazarded, shyly.

But Signor Anselmo immediately interrupted: "There she is: always afraid of her own shadow! It's just foolishness! Forgive me, Silvia, but this goes for you, too. You know the spirit who is your familiar, after all, and you know this is the first time he's . . . Well, it would be a shame—unpleasant as this little incident was, of course . . . Tonight seems a night when the other world is ready to reveal itself with unusual force . . ."

"Too much!" Bernaldez exclaimed, snickering and making the others laugh.

"As for myself," I added, "I wouldn't like to get a fist in this eye of mine . . ."

"*Ni tampoco yo!*" added Pepita.

"Take your seats," Papiano then ordered firmly. "We'll follow the suggestion of Signor Meis. Let's try asking Max to explain. If the psychic phenomena are too violent again, then we'll stop. Everyone sit down now!"

And he blew out the lantern.

In the darkness I sought Adriana's hand; it was cold and trembling. Out of respect for her shyness, I didn't squeeze it at first, but slowly, gradually, I pressed it, as if to warm it, and with that warmth, to reassure her that everything would proceed calmly now. There could be no doubt, in fact, that Papiano had regretted giving way to violence, and had changed his mind. In any case, we would have a truce; then perhaps Adriana and I, in that darkness, would become Max's targets. "Well," I said to myself, "if the game becomes too violent, we'll cut it short. I won't allow Adriana to be tormented."

Meanwhile Signor Anselmo had started talking to Max, just as you would talk to a real person, present in the room.

"Are you there?"

There were two light raps on the table: he was there!

"Now Max," Paleari asked, in a tone of affectionate reproach, "what made you treat Signorina Silvia so roughly? You're always so good, so kind . . . Will you tell us?"

This time the table stirred a bit at first, then three firm, sharp raps were heard in the center of it. Three knocks meant *no*; he wouldn't tell us.

"We won't insist," Signor Anselmo agreed. "Perhaps you just lost your temper for a moment, eh, Max? I understand. I know you . . . yes, I know you. Would you at least tell us if you're satisfied with the way the chain's arranged now?"

Paleari hadn't finished asking the question when I suddenly felt something, the tip of a finger perhaps, strike me lightly on the forehead, twice.

"Yes!" I suddenly exclaimed, reporting the phenomenon, and squeezed Adriana's hand.

I must confess that this unexpected "touching" made a strange impression on me, at first. I was sure that, if I had raised my hand in time I would have caught Papiano's, but still . . . The delicate lightness of the touch and its precision had been, in any case, marvelous. And, as I said, I wasn't expecting it. But why had Papiano chosen me, of all people, to indicate his repentance? Did he want to reassure me with this sign? Or was it a challenge, meaning "Now I'll show you whether I'm satisfied or not."

"Bravo, Max!" Signor Anselmo cried.

And I said to myself:—Bravo indeed! I'd like to punch your head!—

"Now, if you don't mind," my landlord continued, to Max, "please give us a sign that you're not angry with us."

Five raps on the table commanded: *Speak!*

"What does that mean?" Signora Candida asked, frightened.

"We have to speak," Papiano explained calmly.

And Pepita asked: "Who with?"

"Why, with anyone you like, Señorita! Speak with your neighbor, for example."

"Loud."

"Yes," Signor Anselmo said. "This means, Signor Meis, that in the meanwhile Max is preparing some nice manifestation for us. A light perhaps . . . Who knows? . . . Let's talk now. Talk everybody!"

What were we to say? I had already been speaking for quite a while with Adriana's hand, and alas, I could no longer think of anything else! I was making a long, intense, tacit speech to that little hand, pressing it and caressing it, as it listened, trembling and submissive. I had forced it to allow me to enlace my fingers with hers. An ardent ecstasy had seized me, and I delighted in my own effort to repress my furious longings and express them instead with the gentle tenderness necessary for the innocence of that timid and sweet spirit.

Now, as our hands indulged in this deep conversation, I began to notice a kind of rubbing, or scratching, between the two rear legs of my chair. I was upset. Papiano's foot couldn't reach that far, and even if it could, the crossbar between the two front legs would have blocked him. Had he risen from the table and come around behind my chair? But, in this case, Signora Candida—unless she was downright simple-minded—should have glimpsed him. Before I announced this phenomenon to the others, I wanted to explain it somehow to myself; but then I decided that, after all, I had now achieved what I desired, and so I was almost obliged to assist the deceit, which was assisting me. So, to avoid irritating Papiano any further, I should disclose what I had perceived.

"Really?" Papiano exclaimed, from his seat, with an amazement that sounded sincere to me.

Signorina Caporale was equally amazed.

I felt my hair stand up on my head. So this phenomenon was real, then?

"Rubbing?" Signor Anselmo asked anxiously. "In what way? Describe it!"

"Rubbing!" I confirmed, a little annoyed. "And it's still going on! As if there were a dog behind me . . . there!"

A loud burst of laughter greeted my explanation.

"Why, it's Minerva! It's Minerva!" Pepita Pantogada cried.

"Who's Minerva?" I asked, mortified.

"My little dog!" she answered, still laughing. "My poor old dog, Señor, she scratch always under the chair. Please . . . I get her!"

Bernaldez lighted another match, and Pepita stood up to get her dog, whose name was Minerva. She settled the dog in her lap.

"Now I see," Signor Anselmo said, crossly. "Now I see why Max was so irritated. People aren't being serious this evening, that's the trouble!"

People may not have seemed serious to Signor Anselmo that evening perhaps, but they were even less so on the evenings that followed—at least, as far as spiritualism was concerned.

Who could keep up with Max's exploits in the darkness? The table creaked, moved, spoke with raps loud and soft; more raps were heard on the backs of our chairs and on the other pieces of furniture here and there about the room. Scratching and sliding sounds were heard, and strange phosphorescent lights, like will-o'-the-wisps, glimmered in the air for a moment, and the sheet also came alight and swelled out like a sail. A smoking table took several strolls around the room, and once even sprang on to the larger table where we were seated in our chain. The guitar, as if it had sprouted wings, flew from the dresser and began to strum over our heads . . . But I felt that Max displayed his remarkable musical gifts better with the rattles of the dog collar which, at one point, was placed around Signorina Caporale's neck.

To Signor Anselmo this seemed a charming, affectionate jest on Max's part, but the Signorina wasn't very pleased by it.

Obviously Papiano's brother Scipione had come on the scene under cover of darkness, with very special instructions. The boy was an epileptic, but not really the idiot that his brother Terenzio and he himself wanted others to believe. He must have become used to seeing in the dark, from long habit. To tell you the truth, I can't really say how apt he was in those tricks planned beforehand by his brother and Signorina Caporale. For us, that is to say for me and for Adriana, for Pepita and Bernaldez, Scipione could do whatever he liked, and all went well, no mattter how he did it. He had to satisfy only Signor Anselmo and Signora Candida, and he seemed to be succeeding splendidly. True, neither of them was hard to please. Signor Anselmo, indeed, was beside himself with pride and joy; at times he looked like a child at a puppet show. I suffered at some of his infantile exclamations, depressed to see a man who wasn't a fool act like one to such an incredible degree, and also because I felt Adriana's remorse at enjoying herself like this, at the sacrifice of her father's intelligence, taking advantage of his ridiculous good faith.

This was the only thing that occasionally disturbed our joy. And yet, knowing Papiano, I should have suspected that, if he was resigned to leaving me next to Adriana and, contrary to my fears, didn't make the spirit of Max disturb us, but rather favor and protect us, he must have something else up his sleeve. But the untroubled freedom in the darkness made me so happy that I was incapable of suspicion.

"No!" Señorita Pantogada screamed at one point.

And Signor Anselmo said promptly: "Tell us, tell us, Señorita. What was it? What did you feel?"

Bernaldez also urged her to speak up. So Pepita then said: "*Aquí* . . . on my cheek . . . a caress . . ."

"Was it a hand?" Signor Anselmo asked. "Very gentle, eh? Cold, furtive, delicate . . . Oh, when he wants to, Max can be very gentle with the ladies! Come now, Max, can you caress the lady's cheek again?"

"*Aquí está! Aquí está!*" Pepita began to scream at once, laughing at the same time.

"What did you say?" Signor Anselmo asked.

"Again . . . he caress me again!"

"How about a kiss, Max?" Paleari then suggested.

"No!" Pepita screamed.

But a resounding kiss landed on her cheek.

Almost involuntarily I raised Adriana's hand to my mouth; then, still not satisfied, I bent down to seek her lips, and so we exchanged our first kiss, a long, silent one.

What happened next? Confused and ashamed as I was, it was a moment before I could recover my senses in the commotion that broke out suddenly. Had the others been aware of our kiss? They were shouting. One, then two matches were lighted, then the candle inside the red lantern. And everyone sprang to his feet! Why? Why? A loud knock, a terrible one, as if struck by the fist of an invisible giant, thundered on the table, there, in the full light. We were all taken aback, Papiano and Signorina Caporale more than anyone.

"Scipione! Scipione!" Terenzio called.

The epileptic had fallen to the floor and was gasping strangely.

"Sit down!" Signor Anselmo shouted. "He's gone into a trance, too! There! Look, the table's moving. It's rising . . . Levitation! Good for you, Max! Bravo!"

And truly the table, with nobody touching it, rose nearly a foot from the floor, then fell back again heavily.

Signorina Caporale, pale, trembling, terrified, hid her face against my chest. Señorita Pantogada and her duenna ran out of the room, while Paleari shouted in great annoyance: "No, come back! Don't break the chain. The best is yet to come. Max! Max!"

"Max, my foot!" Papiano cried, finally shaking off the terror that had nailed him in his place. He ran to his brother to try to bring him round.

The memory of Adriana's kiss was for a moment erased by my amazement at that really odd and inexplicable revelation I had witnessed. If, as Paleari insisted, the mysterious force that had acted at that moment in the light before my very eyes came from an invisible spirit, that spirit was obviously not Max. One look at Papiano and Signorina Caporale was enough to prove that. They had invented Max themselves. Who had done it then? Who had given the table that terrible blow?

Many things I had read in Paleari's books suddenly came into my mind; and with a shudder I thought of that unknown man who had drowned himself in the millrace, whom I had deprived of his family's tears, of the mourning of strangers.

—Suppose he were the one!, I said to myself. If he had come to seek me out, to avenge himself by revealing the whole story . . . —

Meanwhile Paleari—the only one who hadn't been amazed or alarmed—couldn't understand why such a simple, commonplace phenomenon as the levitation of the table had upset us so, after all the marvels that we had witnessed. The fact that the phenomenon had taken place in the light meant little to him. What he couldn't understand was what Scipione was doing there in my room, while everyone thought he was in bed.

"I'm surprised," he said, "because generally the poor boy pays no attention to anything. But apparently these mysterious meetings of ours have aroused his curiosity. He must have come to spy on us, he sneaked into the room and then . . . bang! . . . carried away! You know, Signor Meis, there's no denying that some of the most extraordinary cases of mediumistic powers have been found in cases of epilepsy, catalepsy, and hysteria. Max draws on everyone, even from us he takes a good part of his nervous energy, which he then uses to produce his phenomena. That's been proved! Don't you feel, too, as if something had been taken from you?"

"Not yet, to tell you the truth."

I tossed and turned in my bed almost until dawn, letting my imagination run riot, thinking about that poor wretch buried in the Miragno cemetery under my name. Who was he? Where had he come from? Why had he killed himself? Perhaps he had wanted the world to know about his sad end; perhaps it had been a reparation, an expiation . . . and I had exploited it! More than once, there in the darkness, I confess I was cold with fear. That invisible fist on the table . . . I wasn't the only one who had heard the blow. Had it been he? And was he still there in the silence, present and invisible at my side? I listened intently for any sound in the room. Then I fell asleep and dreamed horrifying dreams.

The next day I opened my windows and let in the light.

XV. My Shadow and I

More than once, waking in the heart of the night (which, on these occasions, proves it has no heart), I have felt in the silence and darkness a strange wonder, a strange embarrassment at the memory of something I had done during the preceding day, in broad daylight, paying no attention to it. And I've then asked myself whether our actions are also determined by the colors, the appearance of the things around us, the various hubbub of life. Naturally, there's no doubt about it— and who knows how many other things also contribute to the process? Don't we live, as Signor Anselmo says, in relation to the universe? Now apparently this cursed universe makes us commit no end of folly, for which we hold our wretched conscience responsible, though it is impelled by external forces, by a light outside itself. And, at the same time, don't many of our decisions, the plans we lay, the expedients we think up during the night seem futile, collapse, and vanish in the light of day? As day is different from night, so perhaps we are one thing during the daytime, and another after dark: though poor enough material at any hour.

Opening the windows of my room after forty days, I know I felt no joy at seeing the light again. The memory of what I had done in the darkness of those days was too troublesome. All the pretexts, the reasons, the convictions that, in the darkness, had had weight and value, now had none, since the windows were opened, or else their weight and value were completely contradictory. And the poor Me, who had remained for so long with the windows shut and had done everything possible to relieve the furious boredom of his imprisonment, now was as shy as a whipped dog and followed the new Me, who had opened the windows and wakened to the light of day with a frown, stern and impetuous. The first Me tried in vain to drive out the grim thoughts, inviting the second Me to the mirror, to congratulate him on the success of the operation, the regrown beard, and even the pallor which in some way improved his appearance.

"Fool! What have you done? What have you done?"

What had I done? Nothing, in all fairness! I had made love. In the darkness—was it my fault?—I hadn't seen any obstacles, and I had lost that control I had formerly imposed on myself. Papiano wanted to take Adriana from me; Signorina Caporale had given her to me, had placed her beside me, and had got a fist in the mouth for her pains, poor thing. I was suffering and naturally, like every unfortunate (read: *man*), I thought I deserved compensation for my pain. So, when the compensation was at my side, I took it. In the room they were experimenting with death; and Adriana, near me, was life, life waiting only for a kiss to open to joy. Now Manuel Bernaldez had kissed his Pepita in the darkness, so I also . . .

"Ah!"

I flung myself in my chair, my hands covering my face. I felt my lips tremble at the memory of that kiss. Adriana! Adriana! What hopes had I aroused in her heart with that kiss? To be my bride? When the windows were open, everyone should celebrate, eh?

I don't know how long I sat in that chair thinking, at times with my eyes wide, at other times, tight-shut, compressing my whole body angrily, as if to protect myself from some inner fit of pain. At last I could see. In all its cruelty I could see the deceit of my illusion: what had seemed the greatest part of my good fortune in the first bliss of my liberation.

I had already seen how my freedom, which at the beginning had seemed without limitations, was limited in the first place by the scarcity of my money. Then I had realized that, instead

of freedom, it could better have been called solitude and boredom, and that it sentenced me to a terrible punishment: my
own company. Then I tried to approach others, but my
determination to avoid binding the cut threads together, even
weakly, had come to what end? This: the threads had become
knotted together again by themselves; and life, despite my
caution, my opposition, despite everything, life had swept
me off with its irresistible force. Life, which was no longer
for me! Ah, how clearly I saw that now! Now when vain
excuses, puerile fictions, weak, pitiful pretexts couldn't prevent me from consciously admitting my feeling for Adriana,
and couldn't attenuate the import of my intentions, my
words, my actions. Though I hadn't spoken, I had said too
many things to her, as I pressed her hand, and made her lock
her fingers in mine; and a kiss, finally a kiss had set the seal
on our love. Now how could I live up to that promise with
deeds? Could I make Adriana mine? But back there at the
mill, those two excellent creatures Romilda and the widow
Pescatore had thrown me into the water; they hadn't thrown
themselves in, alas! So it was my wife who had remained free,
not I who had assumed the role of a corpse in the illusion
that I could become another man, live another life. Another
man, yes, but on condition that I do nothing. What sort of
a man was I then? The shadow of a man! And what kind of
life was mine? As long as I was content to remain shut up in
myself and watch others live, yes, then I could prolong the
illusion that I was living a new life. But I had come so close
to life that I had managed to pluck a kiss from a beloved pair
of lips, and now I had to draw back in horror, as if I had
kissed Adriana with the lips of a dead man, a dead man who
could not return to life for her! Bought lips, yes—those I
could kiss; but was the flavor of life in such kisses? Oh, if
Adriana were to know my strange situation . . . She? No, no,
it was unthinkable! She, so pure, so timid . . . Even if her
love were stronger than anything, stronger than any social
considerations . . . poor Adriana, could I imprison her, too,

in the emptiness of my fate, make her the companion of a man who could in no way assert himself or prove himself alive? What was I to do?

Two raps on my door made me spring from the chair. There she was, Adriana.

With a violent effort I tried to calm the tumult of my emotions, but I couldn't help seeming at least a little upset to her. She was upset, too, by her modesty, which forbade her to display her happiness, as she would have liked, seeing me cured at last, in the daylight, and happy. Wasn't I? Why not? . . . She glanced up at me briefly and blushed, then she handed me an envelope: "This is for you."

"A letter?"

"I don't think so. It's probably Doctor Ambrosini's bill. His manservant wants to know if there's any answer."

Her voice was unsteady. She smiled.

"I'll settle it at once," I said. But a sudden tenderness gripped me, as I realized that she had come with that bill as an excuse, seeking a word from me that could confirm her hopes. A profound, anguished pity overcame me, for her and for myself, a cruel pity which drove me helplessly to caress her, and to caress in her my own grief, which could find comfort only in her, its cause. And though I knew I was only compromising myself further, I couldn't resist. I held out both hands to her. Trustingly, but with her face aflame, she slowly raised her hands and placed them in mine. Then I drew her little blond head to my breast and ran my hand over her hair.

"Poor Adriana!"

"Why?" she asked, as I caressed her. "Aren't we happy?"

"Yes . . ."

At that moment I felt an impulse to rebel, a temptation to reveal everything and say to her: "Why? I'll tell you why. Listen, I love you, and I can't, I must not love you! But if you want . . ." No, no. What could that gentle creature want? She pressed her head against my chest, and I felt that I would be even more cruel if, from the supreme joy to which she felt love lifting her at that moment, I plunged her into the abyss of my despair.

"Because," I said, letting go of her, "because I know many things that wouldn't make you happy . . ."

She seemed grieved and confused, as she saw herself suddenly released from my arms. After that caress, was she expecting me to call her *tu*? She looked at me and saw my agitation; hesitantly she asked, "These things that you know . . . do they regard yourself . . . or my family here?"

I answered her with a gesture: *here, here*, to reject the temptation gradually overcoming me, to speak, to open my heart to her.

If only I had! Giving her promptly that one, abrupt sorrow, I would have spared her others, and I wouldn't have forced myself into new, worse complications. But my sad discovery was then too recent, I still had to ponder it; and love and pity deprived me of the courage to shatter in a single moment her hopes and my very life, or rather that illusion of life I could still retain, as long as I was silent. And also I felt how hateful was the declaration I would have to make to her, that I still had a wife. Yes, if I revealed to her that I wasn't Adriano Meis, I became Mattia Pascal again: *dead but still married!* How can a man say such things? This was the peak of a wife's persecution of her husband: freeing herself, by identifying him in the body of a poor drowned man, and yet, after his death, still weighing on him, burdening him like this. I could have rebelled, I know, by saying I was alive, but then . . . Who wouldn't have done what I did, in my place? Anyone in my shoes at that moment would have considered himself lucky to be freed, in such an unexpected, unhoped for, inconceivable way, from his wife, his mother-in-law, his debts, and a wretched, languishing existence like mine. Could I then have imagined that, even after my death, I wouldn't be free of my wife? That she would be freed from me, but not I from her? And that the life which seemed to stretch ahead of me, free, free, free, was only a mirage, which could never become real-

ity except superficially, and that I was more than ever en-
slaved, bound by the fictions and lies I was forced to employ
with such disgust, bound by the fear of being discovered,
though I had committed no crime?

Adriana agreed that the situation there in her family was
not a happy one; but now . . . And with her eyes and a sad
smile she asked me if what caused her sorrow could be an ob-
stacle for me. Can it? those eyes asked, and that sad smile.

"Well, let's pay Doctor Ambrosini!" I cried, pretending
suddenly to remember the bill and the manservant who was
waiting in the other room. I tore open the envelope and, immediately, forced a bantering tone. "Six hundred lire!" I said.
"You see, Adriana? Nature plays one of her usual tricks. She
forces me for years to wear an eye that is . . . let's say, dis-
obedient. I suffer and am imprisoned to correct Nature's mistake, and I have to pay for it in the bargain. Does that seem
fair to you?"

Adriana smiled sadly.

"Perhaps," she said, "Doctor Ambrosini wouldn't be
pleased if you told him to ask Nature to pay his bill. I think
he even expects to be thanked, since the eye . . ."

"You think it looks all right?"

She forced herself to look at me, and said softly, quickly
lowering her eyes: "Yes . . . like a different person . . ."

"Just the eye? or me?"

"You . . ."

"Maybe it's this terrible beard . . ."

"No, why? It looks well on you . . ."

I could have dug out that eye with my finger! What did I
care now, that it was in place?

"And yet," I said, "perhaps the eye itself was happier before. Now it bothers me a little . . . Nothing serious. It'll
pass!"

I went to the little cupboard in the wall where I kept my
money. Adriana indicated that she wanted to go. Like a fool,
I kept her there. But how could I have foreseen? In all my

troubles, large and small, as you know by now, Fortune has always come to my aid. And this is how she came then to help me in my despair.

As I opened the cupboard, I noticed that my key wouldn't turn in the lock. I gave the door a little push, and it opened. It was unlocked!

"What?!" I cried. "Can I possibly have left it unlocked?"

Noticing my sudden concern, Adriana became very pale. I looked at her and said: "But look . . . here, Signorina. Somebody's been in here!"

Inside the little cupboard there was great disorder: my bank notes had been taken from the leather case in which I kept them and were scattered over the shelf. Adriana hid her face in her hands, horrified. I feverishly collected the money and began to count it.

"It's not possible!" I cried, after I'd finished counting. I ran my trembling hands over my forehead, beaded with icy sweat.

Adriana was almost fainting, but she grasped a little table, and asked in a voice that no longer seemed her own: "Has something been stolen?"

"Wait . . . wait . . . How can it be?" I said.

And I began to count again, angrily snapping my fingers and that paper as if by twisting those notes, I could force the missing ones to reappear.

"How much?" she asked, overcome with horror and dismay, as soon as I had finished.

"Twelve . . . twelve thousand lire," I stammered. "I had sixty-five . . . now there's fifty-three! Count for yourself . . ."

If I hadn't caught her in time, poor Adriana would have fallen to the floor, as if clubbed. Still, with a supreme effort, she managed to recover herself and, with convulsive sobs, tried to free herself from my arms, as I wanted to help her into a chair. She started to rush to the door:

"I'll call Papa! I'll call Papa!"

"No!" I shouted at her, holding her back and forcing her to sit down. "Don't be upset like this, for heaven's sake. You worry me even more . . . I don't want this. You have nothing to do with it! Please, be calm. Let me first make sure . . . yes, the cupboard was unlocked, but I can't, I won't believe that such a large theft . . . Please, be a good little girl!"

And again, to be absolutely sure, I counted the money another time, and though I knew full well all my money had been there in the cupboard, I began to rummage and search everywhere, even in places where it was impossible for me to have left such a sum unless I had been seized with a fit of madness. As an excuse for this search, which seemed more silly and futile to me every moment, I forced myself to believe that the thief's boldness was incredible.

But Adriana, almost delirious, her hands over her face, moaned and said in a sobbing voice: "It's hopeless! Hopeless! . . . A thief . . . a thief, too . . . Everything planned ahead of time . . . I felt in the darkness . . . I suspected . . . But I refused to believe that he could sink so low . . ."

Papiano. Yes, only he could be the thief; he, thanks to the help of his brother, during our séances.

"But why?" she moaned, in anguish. "Why did you keep so much money here, in the house, like that?"

I turned to look at her, stupidly. What could I answer? Could I tell her why, in my situation, I had to keep my money with me? Could I tell her why I was prevented from investing it in any way, or entrusting it to others? Why I couldn't even deposit it in a bank, since if there had been any trouble about withdrawing it, I had no way of proving it rightfully mine?

Rather than seem stupid, I was cruel: "How could I have imagined . . . ?" I said.

Adriana again covered her face with her hands, moaning, heartbroken: "Oh God! God! God!"

The fright that should have seized the thief in committing the crime now gripped me instead, at the thought of what would happen. Papiano certainly couldn't expect me to blame the Spanish painter for the theft, or Signor Anselmo, Signorina Caporale, the maid, or the spirit of Max. He must have been sure that I would blame him, him and his brother; and yet, he had gone ahead with it, as if to defy me.

And what about me? What could I do? Report him? How? No, nothing! Nothing at all! I felt prostrate, annihilated. This was my second terrible discovery that day! I knew the thief but I couldn't denounce him. What right had I to the law's protection? I was outside the law. Who was I? Nobody! I didn't exist, as far as the law was concerned. Now anyone could steal from me, and I would have to keep quiet!

But Papiano couldn't know all this. What then?

"How could he have done it?" I said, as if to myself. "What made him so sure of himself?"

Adriana raised her face from her hands and looked at me in amazement, as if to say: *Don't you really know?*

"Ah, of course," I said, suddenly understanding.

"But you must report him!" she cried, standing up. "Let me call Papa . . . Please let me call him. He'll report it at once!"

Again I was just in time to restrain her. All I needed now was for Adriana to force me to report the theft! Wasn't it bad enough that they'd stolen twelve thousand lire from me, as if it were nothing? Did I also have to fear that the theft might become known, did I have to pray and beg Adriana not to shout so loud, not to tell anyone about it, for heaven's sake? Ha! Adriana—as I now am well aware—absolutely couldn't permit me to remain silent and force her to be silent too. She couldn't accept what to her seemed my generosity, and for many reasons: first because of her love, then because of the honor of her family, and also because of me and the hatred she bore her brother-in-law.

But at that moment, her just rebellion seemed excessive; exasperated, I shouted at her, "You will remain silent. I insist on this. You won't mention it to anyone, you understand? Do you want to create a scandal?"

"No, no!" poor Adriana protested promptly, weeping. "I want to free my house from the shame of that man!"

"But he'll deny it!" I went on. "And then you and all the rest of the household will be dragged before a judge . . . Don't you understand?"

"Yes, I do. I understand perfectly," Adriana answered fierily, trembling with contempt. "Let him deny it! But we have other things, things of our own, to say against him. Go ahead and denounce him, don't worry about us . . . You'll be doing us a favor, believe me, a great favor! You'll avenge my poor sister . . . You should realize, Signor Meis, that you'll offend me if you don't do it. I want you to denounce him. If you don't, I will! How can you expect me and my father to live with such dishonor . . . No, no, no! And besides . . ."

I took her in my arms; I no longer thought of the stolen money. Seeing her suffer like that, lost and desperate, I promised to do as she wished, if she would only be calm. But . . . dishonor? No, there was nothing dishonorable for her or for her father; I knew who was to blame for that theft. Papiano had decided my love for her was well worth twelve thousand lire, and I had to prove it to him, didn't I? Report him? Very well, I'd do it, but not for myself. I'd do it to free her house from that wretch. But on one condition: that first of all, she would become calm and would stop crying like that . . . yes, and then, that she would swear to me by all she held dearest that she wouldn't mention the theft to anyone, not to anyone at all until I had consulted a lawyer about all the consequences which, in our agitation, neither she nor I could foresee.

"You swear to me? By all that's dearest to you?"

She swore, and her eyes—through their tears—told me by what she was swearing, what was dearest to her.

Poor Adriana!

I stood there in the middle of the room, dazed, drained, destroyed, as if the whole world were meaningless to me. How much time went by before I recovered myself? And how did I recover myself then? Fool! . . . Fool that I was! Yes, like a fool, I went to examine the door of the cupboard to see if there were any traces of violence. No, not a trace. It had been opened cleanly, with a jimmy while I carefully guarded the key in my pocket.

Don't you feel . . . Signor Anselmo had asked me at the end of the final séance, *Don't you feel, too, as if something had been taken from you?*

Twelve thousand lire!

Again, the thought of my utter helplessness, my nothingness assailed me, crushed me. I had never realized before that I could be robbed and forced to remain silent, even fearing that the theft might be revealed, as if I had committed it, and not the thief.

Twelve thousand lire? A mere nothing! They could steal everything from me, even the shirt from my back, and I would have to keep quiet! What right had I to speak? The first thing they would ask me would be: "And who are you? Where did you get that money?" But if without turning him in . . . for instance, if this evening I seized him by the throat and shouted: "Hand over the money you took from my room, you miserable thief!" He'd shout and deny it. Could he be expected to say: "Yes, sir, here it is, I took it by mistake?" And then what? He might even sue *me* for defamation of character. So I must be quiet! Had I once believed that being dead was a stroke of luck? Well, I am really dead. Dead? Worse still, as Signor Anselmo reminded me: the dead can no longer die. But I could: I am still alive for Death, and yet dead for Life. Now what life was left me? The boredom I had known before, solitude, my own company?

I hid my face in my hands and sank into the chair.

Ah, if I had been a rogue at least! Perhaps I could have adapted myself to this state of suspense, at the mercy of chance, exposed to constant risks, with no base, no substance. But no, not I. What was I to do then? Go away? Where? What of Adriana? But was there anything I could do for her? Nothing . . . nothing . . . How could I just go away, though, without any explanation, after all that had happened? She would have sought the motive in that robbery. She would have said: "Why did he want to save the guilty thief, and punish me, the innocent one?" Ah no, no, poor Adriana! But, on the other hand, since I could do nothing, how could I hope to make my behavior towards her less contemptible? I was forced to seem fickle and cruel. The fickleness and cruelty lay in my own fate, and I was the first to suffer from them. Even Papiano, the thief, in committing his crime, had been more logical and less cruel than I, alas, would have to seem.

He wanted Adriana, to avoid repaying his first wife's dowry to his father-in-law. I wanted to take Adriana from him, did I? Then I would have to give Paleari back the dowry.

To a thief's mind, this was completely logical thinking!

Thief? No, he wasn't even a thief. Because the robbery, after all, was more apparent than real. In fact, since he knew Adriana's respectability, he couldn't believe that I planned to make her my mistress. I surely wanted to make her my wife, and therefore my money would be returned to me in the form of Adriana's dowry, and I would receive a wise and good little wife in the bargain. What more could I want?

Oh, I was sure that, if we could wait, and if Adriana had the strength to keep the secret, we would see Papiano keep his promise and return the dowry of his deceased wife even before the end of the year of grace.

That money, true enough, couldn't now come to me, because Adriana couldn't be mine; but it would go to her, if she could follow my advice and keep quiet, and if I could still stay on there a little longer. I would have to be artful, very artful; and at the end Adriana would have gained the restitution of her dowry, if nothing else.

I became a little calmer, at least on her account, as I pondered these things. Ah, not on my own account, though! I was left with the bitter discovery of my illusion; compared with that, the loss of the twelve thousand lire was nothing. Indeed, it was all to the good, if it could work out to Adriana's advantage.

I saw myself excluded from life forever, with no possibility of returning to it. With this mourning in my heart, with this experience behind me, I would now leave that house, to which I had become accustomed, where I had found a little peace, where I had almost settled down. And again I would be on the streets, aimless, without a destination, in the void. The fear of falling again into life's trap would make me stay farther than ever from mankind; alone, utterly alone, distrustful, gloomy; and Tantalus's torment would be renewed for me.

I left the house, like a madman. Some time later I found myself in Via Flaminia near the Milvian Bridge. Why had I gone there? I looked around; then my eyes fell on the shadow of my body, and I stood there for a while, contemplating it. Finally I raised my foot over it angrily. But no, I couldn't trample on my shadow.

Which of us was more of a shadow? It, or I?

Two shadows!

There, there on the ground; everyone could pass over it, crush my head, trample on my heart; and I would be quiet, the shadow would be quiet.

The shadow of a dead man; that was my life . . .

A wagon went by. I remained there, still, on purpose. First the horse, with its four hooves; then the wheels of the wagon.

—There, press down hard! On the neck! Aha! you too, doggie? Fine! Good! Go ahead and raise your leg!—

I burst out in wicked laughter; the dog ran off, frightened. The driver of the wagon turned to look at me. Then I moved, and my shadow moved ahead of me. I hurried along, to force it under other wagons, under the feet of the passers-by, with voluptuous pleasure. An evil fury gripped me, as if digging its talons into my entrails; finally I could no longer see my shadow in front of me; I would have liked to shake it off. I turned, but there: it was behind me now.

—And if I start to run, I thought, it will run after me!—

I rubbed my forehead hard, afraid that I was about to go mad, to be obsessed by this shadow. Yes! This was it: the symbol, the specter of my life. I was there, on the ground, exposed to the mercy of strangers' feet. That was what remained of Mattia Pascal, who died in the millrace: his shadow on the streets of Rome.

But it had a heart, that shadow, and couldn't love; it had money, and anyone could rob it; it had a head, but only to realize that this head belonged to a shadow, and wasn't even the shadow of a head. So it was!

Then I felt that my shadow was a living thing, and I felt its pain, as if the horse and the wagon's wheels and the feet of the passers-by had really crushed it. And I no longer wanted to leave it there, exposed, on the ground. A tram went by, and I boarded it.

When I came into the house . . .

XVI. *The Portrait of Minerva*

Even before I opened the door, I guessed that something serious had happened in the house; I could hear Papiano and Paleari shouting. Signorina Caporale rushed towards me, all distraught: "Is it really true then? Twelve thousand lire?"

I stopped, breathless, dumfounded. Scipione Papiano, the epileptic, at that moment crossed the entrance hall, barefoot, carrying his shoes, pale, and coatless. His brother, in the other room, was shouting: "All right, call the authorities! Go ahead!"

I was immediately seized with fierce annoyance at Adriana, who despite my prohibition and her oath, had told everything.

"Who said that?" I shouted at Signorina Caporale. "It isn't true. I've found the money!"

The Signorina looked at me in amazement.

"The money? Found it again? Really? Ah, God be thanked!" she exclaimed, raising her arms in the air. And, with me following her, she ran into the dining room where Papiano and Paleari were shouting and Adriana, weeping.

Triumphant, the piano teacher announced: "Found! It's been found! Here's Signor Meis! He's found the money again!"

"What?"

"Found?"

"Is it possible?"

All three were stunned: Adriana and her father, with faces aflame; Papiano, on the contrary, ashen, overwhelmed.

I stared at him for a moment. I must have been ever paler than he was, and I was trembling all over. He lowered his eyes, as if frightened, and let go of his brother's jacket. I went over, until I was face to face with him, and held out my hand.

"Please forgive me. You . . . and everyone . . . forgive me," I said.

"No!" Adriana shouted, indignant; but she immediately pressed her handkerchief to her mouth.

Papiano looked at her, and didn't dare take my hand. Then I repeated, "Forgive me . . ." and I held out my hand still farther, to touch his, which was shaking. It was like the hand of a dead man, and his eyes, beclouded and spent, seemed dead, too.

"I'm really very sorry," I added, "about this confusion, the terrible distress I've caused, without meaning to."

"But no . . . or rather, yes . . . to tell the truth," Signor Anselmo stammered. "It was something that . . . yes, was impossible. Delighted, Signor Meis . . . I'm truly delighted that you've found your money again, because . . ."

Papiano let out his breath sharply, ran both hands over his sweating forehead and his head, then turned his back and looked towards the terrace.

"I was like the man in the story . . ." I went on, forcing a smile. "I was looking for my horse, and I was on its back. I had the twelve thousand lire with me, here in my wallet."

But at this point, Adriana could stand no more.

"But I was there," she said, "when you looked in your wallet, and everywhere else . . . the wallet was there in the cupboard . . ."

"Yes, Signorina," I interrupted her, with cold, stern firmness. "But obviously I didn't search carefully, since I've found it again . . . I must especially beg your pardon for my stupidity, since you have had to suffer more than the others. But I hope that . . ."

"No! No! No!" Adriana shouted, bursting into sobs and hurrying out of the room, followed by Signorina Caporale.

"I don't understand," her father said, dazed.

Papiano turned around, angrily: "I'm leaving anyway. This

very day . . . It seems that now there's no longer any need
to . . . to . . ."

He broke off, as if he felt his breath fail him; he wanted to
turn towards me, but he lacked the nerve to look me in the
eye.

"I . . . I couldn't, believe me, I couldn't even say no . . .
when they came after me here . . . I fell on my brother . . .
in his foolishness . . . his illness . . . irresponsible, I thought
. . . who knows? It was possible that . . . I dragged him here
. . . A brutal scene! I had to strip him . . . search him . . .
everywhere . . . his clothes, even his shoes . . . And he! . . .
ah!"

At this point, his throat was choked with tears; his eyes
filled, and as if stifled by his anguish, he added: "So they saw
that . . . But now that you . . . After this, I'm leaving!"

"No, no, not at all!" I said then. "On my account? No, you
must stay here! I'll be the one to go!"

"Why, what are you saying, Signor Meis?" Paleari said sadly.

Even Papiano, prevented from speaking by the tears he was
trying to repress, waved his hand negatively. Then he said: "I
had to . . . had to go away. In fact, all this happened because
I . . . innocently . . . announced that I was planning to go,
because of my brother, who can't be kept at home here. In
fact, the Marchese gave me—I have it here—a letter to the
director of a sanitorium in Naples; I have to go down there
for more documents that he needs . . . And then my sister-in-
law, who . . . quite rightly . . . has such esteem for you . . .
jumped up and said nobody was to leave the house . . . that
we all had to stay here . . . because you . . . I don't know . . .
had discovered . . . To me! To her own brother-in-law! . . .
perhaps because, poor but honest as I am, I still have to repay
my father-in-law . . ."

"Now what are you thinking about?" Paleari exclaimed, in-
terrupting him.

"No!" Papiano insisted proudly. "I do think about it! I

think about it, never fear. And if I'm leaving, it's . . . Poor
Scipione! Poor, poor Scipione!"

Unable to restrain himself any longer, he burst into floods
of tears.

"Yes, but . . ." Paleari said, dazed and moved. "What does
he have to do with it now?"

"My poor brother!" Papiano went on, with such an outburst of sincerity that I, too, was almost moved to compassion.

In that outburst I realized the remorse that, at that moment, he must have felt towards his brother, whom he had
exploited, whom he would have blamed for the theft if I had
reported it, and whom he had just submitted to the humiliation of being searched.

No one knew better than Papiano that I couldn't have
found the money which he had stolen from me. My unexpected declaration had saved him just when, seeing himself
lost, he had accused his brother or at least had implied—obviously following a plan worked out before—that only his
brother could have been the author of the crime. Now my
statement had overwhelmed him. He was weeping out of an
uncontrollable need to unburden his profoundly shaken spirit,
and perhaps too he felt unable to stand there in front of me,
unless he wept. With these tears he was prostrating himself
before me, as if kneeling at my feet, but on condition that I
stuck to my statement about finding the money; and if I had
taken advantage of his present humiliation and tried to re-
nege, he would have risen up against me in a rage. It was
tacitly understood that he knew nothing about the robbery,
and was to know nothing about it; and I, with my statement,
was only saving his brother, because if I had denounced poor
Scipione he would probably have been exonerated anyway,
thanks to his illness. And for his part, Papiano was promising,
as he had already hinted, to return the dowry to Paleari.

All this I thought I sensed in his weeping. Exhorted by

Signor Anselmo and by me as well, he finally grew calm and said that he would soon return from Naples, as soon as he had put his brother in an asylum, *liquidated his share in a certain business he had lately begun down there in partnership with a friend*, and traced the documents that the Marchese needed.

"Ah, by the way," he concluded, turning to me. "I had almost forgotten. The Marchese asked me to say that, if you would like, today . . . with Adriana and my father-in-law . . ."

"Bravo! Good!" Signor Anselmo cried, without allowing him to finish. "We'll all go . . . splendid! We have a good reason to rejoice now, it seems to me. What do you say, Signor Adriano?"

"As far as I'm concerned . . ." I said, holding out my arms indifferently.

"Then, about four . . . Is that all right?" Papiano suggested, definitively drying his eyes.

I retired to my room. My thoughts flew at once to Adriana, who had run off sobbing, after I had contradicted her like that. What if she came to me now for an explanation? Naturally she couldn't believe I had really found the money. What would she imagine then? That, in denying the theft, I had meant to punish her for failing to keep her oath. But why? Obviously because the lawyer, whom I told her I was going to consult before reporting the theft, had warned me that she and everyone else in the house would be held responsible. Yes, but hadn't she told me herself that she would willingly face a scandal? True, but I didn't want that, of course; I had preferred to sacrifice my twelve thousand lire . . . So was she to believe this was all generosity on my part, a sacrifice out of love for her? Here was another lie forced on me by my condition: a disgusting lie, which made me shine in an exquisite, tender proof of love, attributing to me a generosity all the greater since she hadn't requested or even desired it.

Ah, but no! No! What was I dreaming of? Following the logic of that obligatory, inevitable lie of mine, she would come to quite different conclusions! Generosity indeed! Sacrifice?

Proof of love? Ha! Could I continue to deceive that poor girl? No, I had to stifle my passion, never address another glance at Adriana or a single word of love. Then what? How could she reconcile my presumed generosity with the way I was forced to behave towards her from now on? I was therefore obliged to exploit the theft that, against my wish, she had revealed and I had denied. I would use it to break off all relations with her. But where was the logic in this? I had either been robbed or I hadn't; and if I knew the thief, then why didn't I denounce him? Why instead did I stop loving her, as if she were the guilty one? Or if I had really found the money, why shouldn't my love for her continue?

I was choked with nausea, wrath, hatred of myself. If I could at least have told her that my act hadn't been generosity; that I was absolutely unable to report the theft . . . But I would have to give her some reason . . . Was my money stolen property? She might even imagine it was . . . Or should I tell her that I was a victim of persecution, a refugee, who had to live in the shadows and couldn't bind any woman's future to his own? More lies to the poor girl . . . But on the other hand, could I tell her the truth, which now seemed incredible even to me, an absurd fable, a senseless dream? To avoid lying to her now, must I admit that I had told her nothing but lies till now? This is what the revelation of my true condition would mean. And what would be gained by it? It would afford no justification for me, nor remedy for her.

Still, exasperated and indignant as I was at that moment, I might have confessed everything to Adriana, if she had come in person to my room to explain why she had broken her oath. Instead she sent Signorina Caporale.

I already knew the reason: Papiano himself had explained it to me. The Signorina added that Adriana was still beside herself.

"Why?" I asked, with forced indifference.

"Because she doesn't believe you really found your money," she answered.

Then and there I had an idea (which, for that matter, was consistent with my mood, the nausea I felt towards myself): the idea of making Adriana lose all respect for me. Then she could love me no more. I would prove myself false, hard, inconstant, mercenary . . . I would punish myself in this way for the wrong I had done her. At first, I would cause her fresh pain, to be sure; but it was for her own good, to cure her.

"She doesn't believe it? Why not?" I said to Signorina Caporale with a laugh. "Twelve thousand lire, Signorina . . . that's not chicken feed, you know. Do you think I'd be so cool, if the money had really been stolen from me?"

"But Adriana told me . . ." she tried to insist.

"Nonsense! Nonsense!" I cut her off. "Yes, it's true that for a moment . . . I did suspect . . . But I also said to Signorina Adriana that I didn't think robbery was possible . . . And, in fact, you see? Besides, what reason would I have for saying I'd found the money again, if I hadn't found it?"

Signorina Caporale shrugged.

"Perhaps Adriana believes you may have some reason to . . ."

"Oh, no, no!" I hastened to interrupt her. "As I said before, it amounted to twelve thousand lire, after all! . . . If it had been thirty or forty, well . . . But I'm not all that generous, believe me. Good heavens! A man would have to be a hero . . ."

When Signorina Caporale went off to report my words to Adriana, I wrung my hands and even bit them. Did I really have to behave like this? Make use of that robbery, as if with that money I wanted to pay her, compensate her for her disappointed hopes? Ah, how base my actions were! She would surely cry out with anger, there in the other room, and despise me . . . not knowing that her grief and mine were one. Well, so it had to be. She had to hate me and despise me, as I hated and despised myself. And to make her still angrier with me, to increase her contempt, I would now be very tender towards Papiano, her enemy, as if to make amends to him, before her very eyes, for the suspicion that had been cast on him. Yes, and in this way I would confound even my thief; at the end, everyone would think me mad . . . And I'd go even further: Weren't we about to visit the home of Marchese Giglio? Well, that very day I would set myself to court Señorita Pantogada.

"You'll despise me even more now, Adriana!" I moaned, sinking back on my bed. "What else . . . what else can I do for you?"

A little after four Signor Anselmo came and rapped on my door.

"Coming," I said, and pulled on my overcoat. "I'm ready."

"Are you going like that?" Paleari asked, looking at me in amazement.

"Like what?" I asked.

But then I realized at once that I still had on my head a little traveling cap that I was accustomed to wear in the house. I stuck it in my pocket and took my hat from the peg, while Signor Anselmo laughed, laughed as if he . . .

"Where are you going, Signor Anselmo?"

"Just look at me! Look at the way I was about to leave the house!" he answered, still laughing, and pointed to the slippers on his feet. "Go on into the other room. Adriana's there . . ."

"Is she coming with us?" I asked.

"She didn't want to come," he said, going off towards his own room. "But I persuaded her. Go along. She's in the dining room, all ready . . ."

With what a harsh, reproachful gaze Signorina Caporale received me in that room! She, who had suffered from love so much herself and had been comforted so many times by the gentle, unknowing child, now wanted to comfort Adriana, now that the child knew and was hurt; the Signorina was kind, attentive, and she turned against me because it seemed unjust to her that I should make such a good and lovely creature suffer. She herself, the Signorina, was neither good nor lovely, so if men were wicked to her, there was at least a faint excuse for them. But why should Adriana be made to suffer so?

This is what her eyes said to me, bidding me to look upon the girl whose sufferings I caused.

How pale she was! Traces of weeping could still be seen in her eyes. Who could describe the effort, the anguish it had cost her to dress up and go out with me . . .

Despite my state of mind as I went to pay the call, the Marchese Giglio d'Auletta and his house aroused my curiosity.

I already knew that the Marchese lived in Rome because, to his mind, the only hope for a restoration of the Kingdom of the Two Sicilies lay in the outcome of the struggle to reassert the temporal power of the Pope. When Rome had been returned to the Holy See, the unity of Italy would be destroyed, and then . . . who knows? The Marchese didn't want to hazard any prophecies. For the moment his task was clearly defined: a battle without quarter, there, among the clergy. And his house was frequented by the most intransigent prelates of the Curia, the most ardent supporters of the "black" faction.

That day, however, in the vast and splendidly furnished drawing room, we found no one. Or rather: there was in the center of the room an easel with a half-sketched canvas, an unfinished portrait of Minerva, Pepita's little dog, all black, lying on a completely white armchair, her head between her front paws.

"A work of the painter Bernaldez," Papiano announced to us gravely, as if he were making introductions, and expected us to bow deeply.

The first to come in were Pepita Pantogada and her duenna, Signora Candida.

I had seen both of them only in the semidarkness of my room. Now, in the light, Señorita Pantogada seemed another person to me: not completely, that is, but her nose . . . Could she really have had this nose when she was in my room? I had pictured a little, turned-up nose, a saucy nose; instead it was aquiline and sturdy. But she was nevertheless beautiful: dark, with flashing eyes, gleaming black wavy hair, her lips fine, straight, ardent. Her dark dress, with white dots, seemed painted on her slender, shapely body. Beside her, Adriana's mild blond beauty paled.

And at last I could see what Signora Candida wore on her head! A magnificent, tawny, curly wig and—over the wig—a large pale-blue silk kerchief, a shawl really, tied artistically under her chin. The brightness of this frame contrasted with the dreariness of the little, thin, flaccid face inside, though it had been whitened and smoothed and adorned.

Minerva, the old dog, with her loud, hoarse barking, prevented us from exchanging the proper greetings. The poor animal wasn't barking at us, however; she barked at the easel, at the white armchair, which for her must have represented instruments of torture. Hers was the protest, the unburdening of an exasperated spirit. She wanted to drive that cursed apparatus with its three long legs out of the drawing room; but since it stayed there, immobile and menacing, she withdrew herself, still barking, only to jump back at it again with bared teeth, then dart away furiously.

Squat, fat, with her too-small legs, Minerva was really a graceless creature: her eyes were already misted with age, and the hair on her head was white. On her back, where her tail began, she was hairless because of her habit of scratching herself ferociously under shelves or the crossbars of chairs, whenever and wherever she could. As well I knew.

Suddenly Pepita seized the dog by the neck and hurled her into Signora Candida's arms, shouting:

"Silence!"

At that moment, Don Ignazio Giglio d'Auletta came rushing in. Bent, almost broken in two, he ran to his chair by the window and—as soon as he was seated—he placed his cane between his legs and heaved a deep sigh, smiling at his mortal weariness. The tired face, all lined with vertical wrinkles, clean-shaven, was of a cadaverous paleness; but his eyes, on the contrary, were lively, glowing, almost youthful. In an odd way curious clumps of hair fell over his cheeks and temples, like tongues of damp ash.

He received us most cordially, speaking with a marked Neapolitan accent; then he begged his secretary to continue to show us the various mementos that filled the room, attesting his loyalty to the Bourbon dynasty. At the end we were standing in front of a little square frame covered by a green cloth with the gold-embroidered legend: *I do not hide; I protect. Lift me and read.* The Marchese asked Papiano to remove the object from the wall and bring it to him. Beneath the cloth there wasn't a picture, but instead, framed under glass, a letter from the Royal Minister Pietro Ulloa who, in 1860, that is to say during the death throes of the realm, invited the Marchese Giglio d'Auletta to be a member of the Cabinet which was never to be formed. Along with this invitation there was the draft of the Marchese's letter of acceptance: a proud letter that castigated those who refused to accept the responsibility of power in this moment of supreme danger and anxiety with the enemy, the bandit Garibaldi, almost at the gates of Naples.

Reading this document aloud, the old nobleman became so heated and moved that, even though what he read was quite contrary to my sentiments, he nevertheless aroused my admiration. He, too, in his way, had been a hero. I had another proof of his heroism in a story he chose to tell me: the story concerned a lily of gilded wood, also displayed there in the drawing room. On the morning of September 5, 1860, the King rode out of his palace in Naples in a little open landau with the Queen and two gentlemen of the court. When the carriage reached Via Chiaia, it had to stop because a number of wagons and carts were blocking the way, held up in front of a pharmacy which had these golden lilies on its sign. A ladder, propped up against the sign, was preventing the traffic from going on. Some workmen had climbed up the ladder and were removing the royal lilies. The King noticed this, and pointed out to the Queen this pharmacist's act of cowardly caution, this from a man who had once begged for the honor of putting the royal symbol on the front of his shop. The Marchese d'Auletta also happened to be passing by; furious, outraged, he rushed to the pharmacist, seized the coward by his coat collar and showed him the King, there in the carriage. Then the Marchese spat in the man's face and, brandishing one of the lilies that had been removed, he shouted at the crowd: "Long live the King!"

Now, here in the drawing room, the wooden lily reminded him of that sad September morning and one of the King's last drives through the streets of Naples; and our host was almost as proud of that lily as he was of the "Golden Key" he possessed as gentleman in waiting, and his decoration as a Knight of San Gennaro, and all the other decorations that were framed there in the room, under the two great oil portraits of Ferdinando and of Francesco II.

A little later, to carry out my despicable plot, I left the Marchese with Paleari and Papiano, and went over to Pepita.

I realized at once that she was very nervous and impatient. The first thing she asked me was the time:

"Four and a half. *Muy bien!*"

But she wasn't very pleased at it's being half past four; this I judged from her *muy bien*, muttered through clenched teeth, and from the aggressive way she immediately began to speak against Italy and especially against the city of Rome, so swollen with pride in its past. She told me, among other things, that in Spain, too, they had a Colosseum just like ours, just as old; but they didn't set so much store by it: "Dead stone! *Muerta!*"

For them, a *Plaza de toros* was worth much, much more. Yes, and she would have given all the masterpieces of ancient art, for that portrait of Minerva by the painter Manuel Bernaldez, who was late in arriving. Pepita's impatience was caused only by this, and it was now at its peak. She was seething as she spoke; from time to time she nervously rubbed her finger over her nose or bit her lip. She clenched and unclenched her hands, and her eyes kept straying over there, to the door.

At last the butler announced Bernaldez, who arrived sweating, overheated, as if he had run all the way. Pepita immediately turned her back on him and assumed a cold, indifferent manner; but when, after greeting the Marchese, he came to us, or rather to her, speaking to her in her own language, apologizing for his lateness, she could no longer contain herself and she answered him, speaking at a dizzying speed: "First of all, you speak *italiano, porqué* we are in *Roma*, and these *señores* do not understand *español*. So it is bad for you to speak *español con migo*. And I tell you I care nothing if you are late. You need not give excuses."

Deeply mortified, the artist smiled uneasily and bowed; then he asked her if he could resume work on the portrait, since there was still a little light.

"What you please!" she answered, in the same tone and manner. "You may *pintar* without me, or even *borrar lo pintado* . . . what you like!"

Manuel Bernaldez bowed again and turned to Signora Candida, who was still holding the dog in her arms.

For Minerva, the torture began again. But her torturer himself was subjected to worse torment: Pepita, to punish him for his lateness, took to flirting with me so openly that she was going too far even for my own purposes. Glancing secretly at Adriana from time to time, I saw how much she was suffering. So not only Bernaldez and Minerva were being tortured; so were Adriana and I. I felt my face aflame, as if I were gradually becoming drunk with the knowledge of the displeasure I caused that poor young man, though he inspired no pity in me. My pity, in that room, was all for Adriana. And since I had to make her suffer, I didn't care whether he, too, suffered with the same pain. In fact, the more he suffered, the less it seemed to me that Adriana should suffer. Little by little, the violence that each of us was doing to himself increased and became so taut that it had to explode somehow.

Minerva gave the pretext. Since her mistress's gaze wasn't there to make her behave that day, as soon as the painter looked from his subject to his canvas, the dog would quietly rise from the pose, and dig her front paws and nose into the crevice between the back and the seat of the chair, as if she wanted to make a hole there and hide. And in this way she presented the painter with her rump, round as an O, wagging her erect tail as if to mock him. Signora Candida had already put the dog back in the proper pose several times. As he waited, Bernaldez sighed impatiently and overheard some words of mine to Pepita. He would comment on them under his breath. More than once, as I noticed this, I wanted to say to him: Speak up! But finally he was the one who lost all control and shouted at Pepita: "Please: make that beast sit still!"

"Beast! Beast!" Pepita snapped, waving her hands in the air in her excitement. "She may be beast, but you don't say to her!"

"For all that she can understand, poor thing . . ." I happened to say, apologetically, to Bernaldez.

My remark could, in fact, be taken in two ways; I realized this the moment I had said it. What I meant was: Who knows what the poor dog understands of all this? But Bernaldez chose to find another meaning in my words, and with extreme violence, staring into my eyes, he retorted: "She probably understands more than you do!"

At his steady, defiant gaze, in my own emotional state, I couldn't help answering him back: "My dear sir, I understand that you may be a great painter, but . . ."

"What's this?" the Marchese asked, noticing our aggressive attitudes.

Bernaldez, now completely out of control, stood up and came over to me, until we were face to face: "Yes, a great painter . . . Go on!"

"A great painter, yes . . . but not a polite one, it seems to me; a painter who frightens little dogs," I said, determined and contemptuous.

"Very well," he said, "we'll see if it's only dogs that I frighten!"

And he withdrew.

Pepita promptly burst into strange, convulsive sobs, then fell in a faint into the arms of Papiano and Signora Candida.

In the subsequent confusion, as I helped the others settle Pepita on a sofa, I felt someone seize my arm, and there was Bernaldez again. He had come back. I was just in time to grasp the hand that he had raised against me and force it away, but he hurled himself on me a second time and just grazed my cheek with his palm. I fell upon him, furiously; but Papiano and Paleari rushed up to restrain me, as Bernaldez went off, shouting: "Consider your face slapped! I'm at your orders! . . . They know my address here!"

The Marchese had sat up halfway in his chair, shouting angrily at the aggressor. Meanwhile I was vainly struggling between Paleari and Papiano, who prevented me from running after the painter. The Marchese also tried to calm me, saying that, as a gentleman, I was to send two friends to that rogue and give him a good lesson, after he had showed such lack of respect for the house.

My whole body trembling, out of breath, I managed to apologize for the regrettable incident and rush out, followed by Paleari and Papiano. Adriana stayed with the unconscious Pepita, who had been removed to another room.

Now I had to ask my robber to act as my second: he and Paleari. To whom else could I turn?

"Me?" Signor Anselmo exclaimed, amazed and innocent. "Oh, no, never, my dear sir! You're not serious?"—He smiled. "I know nothing about such matters, Signor Meis . . . Come, it's all childish nonsense . . . forgive me for saying so . . ."

"You must do this for me!" I shouted loudly, unwilling to

argue with him at this point. "You and your son-in-law will go and wait upon that gentleman, and . . ."

"But I won't go! . . . What are you saying?" he interrupted. "Ask any other service of me, and I'm yours to command. But no, not that. It isn't for me, first of all. And besides, as I said: it's just childishness . . . You mustn't attach any importance to it . . . What does it matter . . ."

"No, no . . . That's wrong!" Papiano spoke up, seeing the state I was in. "It does indeed matter. Signor Meis has every right to demand satisfaction; in fact, I'd say he's obliged to . . . Yes, he must!"

"Then you can go with a friend of yours," I said, not expecting a refusal from him, too.

But Papiano held out his arms, grief-stricken: "Of course, I'd go with all my heart . . ."

"But you refuse?" I shouted loudly, there in the middle of the street.

"Lower your voice, Signor Meis, please . . ." He explained humbly. "You must see . . . Listen, consider my unfortunate position as an inferior . . . a miserable secretary of the Marchese . . . a servant . . . yes, a servant!"

"What's that got to do with it? The Marchese himself . . . you heard him, didn't you?"

"Yes, I did. But what about afterwards? He's so religious . . . in the eyes of his political party . . . a secretary who gets involved in duels . . . Ah, by God, you can't imagine the pettiness! And then that flirt . . . did you see her? She's mad with love for that painter, the scoundrel . . . Tomorrow they'll make peace, and then where will I be? I'll be the one to pay! Forgive me, Signor Meis, but consider my situation . . . there it is."

"Do you mean to leave me alone at a time like this?" I shouted again, exasperated. "I don't know a soul here in Rome!"

". . . But there's a solution! It can all be remedied," Papiano quickly advised me. "I wanted to tell you right away

. . . Both my father-in-law and I would get everything mixed up; we really wouldn't be the best choice anyway . . . You're right, you're in a fury—I can see: blood isn't water, after all. Well, all you have to do is ask two royal army officers; they can't refuse to represent a gentleman like yourself in a question of honor. You introduce yourself, explain the situation . . . This wouldn't be the first time that they've done such a favor for a stranger."

We had reached the door of our building. I said to Papiano: "All right!" And I left him there with his father-in-law, as I grimly, but aimlessly, strode off.

Once again the thought of my crushing helplessness overcame me. Could I fight a duel in my position? Why couldn't I get it into my head that I was unable to do anything now? Two officers? Yes, but first they would rightly want to know who I was. Ah, anyone could spit in my face or slap me or beat me; and I had to beg them to strike hard, yes, as hard as they liked, but without shouting, without making too much noise . . .

Two officers! If I were to reveal to them even a part of my story—first of all they wouldn't have believed it—and then what would they have suspected? Besides it was useless, as it would have been with Adriana: even if they believed me, they would advise me to return to life again. A dead man, after all, has no obligations to the code of chivalry . . .

Was I to suffer this insult, as I had the robbery, without taking action? Outraged, almost slapped, challenged, was I to sneak off like a coward, disappear into the unbearable darkness of the fate that awaited me, contemptible, odious even to myself?

No! No! How could I live afterwards? How could I stand such a life? Enough! Enough! I stopped. I saw everything sway around me; and I felt my legs fail me as a dark emotion suddenly rose in me, making me shudder from head to foot.

"But first . . . at least," I said to myself, in a delirium, "at least try first . . . why not? Even if it happened . . . at least try . . . so as not to seem such a coward to myself . . . If I could . . . I would be less disgusted with myself . . . I have nothing to lose anyway . . . Why not try?"

I was only a few steps from the Aragno Café. "There! I'll have a try!" And driven by my blind emotion, I went inside.

In the first room there were five or six artillery officers around a little table, and as I stopped near them, confused, hesitant, one of them turned to look at me. I made a brief gesture of greeting and asked, in a broken, gasping voice: "I beg your pardon . . . forgive me . . . Could I have a word with you?"

He was a young man, without a mustache, who must have finished the Academy that year: a lieutenant. He got up at once and very courteously came over to me.

"What can I do for you, sir?"

"First let me introduce myself: Adriano Meis. I'm from out of the city, and I don't know anyone here . . . I've had a . . . well, quarrel . . . and I need two seconds . . . I wouldn't know where to turn . . . If you and some fellow officer of yours could . . ."

Surprised and puzzled, the young man looked me up and down for a moment, then he turned towards his companions and called: "Grigliotti!"

His friend was an elderly lieutenant with handle-bar mustaches, a monocle thrust into his eye; he was licked and pomaded, and he got up, still talking with the others (he rolled his r's, French style). He came over and made me a brief, reserved bow. When I had seen him stand up, I had almost said to my little lieutenant: "Oh no, not that one, for heaven's sake!" But there was no other in the group, as I was later to see, who could have been more suited to the task than this Grigliotti. He had all the articles of the code of honor at his fingertips.

I couldn't repeat here in detail all the things he delighted in telling me about my case, and all the things he required of me . . . I was to telegraph, I don't know how or to whom,

explain, make sure, go to the colonel . . . *ça va sans dire* . . .
as he had done when a similar business had happened to him
once in Pavia before he was in the army . . . Because, according to the code . . . and then he went on and on, with
articles and precedents and controversies and councils of
honor and I don't know what all.

I had begun to feel nervous the first moment I saw him; you
can imagine how I felt later, hearing him go on like this.
Finally I could stand no more; my blood had all rushed to my
head, and I blurted out: "Yes, yes, Lieutenant, I see . . .
You're quite right. But how can I send a telegram now? I'm
alone! I want to fight this duel at once, tomorrow morning if
possible . . . and without all this fuss! What do I know about
it all? I spoke to you in the hope that there weren't so many
formalities, so many details, so much foolishness, if you'll forgive my saying so!"

After this outburst, the conversation almost degenerated
into an argument, then ended abruptly in a burst of loud
laughter from all the officers. I ran out, beside myself, flushed,
as if they had whipped me. I put my hands to my head as if
to hold on to my sanity which threatened to abandon me; and,
pursued by that laughter, I rushed away to hide, to take refuge
somehow . . . Where? At home? The idea horrified me. I
walked on and on, heading nowhere; then gradually I slowed
my pace and finally stopped, breathless, as if I could drag my
soul no farther, lashed as it was by that mockery. Furious, I
was also filled with leaden, grim anguish. For a while I stood
there in a daze, then began to move again, my mind a blank,
suddenly, strangely relieved of all my woe, almost stupefied.
And I began to wander once more, I don't know for how long,
stopping here and there to look in the windows of the shops,
which were gradually closing. They seemed to be shutting me
out, forever. Little by little, the streets became deserted, so
that I was left alone in the night, wandering among silent,
dark houses, all the doors and windows shut, locked against
me. Locked out forever. Life was being locked up, extin-

guished, falling silent with the night; and I already saw it as from afar, as if it no longer had any sense or purpose for me. And then, finally, unconsciously, as if led by the dark emotion that had invaded me, ripening slowly within me, I found myself again on the bridge, the Ponte Margherita, leaning on the railing, staring at the river, black in the night.

"There?"

A shudder of horror went through me, suddenly, furiously arousing all my vital energies, with a feeling of hatred for those who, from the distance, were forcing me to end my days now, as they had wanted before, there in the millrace. They, Romilda and her mother, had got me into this situation. Ah no, on my own, I would never have thought of simulating suicide to be free of them. And now, after two years of roaming like a shadow in that illusion of life beyond death, I saw myself being forced bodily to carry out the sentence *they* had passed. They had really killed me! And they, they alone, were freed of me . . .

I was filled with an impulse to rebel. Couldn't I take my revenge on them, instead of killing myself. Whom was I about to kill? A dead man . . . nobody . . .

I stood there, as if dazzled by a strange, sudden light. Avenge myself! Return there, to Miragno? Free myself from the lie that was stifling me, which had become unbearable now? Return there alive, as their punishment, with my real name in my real condition, with my real and proper sufferings? What about my present troubles? Could I shake them off like this, like a tiresome burden that can be thrown away? No, no! I felt that I couldn't do it. And I wrestled with my conscience there on the bridge, still uncertain of my fate.

Meanwhile, in the pocket of my overcoat, I was touching something, clasping something with my nervous fingers, an object I couldn't identify. Finally, in a fit of anger, I drew it out. It was my little traveling cap, the one I had carelessly thrust in my pocket as I left the house to visit the Marchese Giglio. I started to throw it into the river, but then—as I was about to do it—I had an idea. A notion of mine, a thought I'd had on the journey from Alenga to Turin now came clearly back into my mind.

"Here," I said, almost mechanically, to myself. "On this railing . . . the hat . . . my cane . . . Yes! Just like those women there at the mill found Mattia Pascal; here, now, Adriano Meis . . . Turn and turn about! I'll come alive again. I'll avenge myself!"

A sudden joy, or, rather, madness seized me, uplifted me. Yes! Of course! I needn't kill myself, a dead man; I should kill that mad, absurd fiction who had racked and tortured me for two years, that Adriano Meis, condemned to being a coward, a liar, a wretch; I should kill that Adriano Meis who, with a false name like his, must also have had a brain of straw, a heart of papier-mâché, veins of rubber in which a little colored water flowed in place of blood. All right! Away with the loathsome puppet! Drown him there, like Mattia Pascal! Turn and turn about! That shadow of a life, born from a macabre lie, would end worthily, like this, in another macabre lie! And I would settle everything! What other satisfaction could I have given Adriana for the wrong I had done her? Did I have to swallow the insult of that scoundrel, though? He had struck me sneakily, the coward! Oh, I was sure I wasn't afraid of him. No, not I—it was Adriano Meis who had received the insult. And now, lo and behold! Adriano Meis was going to kill himself.

There was no other way out for me!

A trembling had gripped me again, as if I really were going to kill somebody. But my brain was suddenly clear, my heart light, and I felt an almost joyous lucidity of spirit.

I looked around. I suspected that over there, on the street along the river, there might be someone, a policeman, who might have noticed me standing there on the bridge for some time. Perhaps he was keeping an eye on me. I had to make sure. I walked away and looked first in Piazza della Libertà, then in the street below it. Nobody! Then I turned back, but before stepping onto the bridge again, I stopped for a moment under the trees, near a street lamp. I tore a page from my notebook and wrote in pencil: *Adriano Meis*. What else? Nothing. The address and the date. That was enough. All of Adriano Meis was there, in that hat and that cane. I would leave everything behind at the house, clothes, books . . . Since the robbery, I had kept the rest of the money with me.

I went back on the bridge, silently, bending over. My legs were trembling, and my heart was pounding wildly in my breast. I chose the spot where the street lamp's light was dimmest, and I promptly took off the hat, put the folded paper in its band, then set it on the railing with the cane near it. I put on the providential traveling cap that had saved my life, and off I went, keeping to the shadow like a thief, never looking back.

XVII. Reincarnation

I reached the station in time to catch the 12:10 train for Pisa.

I bought my ticket, huddled up in a second-class compartment with the visor of my cap pulled down over my nose, not so much to hide myself as to keep from seeing. But, in my mind's eye, I saw all the same: that hat and the cane left on the railing of the bridge were a nightmare. Perhaps at this very moment, somebody was passing by and would notice . . . Or perhaps some policeman on his rounds had already rushed back to the station to give the alarm . . . And I was still in Rome! What would happen? I couldn't breathe . . .

At last the train got under way. Luckily I was still alone in the compartment. I sprang to my feet, raised my arms, and heaved an endless sigh of relief, as if a boulder had been lifted from my chest. Ah! I was returning to life, I was myself again, Mattia Pascal. I wanted to shout it aloud to the whole world: "I am Mattia Pascal! Here I am! I'm not dead! Look at me!" And I wouldn't have to lie any more or be afraid of discovery! Not quite yet, to tell the truth; not till I reached Miragno . . . There, first I would have to reveal myself, make them recognize that I was alive, graft my life on to its buried roots again . . . Madman that I was! How could I have believed that a trunk can live when cut off from its roots? And yet, now I remembered the other journey, the one from Alenga to Turin. Then, too, I had believed myself happy, in this same way. What folly! Liberation, I had said then . . . That had seemed a liberation! Yes, with a leaden hood of lies over my head . . . A leaden hood over a shadow . . . Now I would have my wife on my head again, true enough, and my mother-in-law . . . But hadn't they weighed on me also when I was dead? Now I was alive at least, and ready to face them. Ah, now we would see!

When I thought back now, it seemed incredible, the fool-hardiness with which I had cast myself out of every walk of life, haphazardly. And I could see myself again, in the first days, blissful in my ignorance, or rather my madness, first in Turin, and then in the other cities during my pilgrimage, grad-ually more silent, alone, shut up in myself, in what still seemed my happiness; and there I was in Germany, on the Rhine, on a steamer: Was this a dream? No, I had really been there! Ah, if I could have gone on forever under those conditions, a foreigner in life . . . But in Milan then . . . that poor little puppy that I had wanted to buy from the old peddler . . . I was already beginning to realize . . . And afterwards . . . Ah, afterwards!

In my thoughts I was forced back to Rome; like a shadow I entered the house I had abandoned. Were they all asleep? No, perhaps not Adriana . . . she was still waiting for me, waiting to hear me come in; they would have told her that I had gone out to engage seconds, to fight a duel with Bernaldez . . . Not hearing me come in, she would be afraid and would weep . . .

I pressed my hands to my face, as my heart contracted in anguish.

"But if I could never be alive for you, Adriana," I groaned, "it's better for you to know now that I am dead! Dead, the lips that took the first kiss from your mouth, poor Adriana! . . . Forget me! Forget!"

Ah, what would happen in that house the next morning when someone from the police appeared with the news? What motive, after the first shock had passed, would they think up for my suicide? The imminent duel? Ah, no! It would be very strange, to say the least, for a man who had never showed any signs of cowardice to kill himself for fear of a duel . . .

Well then, why? Because I couldn't find any seconds? A poor excuse! Or perhaps . . . who knows? Was there possibly some mystery behind that strange existence of mine?

Oh yes, they would surely think there was! I had killed myself like that, for no apparent reason, without having given any signs of my intentions beforehand. Yes: I'd done some strange things, more than one, in those days. That whole business of the robbery, first suspected, then suddenly denied . . . Could that money not have been mine? Did I have to give it back to someone? Had I embezzled some of it, then tried to pass myself off as the victim of a robbery, only to repent later and finally kill myself? Who could say? To be sure, I had been a very odd man: never a friend or a letter, not one, from anywhere . . .

It would have been wiser for me to write something on that paper, in addition to the name, the date, and the address: some kind of motive for the suicide. But at a moment like that? . . . And besides, what would have been the use?

My thoughts wandered wildly: "I wonder how the newspapers will go on in the next few days about this mysterious Adriano Meis? No doubt my old cousin, that Francesco Meis, the clerk from Turin, will spring up, and give his information to the police. They'll follow up that information, and who knows what will come out? Ah, but what about my money? The inheritance? Adriana saw all those bank notes . . . I can just imagine Papiano! An assault on the cupboard! But he'll find it empty . . . Lost? At the bottom of the river? What a terrible shame! The police will confiscate my clothes, my books . . . Who will get them finally? Ah, a souvenir at least to poor Adriana! What will she think, now, when she looks at my deserted room?"

Questions, suppositions, thoughts, emotions revolved in my mind, as the train rumbled through the night. They gave me no peace.

I thought it was wisest to stay in Pisa for a few days to avoid establishing any connection between the reappearance of Mattia Pascal at Miragno and the disappearance of Adriano Meis in Rome, a connection which could easily have seemed obvious, especially if the Roman papers had talked too much about the suicide. I would wait in Pisa for the Rome papers, the evening ones and the ones of the next morning. Then, if they weren't making too much fuss, I would start for Miragno, stopping off first at Oneglia at my brother Roberto's to test the effect of my resurrection on him. But I had to forbid myself even the slightest hint of my stay in Rome, the adventures and situations that I had lived through there. For the two years and odd months of my absence, I would invent fantastic information of distant journeys . . . Ah, now that I was going to be alive again, I could even enjoy telling lies, lots and lots of them, as big as those of Cavalier Tito Lenzi. Even bigger!

I still had more than fifty-two thousand lire. My creditors, thinking I died two years ago, had surely been satisfied with Hen Coop farm and the mill. When both were sold, the creditors would take what they could; they wouldn't bother me any more now. I'd see to that. And with fifty-two thousand lire in Miragno, I would live, well, perhaps not in luxury, but comfortably at least.

When I got off the train in Pisa, I went first to buy a hat, the size and shape of the hats Mattia Pascal always used to wear. And I immediately had the locks of that idiot Adriano Meis shorn away.

"Nice and short, mind you!" I said to the barber.

My beard had already grown out a little and now, with my hair short, I began to resume my former appearance, much improved, though, more refined . . . yes, more gentlemanly. My eye wasn't crooked any more, in the first place; that was no longer the most obvious feature of Mattia Pascal.

So something of Adriano Meis would still remain in my face. But I also looked more like Roberto now—more than I would ever have imagined possible.

There was a little mishap after I had rid myself of all that hair: I put on the hat I had just bought, and it slipped down over my eyes! With the barber's help, I adjusted it, putting a fold of paper inside the lining.

I didn't want to go into a hotel empty-handed, so I bought a suitcase. For the moment I would put inside it the suit and the overcoat I had been wearing. I had to buy a whole new wardrobe; I could hardly hope that, after all this time, my wife would still have any of my suits or linen there at Miragno. I bought a ready-made suit in a shop and put it on; with my new suitcase I went to the Hotel Nettuno.

I had been to Pisa before, when I was Adriano Meis, and I had stayed at the Albergo di Londra. I had already admired all the art treasures of the city; now, exhausted by my violent emotions, fasting since the preceding morning, I was dying of sleep and hunger. I ate something, then slept until evening.

As soon as I was awake, however, I fell prey to an obscure, mounting anxiety. That day, which had passed almost without my noticing it, what with my first concerns and then that deep sleep—how had it been spent meanwhile there at the Paleari home? Bustle, amazement, morbid curiosity of outsiders, hasty investigations, suspicions, wild hypotheses, insinuations, futile searches; my clothes, my books examined with that consternation inspired by objects belonging to someone who has died tragically.

And I had slept through it all! Now, in my anxious impatience, I would have to wait till the morning of the next day, to learn something from the Rome newspapers.

Meanwhile, since I couldn't rush to Miragno or even to Oneglia, I had to remain in a fine situation, this parenthesis of two or three days, or perhaps even more: still dead, there at Miragno, as Mattia Pascal; and now dead, on the other hand, in Rome, as Adriano Meis.

Not knowing what to do, hoping to find some distraction from all my worries, I took these two dead men out for a walk in Pisa.

Oh it was a charming stroll! Adriano Meis, who had been there before, wanted to act as guide to Mattia Pascal. But

Mattia, upset by the things that he kept turning over in his mind, shook off his companion rudely, waving his arm as if to drive away that nasty long-haired shade, with his frock coat, his broad-brimmed hat, and his glasses.

"Go away! Go! Back to the river and stay drowned!"

But I remembered how Adriano Meis, two years before, while strolling through the streets of Pisa, had been annoyed in the same way by the equally nasty shade of Mattia Pascal. And Adriano then wanted to drive him off with the same gesture, flinging him back into the millrace. The best course was to pay no attention to either one. O white campanile, you could lean to one side; but I, between those two, could move neither to left nor right.

Thank God, I finally managed to get through that second, endless night of suffering and, the next morning, hold the Rome papers in my hands.

I won't say that, on reading them, I was any calmer; I couldn't be. But my suspense was at least dispelled when I saw that the newspapers had given my suicide only the space of a routine event. All of them said more or less the same thing: the hat and the cane found on the Ponte Margherita, with the brief note. I was from Turin, a rather strange man, and no one knew the motive that had driven me to take the tragic step. One paper ventured the supposition that it was a "personal matter," basing this on the "quarrel with a young Spanish painter in the home of a figure prominent in clerical circles."

Another paper said that it was "probably because of financial reverses." Vague news, in other words, and laconic. Only a morning paper, which habitually relates events at greater length, mentioned the "surprise and grief of the family of Cavalier Anselmo Paleari, former clerk at the Ministry of Education, now retired, in whose home Meis was living, and where he was much esteemed because of his discretion and his unfailing courtesy." Well, thanks for that, at least! This paper also reported the challenge of the Spanish painter M.B. and hinted that the motive of the suicide was to be attributed to a secret love affair.

I had killed myself for Pepita Pantogada, in short. Well, perhaps this was best, after all. Adriana's name hadn't emerged, nor had there been any mention of my bank notes. The police would continue to investigate secretly. But following what traces?

I could leave for Oneglia.

I found that Roberto was at his country villa, for the vintage. You can easily imagine what I felt on seeing my lovely coast once more; I had feared I would never again set foot there. But my joy was marred by my impatience to arrive and my fear of being recognized by some outsider along the way before I reached my family. In addition to this worry, there was my gradually increasing emotion at the thought of what they would feel in seeing me alive, all of a sudden, before them. My eyes became moist at the thought; the sky and the sea turned dark, my blood raced in my veins, my heart beat wildly. And I thought I would never get there!

When the manservant finally came and opened the gate of the charming villa Berto had received as part of his wife's dowry, I thought, as I walked up the path, that I really was returning from the other world.

"This way, please," the servant said, motioning me ahead of him into the villa. "Whom shall I announce?"

I could hardly find the voice to answer him. Concealing my effort with a smile, I stammered: "Just say . . . tell him . . . it's a friend . . . an old friend . . . who has come from far off . . . that's all."

The servant must have believed that I was a stutterer, at the very least. He set my suitcase beside the coat rack and showed me into the living room off the hall.

I trembled as I waited, laughing, sighing, looking around in that bright, well-arranged room, with its new furniture in pale green lacquer. I suddenly saw, at the doorway where I had come in, a handsome boy of four with a little watering can in one hand and a rake in the other. He was staring at me, wide-eyed.

I felt an indescribable tenderness: this must be my little nephew, Berto's oldest child. I bent down and waved to him to come closer. But I frightened him and he ran off.

At that moment I heard the other door of the living room open. I stood up, tears in my eyes, as a kind of nervous laughter rose in my throat.

Roberto was facing me, upset, as if stunned.

"With whom have I . . . ?" he said.

"Berto!" I shouted at him, opening my arms. "Don't you recognize me?"

He turned deathly pale at the sound of my voice; he rubbed his hand briefly over his forehead and his eyes, then stammered, swaying: "How . . . How can this be? . . ."

I was prompt to catch him, though he had moved back, as if from fear.

"It's me! Mattia! Don't be afraid. I'm not dead . . . Can't you see me? Touch me! It's me, Roberto. I've never been more alive than I am now! Come, come . . ."

"Mattia! Mattia! Mattia!" poor Berto began to say, still unable to believe his eyes. "How is this? You? Oh God . . . what's happened? My brother! Oh, my dear Mattia!"

And he embraced me, clasping me to him. I began to cry like a child.

"How can this be?" Berto started asking again, weeping as I was. "How did this happen?"

"Here I am . . . You see? I've come back . . . no, not from the other world . . . I've always been in this grim world of ours . . . Come . . . I'll tell you . . ."

Holding my arm tight, his face filled with tears, Berto led me off, still dumfounded: "But how . . . at home they . . . ?"

"That wasn't me . . . I'll explain . . . They mistook me . . . I was far away from Miragno, and I learned from the newspapers—as perhaps you did—about my suicide at the mill."

"So it wasn't you?" Berto cried. "And then what did you do?"

"I played dead. Wait: I'll tell you the whole story. But I can't now. I'll just tell you this much: at first I wandered here and there, believing I was happy . . . You understand? And then . . . because of . . . because of various things that occurred, I realized I had made a mistake, and that playing dead isn't a very pleasant profession. So here I am. I'm returning to life."

"*Mattia!* I always used to say: *mad Mattia* . . . Mad! Mad! Mad!" Berto cried. "Ah, how happy you've made me! Who could have imagined such a thing? Mattia alive! . . . here! . . . You know? I still can't believe it. Let me look at you . . . You look like a different person!"

"I've had my eye fixed, too. You see?"

"Ah yes, of course . . . that's why I thought . . . I don't know . . . I looked and looked at you! Let's go into the other room, to my wife . . . Oh! But wait! . . . you . . ."

He stopped suddenly and looked at me, distraught:

"You plan to go back to Miragno?"

"Of course. This evening."

"Then you don't know anything?"

He put his face in his hands and groaned: "Poor Mattia! What have you done? . . . What have you done? . . . You don't know that your wife . . . ?"

"Is she dead?" I cried, stunned.

"No, worse! . . . She's . . . she's married again!"

I started.

"Married?"

"Yes, to Pomino. I received an announcement. It must have been over a year ago."

"Pomino? Pomino the husband of . . ." I stammered, but soon a bitter laughter, like a regurgitation of bile, rose in my throat. I laughed, I laughed out loud.

Roberto looked at me in amazement, perhaps afraid I had gone out of my mind.

"You can laugh?"

"Of course! Of course!" I shouted at him, shaking his arm. "All the better! This is the climax of my good luck!"

"What are you saying?" Roberto snapped, almost angrily. "Good luck? But if you go there now . . ."

"I'll run all the way!"

"Don't you realize that you'll have to take her back?"

"What? Me?"

"Of course!" Berto insisted, as I looked at him, now amazed in my turn. "The second marriage is annulled, and you're obliged to take her back."

I was overwhelmed.

"What? What kind of law is that?" I shouted. "My wife takes a new husband, and then I . . . No! Don't say that! It's impossible!"

"No, I tell you that's how it is!" Berto was firm. "But wait, my brother-in-law is here. He's a lawyer; he can explain it to you better than I can. Come . . . Or rather, no; wait here a moment. My wife is pregnant, I wouldn't want her to be upset . . . a shock, even though she doesn't really know you . . . I'll go and prepare her . . . Wait, eh?"

And he held my hand until he reached the door, as if he were afraid of leaving me alone for a moment, afraid that I might disappear all over again.

When I was alone in that little living room, I began again to pace back and forth. Married again! And to Pomino! But of course . . . He had loved her before, after all . . . It must have seemed too good to be true . . . To him and to her, too . . . I can imagine! She'd be rich, the wife of Pomino . . . And while she calmly remarried, there I was in Rome . . . And now I was supposed to take her back? Could that be?

A moment later Roberto came, all exultant, to call me. But I was now so shaken by this unexpected news that I could hardly respond to the festive welcome of my sister-in-law and her mother and brother. Berto noticed this, and immediately asked his brother-in-law about the matter I was so anxious to know.

"But what kind of a law is that?" I shouted again. "Forgive me for saying so, but that law would be all right for the Turks!"

The young lawyer smiled, adjusted his spectacles on his nose with a superior air.

"Nevertheless, that's how it is," he answered. "Roberto's right. I don't remember the exact number of the article, but the situation is dealt with in the constitution. The second marriage is null, when the first husband or wife reappears."

"And I have to take her back," I exclaimed angrily, "a woman who, to everyone's certain knowledge, has lived with another man for a full year as his wife. A man who . . ."

"But the fault is yours, Signor Pascal, if you'll forgive me for saying so!" the lawyer interrupted me, still smiling.

"My fault? How?" I asked. "First of all that woman makes a mistake and identifies some poor wretch who's drowned himself as me. Then she quickly takes a second husband. And it's my fault? And I have to take her back?"

"Of course," the young man answered, "since you, Signor Pascal, didn't choose to correct your wife's error in due time, that is to say within the limit set by the law before a second marriage can be contracted. Mind you, I'm not saying that her error couldn't have been in bad faith. But you accepted that mistaken identification, and made use of it . . . Oh, as far as I'm concerned: I praise you for it. I think you did the right thing. In fact, I'm astonished that you should come back and involve yourself in the complexities of these laws of ours. If I had been in your shoes, I'd never have come back . . ."

The calm, the bold self-assurance of this freshly minted lawyer irritated me.

"That's because you don't know anything about it," I answered, shrugging.

"What?" he said. "Can there be a greater piece of luck, a greater happiness than that?"

"Just try it for yourself," I exclaimed, turning towards Berto, to be rid of the young man and his presumption.

But I found troubles on that side, too.

"Oh, by the way," my brother asked me. "How did you manage all this time . . . for . . . ?"

And he rubbed his thumb and index finger together, indicating: *money.*

"How did I manage?" I answered. "A long story! I'm in no condition to tell it all to you now. But I had plenty, you know? And I still have some. You needn't think I'm going back to Miragno because I'm short of funds."

"Ah, you insist on going back there?" Berto went on. "Even after this news?"

"Of course I'm going back!" I cried. "Do you think I want to go on playing dead, after everything I've gone through? No, my dear Berto. I want to have my papers in order. I want to feel alive again, completely alive, even if it means having to take back my wife. By the way, is her mother still alive, the widow Pescatore?"

"Ah, I don't know," Berto answered. "After the second marriage, you understand, I . . . But yes, I think she's still alive . . ."

"Now I feel better!" I said. "But it doesn't matter. I'll avenge myself! I'm no longer the man I was before, you know. I'm only sorry to bring this stroke of luck to that imbecile Pomino!"

They all laughed. The manservant came to announce that dinner was served. I had to stay for the meal, but I was so impatient I hardly noticed what I was eating. I sensed, however, that at last I had finished devouring my food. The beast in me had been nourished, to prepare himself for the coming attack.

Berto urged me to stay at the villa overnight at least, then we would go to Miragno together the next day. He wanted to enjoy the scene of my unexpected return to life, my falling like a hawk on Pomino's nest. But I was too restless; I wouldn't hear of waiting. I begged him to let me go alone, that very evening, with no further delay.

I left on the eight o'clock train. It was half an hour to Miragno.

XVIII. *The Late Mattia Pascal*

In my anxiety and my rage (I didn't know which drove me hardest, but perhaps they were a single thing: anxious rage, or raging anxiety) in this state, I no longer cared whether anyone else recognized me before I got off at Miragno or immediately after I arrived.

My only precaution was to take refuge in a first-class carriage. It was evening, and for that matter, the experiment with Berto had reassured me. The certainty of my sad death more than two years ago was now deeply rooted, nobody would ever suspect that I might be Mattia Pascal.

I tried sticking my head out of the window, hoping the sight of these familiar places would inspire some more peaceful emotion in me; but it only increased my anxiety and rage. In the distance I could see the slope behind the mill in the moonlight.

"Murderesses!" I hissed. "There it was . . . but now!"

In my daze after the unexpected news, I had forgotten all sorts of things I had meant to ask Roberto! Had the farm and the mill really been sold? Or were they still being run by a temporary management, in agreement with the creditors? Was Malagna dead? And Aunt Scolastica?

I could hardly believe that only two and a half years had gone by; to me it seemed an eternity, and since I had had so many strange adventures, I felt that similar ones must have taken place at Miragno. Yet perhaps nothing had happened there, except for that marriage, Romilda's with Pomino, which in itself was normal enough and would become abnormal only now, with my reappearance.

Where would I go first, after I got off at Miragno? Where would I find the little nest of the new couple?

Pomino was rich and an only child; the house where I had lived in my poverty would be too humble for him. And besides, the tenderhearted Pomino would surely have been uncomfortable there, with all the inevitable reminders of me. Perhaps he had settled down with his father in the Palazzo Pomino. Ah, I could just imagine the widow Pescatore now. A real matron! And poor Cavalier Pomino, Gerolamo I, so gentle and kindly and mild, in the clutches of that shrew! The scenes! Neither father nor son would have the courage to throw her out. But now, of course—it made me furious to think of it!—I would come along and liberate them . . .

Yes, that's where I should go first, the Pomino house. Even if I didn't find them there, the concierge could tell me where to look next.

The moon was bright that evening, so all the street lights were out, as usual. The streets were almost deserted, since this was the supper hour for most people.

In my nervous state, I could hardly feel my legs; I walked along as if I weren't touching the ground. I couldn't now describe my mood at that moment. All I can remember is that, in my emotion, a kind of immense, Homeric laughter racked my entrails, unable to burst out freely. If I had allowed it to explode, it would have knocked out my teeth, shaken the houses, uprooted the cobblestones of the streets.

In no time I was at the Pomino house. But in that kind of glass case which, in the Palazzo, serves as porter's lodge, I couldn't find the old concierge. Seething with impatience, I waited for a moment or two, then I noticed a mourning wreath, faded and dusty, hanging beside the entrance, obviously nailed there some months before. Who had died? The widow Pescatore? Cavalier Pomino? One of the two, certainly. The Cavalier perhaps . . . In that case, I would find my two turtledoves upstairs beyond any doubt, installed in the Palazzo. I couldn't wait any longer. I rushed up the steps. At the landing there was the concierge.

"Cavalier Pomino?"

From that old tortoise's surprise, I realized that it was, indeed, the Cavalier who had died.

"The son, I mean. The son!" I hastily corrected myself, and continued to run upstairs.

I don't know what the old woman muttered to herself there on the steps. At the foot of the last flight I had to stop. I was out of breath. I looked up at the door and thought: "Perhaps they're still at supper, all three around the table . . . without the slightest suspicion. In a few moments, as soon as I've knocked on that door, their lives will be turned inside out . . . Ah, the fate that hangs over them is still in my hands."

I went up the last steps. With the bell rope in my hand, as my heart leaped to my throat, I listened. Not a sound. And in the silence I heard the slow *ding-ding* of the bell, which I pulled ever so gently.

My blood had all gone to my head, and my ears began to hum as if that faint tinkle, which had already died in the silence, were booming furiously, stunning me.

A little later, with a start, I recognized the widow Pescatore's voice from the other side of the door.

"Who's there?"

At first I couldn't answer. I held my clenched fists to my chest, as if to keep my heart from leaping out. Then, in a sinister voice, almost spelling the words, I said slowly: "Matti-a Pas-cal."

"Who?" screamed the voice inside.

"Mattia Pascal," I repeated, my voice even more cavernous.

I heard the old witch run off, terrified no doubt, and I promptly imagined what was happening at that moment beyond the door. Now Pomino would come, the man of the house, the brave one.

But first I would have to ring again, very faintly, as before.

Pomino flung the door open furiously, then saw me, erect,

my chest out, facing him; he stepped back, filled with horror.

I moved forward, shouting: "Mattia Pascal. From the other world."

Pomino fell on the floor with a great thud, in a sitting position, his arms behind him for support, his eyes wide.

"Mattia? You?"

The widow Pescatore, who had run in with a lamp in her hand, let out a shrill scream, as if she were in labor. I kicked the door shut behind me and, with one bound, grabbed the lamp away from her as it was about to drop from her hand.

"Shut up!" I shouted in her face. "Do you really take me for a ghost?"

"Alive?" she said, aghast, her hands in her hair.

"Alive! Yes, alive! Alive!" I went on, with ferocious joy. "You identified me as a dead man, didn't you? Drowned out there?"

"Where have you come from?" she asked in fright.

"From the mill, you witch!" I shouted at her. "Here, take your lamp. Look at me carefully. Am I Mattia? Do you know me? Or do I look like that poor wretch who drowned himself in the millrace?"

"Wasn't it you?"

"Go to hell, you old shrew! I'm here, alive! And you, you're a fine one, Pomino. Get up! Where's Romilda?"

"Please, please . . ." Pomino moaned, hastily standing up. "The little one . . . I'm afraid . . . the milk . . ."

I seized him by the arm. Now it was my turn to be amazed. "What little one?"

"My . . . my daughter . . ." Pomino stammered.

"Ah, you criminal!" the widow shouted.

I still couldn't answer, I was so dazed by this news.

"Your daughter?" I murmured. "A daughter, too? . . . And now . . ."

"Mamma, please, go to Romilda," Pomino begged her.

But it was too late. Her blouse unbuttoned, the infant at

her breast, Romilda came forward, all disheveled as if she had got up in a hurry. She glimpsed me.

"Mattia!" And she sank into the arms of Pomino and her mother, who dragged her away. In their confusion, they left the baby in my arms.

I stayed there in the dark vestibule with that fragile little girl in my arms; she cried, her voice still bitter with milk. Upset, dismayed, I heard again in my ears the scream of that woman who had been mine and who now was the mother of this child which was not mine. Not mine! Whereas mine, my child—her mother had not loved her then! And therefore, no . . . not now, by God! I was not to have pity on this child, nor on them. She had a new husband, hadn't she? And now I . . . But the little creature went on crying, crying . . . What was I to do? To calm her, I held her against my chest and began to pat her lightly on the back and rock her a little as I walked up and down. My hatred died away, my violence vanished. And little by little the baby became silent.

In the darkness, Pomino cried, alarmed: "Mattia! . . . The baby! . . ."

"Hush. I've got her," I answered.

"What are you doing?"

"I'm eating her, what do you think? . . . You threw her in my arms . . . Now leave her here. She's gone to sleep. Where's Romilda?"

Trembling and uncertain, like a bitch who sees her puppy in her master's arms, he came over to me.

"Romilda? Why?" he asked me.

"Because I want to talk to her," I answered rudely.

"She fainted, you know?"

"Fainted? We'll bring her to."

Pomino stood in my path, imploringly: "For God's sake . . . listen . . . I'm frightened . . . how can this be? You? . . . Alive? . . . Where have you been? For heaven's sake, couldn't you . . . couldn't you talk to me?"

"No!" I shouted at him. "She's the one I have to talk to. You don't represent anything around here any more."

"What? Me?"

"Your marriage will be annulled."

"What? What are you talking about? The baby . . ."

"The baby . . . the baby . . ." I ruminated. "Shame on you! In only two years, you married her and had a baby, too. Hush, dear, hush! Now we'll go to Mamma . . . Show me the way? Where do I go?"

When I came into the bedroom with the baby in my arms, the widow Pescatore was ready to leap on me like a hyena.

I pushed her away with my arm furiously. "Go into the other room, you! Your son-in-law's here! If you want to yell, you can yell with him. I don't know you!"

I bent towards Romilda, who was weeping desperately, and I handed her the child: "Here . . . take her . . . Are you crying? Why? Crying because I'm alive, eh? Did you prefer me dead? Look at me . . . yes, look me in the eye. Alive or dead?"

She tried, through her tears, to look up at me; and in a voice choked with sobs, she stammered: "But . . . how . . . you . . . What have you done?"

"What have *I* done?" I sneered. "You ask me what I've done? You've taken a new husband . . . that idiot over there . . . and you've brought a daughter into the world, and you have the nerve to ask *me* what I've done?"

"Now what?" Pomino moaned, covering his face with his hands.

"But you, you . . . where have you been? You played dead and ran off . . ." the widow started screaming, coming forward with her arms upraised.

I seized one of her arms, twisted it, and shouted back at her. "Shut up," I said, "you keep your mouth shut, because if I hear a sound out of you, I'll forget the pity that this idiot son-in-law of yours inspires in me, and that poor little child; and then I'll have the law on you all. You know what the law says? It says I have to take Romilda back . . ."

"You? My daughter? You're mad!" she spat, venomously.

But at my threat, Pomino went over to her at once and begged her to be quiet, to calm down for the love of God.

The shrew turned away from me and began to inveigh against him: stupid, helpless, good for nothing, incapable of anything but crying like a woman . . .

I burst out laughing; I laughed until my sides ached.

"Stop it!" I shouted, when I regained control of myself. "I'll leave her to you. I'll leave her to you gladly. Do you really think I'm so mad that I could want to be your son-in-law again? Ah, poor Pomino. My poor friend, forgive me. I'm sorry I called you an idiot. But then so did your mother-in-law. You heard her? And I can swear that, in the past, the same word was used by Romilda, our wife . . . yes, Romilda. She thought you were silly, a fool, insipid . . . and I don't know what else. Isn't that true, Romilda? Tell him the truth . . . Now, now, stop crying, dear. Pull yourself together. Mind, you'll hurt the baby like that . . . I'm alive now, you see? And I want to be happy . . . *Be happy*, as a certain drunk said, a friend of mine . . . Be happy, Pomino! You think I want to leave a little child without her Mamma? Come! I already have a little boy without a father . . . You see, Romilda? We're even. I have a son, who's the son of Malagna. And you have a daughter now, who's the daughter of Pomino. God willing, we'll marry them one of these days. That boy shouldn't upset you any more now . . . Let's talk about happy things . . . Tell me how you and your mother managed to identify my body there at the mill . . ."

"Oh, but so did I!" Pomino cried, provoked. "So did the whole town. Romilda and her mother weren't the only ones!"

"Good for you! Good for you all! Did he really look so much like me?"

"He was your same height . . . your beard . . . dressed in black like you . . . and then you had been missing for so many days . . ."

"Of course. I had run off. You heard that? As if those two hadn't been the ones to make me run off . . . her . . . and her . . . And yet I was on my way back, you understand? Yes, my pockets full of money, too! But then . . . shall I? shan't I? . . . dead, drowned, putrefied . . . and identified, in the bargain! Thank God, I didn't stint myself for two years. And in the meanwhile, you, here: engagement, wedding, honeymoon, celebrations, joy, baby . . . Let the dead bury the dead, eh? Life is for the living . . ."

"But now? Now what are we going to do?" Pomino moaned again, on pins and needles. "That's what I'm asking!"

Romilda stood up and settled the baby in its crib.

"Come, we'll go into the other room," I said. "The baby's fallen asleep again. We'll discuss things in there."

We went into the dining room, where the remains of supper were still on the table. Trembling, staring, overcome, deathly pale, Pomino blinked constantly; his eyes seemed to have turned white, with two little black holes in their centers. He scratched his forehead and said, as if in a delirium: "Alive . . . alive . . . What's to be done? What's to be done?"

"Don't bore me!" I shouted. "We'll see, I tell you."

Putting on a house robe, Romilda came and joined us. I stood and looked at her in the light, surprised. She had become beautiful again, as she had once been; indeed, she was even more shapely now.

"Let me have a look at you," I said to her. "You don't mind, Pomino? There's no harm in it. I'm her husband, too; in fact, I came first. Now don't be modest, Romilda! Look at Pomino! See how he's squirming. But what fault is it of mine, if I'm not really dead?"

"Things can't go on like this," Pomino blurted, livid.

"He's getting nervous," I said to Romilda, with a wink. "No, no, calm down, Pomino . . . I told you you can keep her; and I'm as good as my word. But wait just a minute . . . if you don't mind!"

I went over to Romilda and planted a resounding kiss on her cheek.

"Mattia!" Pomino shouted, beside himself.

I burst out laughing again.

"Jealous? Of me? Come! I have my rights, by precedence. No, Romilda, rub it out . . . forget it . . . You see, as I was coming here, I imagined—forgive me, Romilda—I imagined, dear Mino, that I'd be doing you a great favor by freeing you of her. And I'll admit that this thought depressed me very much, because I wanted to avenge myself, and I would still like to now mind you, by taking Romilda from you, now that I see that you love her and that she . . . yes, it's almost a dream, she seems the Romilda of so many years ago . . . You remember, eh, Romilda? Yes, those were the days . . . gone forever . . . Ah well, now you have a little girl, and we won't talk about it any more. I'll leave you in peace, after all!"

"But will the marriage be annulled?" Pomino shouted.

"What if it is?" I said to him. "The annulment will be a matter of form, if anything. I won't insist on my rights, and I won't even have myself declared legally alive, if they don't force me to. All I want is for everyone to see me and to know that, in fact, I *am* alive; so that I can escape from this death —which is real death, believe me. You can see for yourself. Romilda here has been able to become your wife . . . the rest doesn't matter. You married her in public; and it's a well-known fact that, for a year, she has been your wife . . . and so she shall remain. Who's going to bother about the legal status of her first marriage? Water under the bridge . . . Romilda *was* my wife; now for the past year she has been *yours*, she's the mother of your child. In a month's time people will already have stopped talking about it. Am I right, double mother-in-law?"

Grimly frowning, the widow nodded her head, agreeing. But, in his mounting emotion, Pomino asked: "And you're going to stay here in Miragno?"

"Yes. And now and then I'll drop by your house in the evening for a cup of coffee, or to drink your health with a glass of wine."

"No. That, no!" the widow snapped, jumping to her feet.

"He's only joking . . ." Romilda said, her eyes cast down.

I had started laughing again, as before.

"You see, Romilda?" I said to her. "They're afraid we'll start making love again . . . Not a bad idea, after all! No, no, let's not torment Pomino . . . If he doesn't want me in the house, then I'll just stroll up and down in the street, below your windows. How's that? And I'll sing you some beautiful serenades."

White, trembling, Pomino paced up and down the room, muttering: "It's not possible . . . not possible . . ."

At a certain point he stopped and said: "The fact is that she . . . with you here, alive . . . wouldn't be my wife any more . . ."

"You can pretend I'm dead," I answered him calmly.

He went back to his pacing. "I can't pretend that any more."

"Then don't . . . Come now, do you really believe," I went on, "that I'll bother you, if Romilda doesn't want me to? She's the one who must say . . . All right, Romilda, who's the more handsome? Him? or me?"

"I'm talking about the law! The law!" he shouted, stopping again.

"In that case," I pointed out to him, "I feel I have more right to be resentful than any of you, since from now on I'll have to see my beautiful quondam other half living with you connubially."

"But Romilda, too," Pomino replied, "since she's no longer my wife . . ."

"Now really!" I said impatiently. "I wanted to avenge myself, and I'm not going to. I'm leaving you my wife, and I'm leaving you in peace. Isn't that enough for you? Come, Romilda, get up! We're going away, the two of us! I'm inviting you on a nice little wedding trip . . . We'll have a wonderful time! Leave this pedantic bore behind! Now he wants me to go and actually throw myself in the millrace!"

"That isn't what I want!" Pomino yelled, in a fever of exasperation. "But go away, at least! Since you enjoyed having people think you were dead, go away from here! Right now, go far away, before anybody sees you. Because with you, here, alive . . . I . . ."

I stood up. I slapped him on the back to calm him down and told him that, first of all, I had already been to see my brother in Oneglia and everybody there by this time knew I was alive again; and tomorrow morning the news would surely reach Miragno. And besides:

"Dead again? Far from Miragno? You're joking, my friend!" I exclaimed. "Come, come. Just go on quietly being a good husband, without giving it so much thought . . . One way or another, your marriage was celebrated. Everybody will approve, since there's a child involved. I solemnly promise that I won't come bothering you any more, not even for a miserable little cup of coffee, not even to enjoy the edifying, heartwarming sight of your love, your harmony, your happiness which was constructed on my death . . . Ingrates! I bet that not one of you, not even you, my bosom friend, has gone to put a wreath, or a single flower on my grave there in the cemetery . . . Am I right? Answer me!"

"You're in a joking mood," Pomino said, shrugging.

"Joking? Not in the least! There really is a dead man there, and that's nothing to joke about! Have you been there?"

"No . . . I didn't . . . I lacked the courage . . ." Pomino blurted.

"But you had the courage to take my wife, you scoundrel!"

"What about you?" he said promptly. "Didn't you take her from me first, when you were still alive?"

"Me?" I cried. "Now, now! She was the one who didn't want you! Do I have to repeat the fact that she considered

you an idiot? You tell him, Romilda, please. You see? He's
accusing me of treachery . . . Now what does that have to do
with the situation. He's your husband, and what's past is
past . . . Don't worry. Tomorrow I'll go to that poor
man's grave, abandoned there without a flower, without a
tear . . . Tell me something, though: Is there a tombstone
at least?"

"Yes," Pomino answered in haste. "City Hall paid for it
. . . poor Papa . . ."

"He made the speech at my grave, I know. If that poor man
heard . . . What's written on the stone?"

"I don't know . . . Skylark wrote it."

"I can just see it!" I sighed. "Oh well, let's change this subject, too. But tell me how you happened to be married so
quickly . . . Ah, my dear little widow, you didn't weep for me
very long . . . Perhaps not all all, eh? Speak up. Won't you let
me hear your voice? Look, it's already late at night . . . as
soon as day breaks, I'll leave, and it'll be as if we had never met
. . . So let's make the most of these few hours. Now tell
me . . ."

Romilda shrugged, looked at Pomino, smiled nervously.
Then she lowered her eyes, staring at her hands, and spoke:
"What can I say? Of course I wept for you . . ."

"More than you deserved!" muttered the widow Pescatore.

"Thanks . . . but, after all, it wasn't for very long, was it?"
I continued. "Those lovely eyes, so easily deceived, weren't
very red, I dare say."

"We were in a bad way," Romilda said, as if to explain, "and
if it hadn't been for him . . ."

"Pomino! Bravo!" I exclaimed. "But that swine Malagna
. . . nothing from him, eh?"

"Nothing," the widow Pescatore said, hard and curt. "He
did everything . . ."

And she pointed to Pomino.

"That is to say . . ." he corrected, "my poor Papa . . . You remember he was at City Hall? Well, he arranged for a pension given first, since it was a tragic case . . . and then . . ."

"He consented to the marriage?"

"He was overjoyed. And he insisted that all of us come here to live with him . . . But . . . two months ago . . ."

Then he started telling me about his father's illness and death, about the old man's love for Romilda and his little granddaughter, and how the whole town had mourned him. I asked for news of Aunt Scolastica, who was such a friend of Cavalier Pomino's. The widow Pescatore, who still remembered that wad of dough the fearsome old woman had slammed in her face, began to writhe in her chair. Pomino answered that he hadn't seen my aunt for two years, but she was still alive. Then, in his turn, he asked me what I had done, where I had been, etc. I told him what I could, without naming names, without mentioning people or places, to prove that I hadn't enjoyed myself at all in those two years. And so, conversing like this, we waited for the dawn of the day on which I was publicly to affirm my resurrection.

We were tired from our vigil and from our strenuous emotions; we were also cold. To warm us a little, Romilda insisted on preparing some coffee with her own hands. As she handed me my cup, she looked at me, with a brief, sad, almost distant smile on her lips, and said: "No sugar, as usual?"

What did she read in my eyes at that moment? She looked away at once.

In that livid dawn's light, I felt an unexpected lump in my throat, and I looked at Pomino with hatred. But the coffee was steaming under my nose, its aroma intoxicating me; and I began to sip it slowly. Then I asked Pomino's permission to leave my suitcase at his house until I had found lodgings. I would send someone to collect it then.

"Of course, of course," he said eagerly. "But don't bother. I'll have it delivered to you . . ."

"Oh," I said, "it's empty, for that matter . . . By the way,

Romilda, you don't have any of my things around by any chance? Clothes? Linen?"

"No, nothing . . ." she answered sadly, holding her hands out helplessly. "You understand . . . after the tragedy . . ."

"Who could have imagined?" Pomino exclaimed.

But I could swear that he, that miserly Pomino, was wearing an old silk scarf of mine around his neck.

"Ah well, good-by then, and good luck!" I said, with a wave, my eyes fixed on Romilda, who refused to look at me. But her hand trembled as she waved back. "Good-by! Good-by!"

When I was down in the street again, I was once more at a loss; even here in my little native town: alone, without a home or a destination.

"Now what?" I asked myself. "Now where shall I go?"

I started off, looking at the people who went by. No! Not one of them recognized me. And yet I was the same man now; seeing me, they might at least have thought:

—Why, look at that stranger there! He's the image of poor Mattia Pascal. If his eye were only a little crooked, you could swear it was Mattia!—

No, no. Nobody recognized me, because nobody thought of me any more. I didn't even arouse curiosity, much less any surprise . . . And instead I had pictured an outburst, cries in the streets, as soon as I showed myself. Profoundly disillusioned, I was annoyed, depressed, embittered more than I can say. And my annoyance and bitterness restrained me from attracting the attention of those people whom, for my part, I recognized perfectly well . . . Ah, this is what being dead means. Nobody, nobody remembered me any more, as if I had never existed . . .

Twice I walked the length and breadth of the town, and no one stopped. In a towering rage, I thought of going back to Pomino and saying that I had made a bad bargain, and I would take my revenge on him individually for the insult I felt the whole town was giving me by not recognizing me any more. But Romilda would never have come away with me peaceably, and for the moment I wouldn't have known where to take her. First I had to find myself a house at least. I thought of going to City Hall, to the registrar's office, to have my name immediately taken off the list of deaths. But as I turned to go there, I changed my mind and instead I came back to this library of Santa Maria Liberale, where I found my reverend friend Don Eligio Pellegrinotto in my old place. He didn't recognize me either, for a moment. Don Eligio, to tell you the truth, insists that he knew me at once and was only waiting for me to say my name before throwing his arms around me. It seemed impossible to him that I could be myself, and he couldn't spontaneously embrace a man who *seemed* to be Mattia Pascal. Perhaps that's how it was. But, in any case, my first welcome—and a very warm one it was— came from him. Then he insisted on taking me back to the town, to erase from my spirit the bad impression that the forgetfulness of my fellow citizens had made on me.

But, out of pique now, I won't describe what followed, first at Brisigo's pharmacy, then at the Caffè dell'Unione when Don Eligio, still exultant, presented me, back from the dead. The news spread in a moment, and everyone ran to see me and to deluge me with questions. They wanted me to tell them who the man was who had drowned at the mill, as if they hadn't identified me, one and all. So it was me? Really me? Where had I come from? From the other world! What had I been doing? Playing dead! I decided to give only those two answers, and to let them all burst with curiosity. This continued for many days. And my friend Skylark was no more fortunate than the others, when he came to "interview" me for *Il Foglietto*. He tried in vain to move me, to make me talk by bringing a copy of the issue of two years ago, with my obituary. I told him I knew it by heart, since *Il Foglietto* had a large circulation in Hell.

"Ah, yes, it does! Thank you, my friend! For the words on the tombstone, too . . . I must go out and read them . . ."

I will refrain from copying out here his leading article the following Sunday, printed under a huge headline:

MATTIA PASCAL IS ALIVE!

Among the few who didn't come to see me, outside of my creditors, was Batta Malagna, even though—I was told—he had displayed great sorrow at my tragic suicide two years earlier. I can believe that. All that sorrow then, knowing that I was gone forever, and as much sorrow now, learning that I had come back to life. I can understand the reason for both sorrows.

What about Oliva? I met her on the street, after Mass a few Sundays later, leading a little boy of five by the hand, plump and handsome as herself—my son! She looked at me with laughing, affectionate eyes, which told me many things in an instant . . .

Enough. I live peacefully now with my old Aunt Scolastica, who took me into her home. My mad adventure suddenly raised me in her esteem. I sleep in the same bed in which my poor mother died, and I spend a great part of my day here in the library with Don Eligio, who is still far from having put the dusty old books in any kind of order.

It's taken me about six months to write this strange story, with his help. He will keep the secret of everything written here, as if he had heard it all in the confessional.

We have discussed my life at length, and I have often told him that I can't see how it can be made instructive.

"In the first place," he says, "it proves that outside of the law, and without those individual characteristics which, happy or sad as they may be, make us ourselves, we cannot live, dear Signor Pascal."

But then I point out to him that I am far from being in a sound legal position, nor have I regained my individual characteristics. My wife is the wife of Pomino, and I can't really say that I'm myself. I don't know who I am.

In the Miragno cemetery, over the grave of the poor stranger who killed himself in the millrace, there is still the stone with Skylark's words on it:

UNDER THE BLOWS OF ADVERSE FATE

MATTIA PASCAL

LIBRARIAN
GENEROUS HEART — NOBLE SOUL
RESTS HERE
BY HIS OWN DESIRE
HIS GRIEVING FELLOW CITIZENS
PLACED THIS STONE HERE
IN HIS MEMORY

I took the wreath of flowers, as I had promised, and every now and then I go out there to see myself dead and buried. Occasionally a curious passer-by follows me for a while at a distance, then walks back with me and smiles, considering my situation, when he asks:

"Who are you, after all?"

I shrug, shut my eyes for a moment, and answer: "Ah, my dear friend . . . I am the late Mattia Pascal."

A Warning
on the Scruples of the Imagination

Mr. Albert Heintz, of Buffalo, U.S.A., torn between the love of his wife and that of a young lady of twenty, decides to invite both to a meeting, at which they can, with him, come to some decision.

The two ladies and Mr. Heintz meet punctually at the appointed place. They argue for some time and, at the end, they reach an agreement.

They decide, all three of them, to kill themselves.

Mrs. Heintz goes home, shoots herself with a pistol and dies. Then Mr. Heintz and the young lady of twenty realize that, with the death of Mrs. Heintz, all obstacles to their union have been removed. They discover that they no longer have any motive to commit suicide, so they make up their minds to remain alive and to be married. The authorities, however, come to a different decision and they are both arrested.

A very vulgar conclusion.

(See the New York newspapers, morning edition, for January 25, 1921.)

Let's suppose a poor playwright has the unfortunate idea of putting such a situation on the stage.

In the first place, his scrupulous imagination will surely think up heroic remedies to repair the absurdity of Mrs. Heintz's suicide, to make it in some way believable.

But you can also be sure that, no matter how many heroic remedies the playwright invents, ninety-nine drama critics out *of a hundred will declare that the suicide is absurd and the play, unbelievable.*

For life, happily filled with shameless absurdities, has the rare privilege of being able to ignore credibility, whereas art feels called upon to pay attention to it.

Life's absurdities don't have to seem believable, because they are real. As opposed to art's absurdities which, to seem real, have to be believable. Then, when they are believable, they are no longer absurd.

An event in life may be absurd; a work of art, if it is a work of art, cannot be.

It therefore follows that to criticize, in the name of life, a work of art for being absurd and unbelievable is sheer stupidity.

In the name of art, yes. But not in the name of life.

In natural history there is a field called zoology because it is inhabited by animals.

Among the many animals who inhabit it there is also man.

The zoologist can talk about man *and can, for example, say that he is not a quadruped, but a biped, and that he has no tail like, for example, the monkey or the ass or the peacock.*

The man of whom the zoologist speaks can never suffer the misfortune of losing a leg, for example, and having to replace it with a wooden one; or of losing an eye and replacing it with one of glass. The zoologist's man always has two legs, neither of wood, and two eyes, neither of glass.

And it's impossible to contradict the zoologist. Because the zoologist, if you introduce him to a man with a wooden leg or a glass eye, will tell you that he doesn't recognize him, because this is not man. *It is* a *man.*

It's also true, however, that we can answer the zoologist by saying that the man *he knows doesn't exist, and that instead* men *exist, of whom none is exactly like another, and some unfortunately may even have wooden legs and glass eyes.*

Now the question is whether certain gentlemen want to be zoologists or literary critics. I mean the gentlemen who judge a novel or a story or a play, condemning this or that character, the way an event or an emotion is depicted, in the name of humanity which they seem to know perfectly. As if humanity really existed in the abstract, not as that infinite variety of men who are capable of committing all the above-praised absurdities, because these men don't have to seem believable, inasmuch as they are real.

Meanwhile, from my own experience of this kind of criticism, I'd say the odd thing is this: while the zoologist admits man is distinct from the other animals because he can reason, and the other animals can't, the process of reasoning (that is to say, man's distinctive quality) in many of my far from happy characters to the critical gentlemen often seems not so much an excess of humanity as a lack of it. Because apparently humanity, for them, is something that consists more in feeling than in reasoning.

Still, to speak abstractly like these critics, isn't it perhaps true that man never reasons so passionately (or so wrongly—not that that changes anything) as when he is suffering? He wants to arrive at the root of his sufferings, he wants to discover who causes them, and whether they are deserved. But when man is happy, doesn't he accept his happiness without reasoning about it, as if it were his right?

The duty of animals is to suffer irrationally. He who suffers and reasons (precisely because he suffers), for the critics, isn't human; because it seems that he who suffers must be merely an animal, and that it is only when we are bestial that, for the critics, we become human.

Recently, however, I found a critic to whom I am very grateful.

On the subject of my inhuman and apparently incurably "cerebral" nature and the paradoxical incredibility of my fables and my characters, this critic asked his colleagues where they found the criteria for judging the world of my art in this way.

"In what is called normal life?" he asked. "But what is that except a system of relationships which we select from the chaos of daily events, and then arbitrarily call normal?" And he concluded: "We cannot judge an artist's world with criteria derived from any place except that world itself."

I must add, to save this critic's standing with other critics, that despite what he wrote, or because of it, he then went on to judge my work unfavorably. It seems to him that I am unable to give a universally human significance and value to my fables and my characters, and therefore the person who must judge them remains puzzled, wondering if perhaps I didn't intentionally limit myself to the narration of certain cases, certain very special psychological situations.

But what if the universally human significance and value of some of my fables and my characters set in the contrast, as he points out between reality and illusion, between the individual's countenance and society's view of it, consisted first of all in the significance and value to be assigned that first contrast that, thanks to one of life's constant jests is always revealed as non-existent? Alas, today's every reality is necessarily destined to prove an illusion tomorrow, but a necessary illusion, since outside of it, unfortunately, there is no other reality for us. What if the significance consisted precisely in this, that a man or woman placed, by himself or by others, in a painful situation, socially abnormal, absurd if you like, remains in it, bears it, plays it out in front of others as long as he himself doesn't see it, whether through blindness or through incredible good faith? As soon as he sees it, as if a mirror had been set in front of him, he can no longer bear it, he feels all its horrors, and he breaks it, or if he can't break it, he feels that it will kill him. Or if the significance consisted in this: that a socially abnormal situation is accepted, even when seen in a mirror, which in this case holds our own illusion up to us; and then we play it out, suffering all its pain, as long as the performance is possible behind the stifling mask that we have put on ourselves or that others, or cruel necessity, have forced on us; in other words, as long as beneath this mask some keenly felt feeling of ours isn't hurt there? Then the rebellion finally breaks out, and that mask is torn off and trampled underfoot.

"Then, all of a sudden," the critic says, "a flood of humanity invades these characters, the marionettes suddenly become creatures of flesh and blood, and words which sear the spirit and break the heart come from their lips."

I should hope so! They have bared their naked individual faces from beneath that mask which made them the marionettes of themselves or in the hands of others, which made them seem at first hard, wooden, stiff, without refinement or tact, complicated and impetuous, like all things composed not freely but by necessity, in an abnormal, unbelievable, paradoxical situation; a situation, in short, which they can't bear and which they finally shatter.

The mischief then, if it exists, is there by desire; the mechanism, if there is one, is also there by desire, but not by my desire. The fable itself, the characters themselves demand it. And this is soon discovered, in fact. Often the mechanism is constucted on purpose and put before your eyes while it is being built. It is the mask for a performance, a game of roles: what we would like to be or what we should be, what we appear to others. What we really are, even we ourselves don't know beyond a certain point. The clumsy, inadequate metaphor of ourselves; the product, often badly put together, that we make ourselves, or that the others make of us. Yes, there is a mechanism in which each person is, purposely, the marionette of himself, as I said before; and then at the end, comes the kick that knocks the whole theatre apart.

I believe my imagination is only to be congratulated if, with all its scruples, it has managed to make the defects it chose seem real, the defects of that fictitious construction the char-

acters themselves have built of their personalities and their lives, or that others have built for them: the defects, in short, of the mask *until it is revealed as naked.*

But I received an even greater consolation from life itself, or rather from the newspaper accounts of life, about twenty years after the first publication of this novel of mine, The Late Mattia Pascal, which is now being republished once again.

This book, too, when it first appeared, was almost unanimously hailed as unbelievable.

Well, life has chosen to give me a proof of its truth to a really exceptional degree, even down to certain minute details which were invented by my imagination.

The following article was to be read in the Corriere della Sera on March 27, 1920:

A Living Man Visits His Own Grave

A singular case of bigamy, caused by the declared but non-existent death of a husband, has been recently revealed. First we will summarize the previous history. In the Calvairate district on December 26, 1916, some peasants found in the ditch known as Five Locks the body of a man wearing a sweater and brown trousers. The police were advised of the discovery and began their investigations. A short time later the body was identified by a certain Maria Tedeschi, a still-attractive woman of about forty, and by one Luigi Longoni and one Luigi Majoli, as that of the electrician Ambrogio Casati, born in 1869, husband of Maria Tedeschi. In fact, the drowned man bore a striking resemblance to Casati.

That identification, according to recent revelations, had an ulterior motive, especially for Majoli and for Maria Tedeschi. The true Casati was still alive! He was, however, in prison, and had been since February 21 of the preceding year for a crime against property. He had been separated, though not legally, from his wife for some time. After seven months of mourning, Maria Tedeschi was married again, to Luigi Majoli, encountering no legal difficulties. Casati finished serving his sentence on March 8, 1917, but learned only a few days ago that he is . . . dead, and that his wife had married again and vanished. He learned all this when he went to the registrar's office in Piazza Missori, to ask for a certificate. The clerk at the window said inexorably to him: "But you are dead. Your legal residence is the Musocco Cemetery, lot 44, grave number 550 . . ."

All protests of the man who wanted to be declared alive

proved vain. Casati now insists on his right to . . . resurrection, and as soon as this error is corrected, the presumed widow will find her second marriage annulled.

Meanwhile the odd mishap has not disturbed Casati in the least. In fact, it seems to have put him in a good humor. And, as if to seek new emotions, he decided to make a little visit to . . . his grave, and, as a tribute to his own memory, he set a fine bunch of flowers on the tomb and lighted a votive candle!

The presumed suicide in a ditch, the corpse taken out and identified by the wife and by the man who is to be her second husband, the return of the false dead man, and even the visit to his own grave! All the facts, naturally, without any of the rest, without what should give a universally human significance and value to the event.

I can't suppose that Signor Ambrogio Casati, electrician, had read my novel and had taken the flowers to his grave to imitate Mattia Pascal.

Life, meanwhile, with its blissful contempt for verisimilitude, had found a priest and a mayor to unite in matrimony Signor Majoli and Signora Tedeschi without bothering about another fact—which it would have been easy to discover—the fact that the first husband, Signor Casati, was in jail, not below the ground.

Imagination would have had scruples, of course, and would have omitted that fact. And now, remembering the old accusation of incredibility, imagination takes pleasure in proving how incredible life can be, even in such novels that, without meaning to, she copies from art.

TITLES IN SERIES